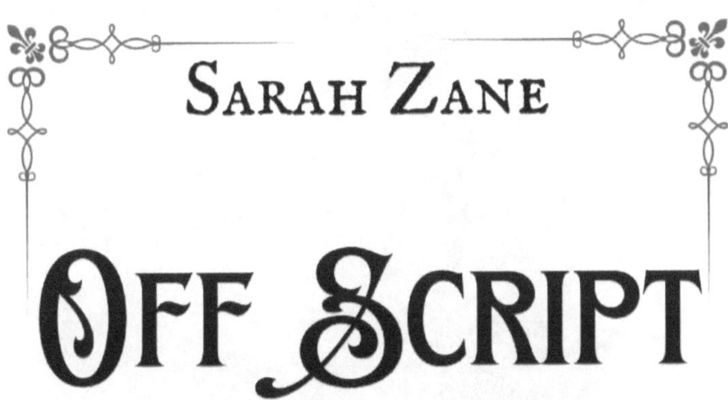

Sarah Zane

Off Script

A Book Ball Fantasy Adventure

To Jordan, Kodie, and the rest of the Books Gowns and Crowns team for making so many people's dreams come true. I'm so proud to be a part of the Books Gowns and Crowns family.

And to my bookish found family who really made this story come to life.

"Perhaps the story in the book is just the lid on a pan: It always stays the same, but underneath there's a whole world that goes on – developing and changing like our own world."

Inkheart by Cornelia Funke

PROLOGUE

I glared down at my screen, hoping the voices in my head would stop. I had just typed 'The End' and could feel Serena screaming at me about how wrong the ending was.

I had written and rewritten her story more ways than I could count, but this was the only ending that made sense, and she would have to live with it. I shook my head, trying to ignore the voices; Inez had joined her now, outraged about the ending. I was sure Tristan would have, too, had he been able.

I wondered, not for the first time, if other authors suffered at the hands of their characters like this. It didn't matter how many carefully constructed plans I laid, the characters tried to do their own thing whenever possible. They were always stubbornly going off script, and when I penned them back into submission, they wreaked havoc on my mind.

I had all but promised my characters and my readers a happy ending, and looking down at my screen, I knew I hadn't delivered.

I knew Serena and Inez's anger was me projecting how the readers would react to the ending, but the happy ending I had in mind hadn't been realistic. At the end of the previous story, Serena had been kidnapped and was being held prisoner by King Damien of Bancroft. He hadn't been able to take control of her mind yet, but with his power, it was only a matter of time, and with her fighting at his side, the duo would be unmatched.

Tristan, Inez, Draco, and Bella were supposed to band together and rescue her, but Draco wouldn't go into an unwinnable fight and would find a way to stop Bella from doing so, too. As much as it would kill him to see her hurting over the loss of her sister, it was better than burying Bella.

Inez wouldn't risk herself for the princess who broke her heart, for the friend who betrayed her by not loving her back, by choosing a prince over her. That prince, Tristan, would go to her, he would take up arms against his uncle to try to rescue Serena, but he wouldn't succeed, and he would never ever make it home.

I felt Serena's pain at the ending and Inez's outrage at the choices her character made, but it was what was meant to happen. Inez, just like the so-called friend I modeled her after, would abandon her friend the moment the friendship became inconvenient, just like Kay did to me. Inez would abandon her to her fate. She wouldn't risk her life against the nearly insurmountable odds to rescue Serena.

Serena was supposed to find her inner strength and fight back long enough for them to rescue her. She was supposed to fight him and resist the pull of his control, fight from sinking into the darkness, into the blissful quiet and peace that beckoned her. She didn't know that once she gave in to him, she would never know a moment of peace. She didn't know what she would be made to do; she only knew she was tired of fighting a battle she didn't feel she could win.

This was their ending. Whether the characters liked it or not, it was how the story was meant to end, the only way it could, with evil prevailing and sinking to new lows, doing whatever it took to win. That's the thing about villains. They're willing to do whatever it takes to get what they want. There wasn't anything Damien wouldn't do to win, no line he wouldn't cross. He was too desperate to have uncrossable lines, and that's why he was always destined to win.

I could still hear Serena's outrage and pleas for things to change and could hear Inez's creative swearing as I closed my laptop. I could only hope my readers would have more appreciation and understanding for the ending than my characters did.

ONE

I screamed so loud I was sure the neighbors had heard. My phone fell out of my hand and went crashing to the floor. I should have worried they might call the cops, but I couldn't bring myself to care.

Could this be real? I had just been checking my email, more out of habit than any positive expectation, and there it was. Filed in with the junk mail, there was an email from "Kodie". It sounded vaguely familiar, but I couldn't place the name. I would have remembered that unique spelling. It was probably actually junk, after all. I glanced at the subject line and saw, **You've been invited...**

It had to be junk mail. I was wasting my time; I knew I was, but there was something about ellipses that I just couldn't ignore. So I did the unthinkable and clicked on the message. I couldn't have been more surprised by what I read than if it had been spam.

"Sadie Hawthorne, you've been selected as a featured author for the upcoming Books, Gowns, and Crowns event in Portland, Oregon. Congratulations! Get your gown and crown ready for a weekend of books, fairytales, whimsy, and a touch of magic."

That was when I had started screaming.

I couldn't believe it! I had applied months ago, the moment I heard about the event, but I hadn't been chosen. I had forgotten I was even on a waitlist. With everything going on lately, it hadn't crossed my mind in the past few weeks. I had been religiously checking my email until I finally gave up hope. But here it was. I skimmed the email again searching for the date. It was only a few weeks away!

I glanced down at the manuscript I had been editing, and closed the tab. The manuscript would have to wait. Instead, I pulled up a search for plane tickets.

I would have to cross the country in a few weeks for this, which meant a plane and a hotel that I couldn't afford, all to probably sell a few measly books, but I couldn't turn down this opportunity. I had been so excited about it and I owed it to myself to go; to experience this once in a lifetime magical opportunity.

It wasn't like I had many other demands on my social or professional calendar. Even my family was getting sick of me lately. It wasn't my fault. They always asked how I was doing, and I'm nothing if not honest. They always asked but never seemed to want to actually know.

At least the next time someone called, I'd have some good news for once. It felt like I hadn't had anything positive to say in months. It was crazy to think about how this time, a couple of years ago, I would have been calling my best friend about the news. We would have been jumping up and down screaming and she would've boughten herself a ticket immediately to be there to support me. She had always been the first one to volunteer to go to the coffee shops with me to do writing sprints, the first one to talk me through the frustrating plot holes, and to hype me up when my anxiety or depression got too bad. When I felt at my worst, she was always there.

Now it was just me.

That's a tad over dramatic. I had people who cared about me and friends that were willing to listen if I needed them, but it wasn't the same. I missed her more than I'd like to admit. Realistically, my life wasn't going all that bad, but that's the thing about depression and anxiety. It doesn't matter how good things are when your brain continually harasses you with the thought that they are about to get worse.

Objectively, I had a lot of things going for me. I had been relatively successful as a self-published indie author, and I had a few fans who were ever so patiently waiting for the end to Serena's story. Yes, it wasn't the success that I had dreamed about when I was a little girl who wanted to be a famous actress by day and a famous author by night, but I was getting by. I had quickly thrown out the actress dream; it was never for me, but the dream of being an author had stuck with me.

I wasn't a famous author by any means; I hadn't hit any of the bestselling lists and didn't have hordes of fans, but I was a published author, which I had to admit was a huge accomplishment I never thought I would reach. I was incredibly privileged to have even made it this far, but I was struggling with how to bring the story to an end, especially since my best friend wasn't around to talk to about it. I had written and rewritten the final 100 pages over and over again and nothing felt right. I had been set on giving Serena a happy ending; I wanted it so badly for her, but it just wasn't working.

I glanced at the email again and looked over the details. A few minutes later, the thought hit me that I would have to face my fans and readers, assuming anyone even knew who I was. I would have to face them all, and I was sure everyone would ask when the ending was coming and what was next for Serena.

I wish I knew.

That would hardly be an acceptable answer. I needed to get back to work. I sighed, turned back to my manuscript, and rolled up my sleeves. Maybe this would give me the motivation I needed. I doubted it, but I hoped it would.

TWO

The first thing I saw when I exited the plane to the airport terminal was a "Keep Portland Weird" poster. I couldn't help the chuckle that escaped my lips. I still couldn't believe I was here. That I had flown across the country for a book signing. The whole situation felt wild to me, and I couldn't wait to explore Portland.

I couldn't wait to meet the girls I'd be exploring it with. I was nervous, but also excited.

We had been talking for a month or so, since I found out I was going and started looking for others that were, too. They were also going alone and wanted to meet up. Conveniently, their planes arrived around the same time as mine, so we planned to meet up at baggage claim.

Now that I was here, I realized there were a few problems with that plan. The first being, I had only ever seen a single picture of each of them. If they were real, and I don't know why they would have gone to the trouble of making fake profiles for this, then would I even recognize them? How would we know each other? We should have arranged some sort of meeting point. I mean, we did, but it should have been somewhere more specific than just "at baggage claim". We should have coordinated what color to wear or even shared what we would be wearing. I was worried about not finding them, but equally worried about finding them, for different reasons. What if they were disappointed by me? What if they arranged the meeting because they wanted a fancy author friend and then were disappointed that I was just me? Disappointed that I was as ordinary as I am. With a sigh, I couldn't help but think I didn't have the best track record for keeping friendships. I would probably disappoint them eventually, anyway. It was probably better to get it over with.

I had been too lost in thought to notice the luggage conveyor belt had started running. As luck would have it, when I glanced down, I saw both of my bags headed my way. I breathed a sigh of relief. Things were going pretty well in Portland so far.

A few minutes later, having secured my bags, I headed to the other side of baggage claim, searching for the others.

My eyes roamed aimlessly over my fellow travelers, looking for someone familiar. There was a pretty girl who I thought might have been Hanna, but was too tall. There was a spectacled man who looked like an old history teacher of mine, but it wasn't him, and it wasn't a helpful observation. There were a couple of girls who looked like sisters who could possibly be going to the event based on the book one of them was holding, but neither looked familiar, so I kept searching.

I did a double take when I saw *him*. It wouldn't be dramatic to say I had to check to make sure I wasn't drooling; it was that bad. He must have stood around 6-feet tall, with dark hair and darker eyes. He was wearing a full three-piece suit, charcoal black, and his patent leather shoes were shiny enough I noticed from over fifty feet away. His forearms strained against his jacket, and I couldn't help but wonder what he would look like without the shirt on.

When my eyes settled on his face for a slightly longer moment, I noticed he was staring at me. My face flushed deeply when I noticed his smirk, but my heart stopped cold at the look in his eyes. He was gorgeous, drop dead, could-get-anyone-to-do-anything-he-pleased-and-they-would-thank-him-for-it handsome, but there was something about those eyes. A moment later, I realized with a shiver what it was. He reminded me of Damien, the Murderous King of Bancroft, quite possibly one of the worst villains I had written to this day. Well, the only villain I had written so far, but he was one of the worst I had been able to imagine. Yes, there was more to him than met the eye, but it was buried down deep, way, way deep, certainly deeper than the bodies he'd buried.

He had his reasons, but some of the things he had done weren't things a person usually came back from. I had been debating a lot whether he deserved any sort of redemption. When I started the series, I hadn't thought he would get one, but as I'd written more, I noticed I had been softening him. The readers were intrigued by him, and that intrigue had caused me to change directions with a few of his more evil scenes. He had been evil without cause, deranged without boundaries. Some people were just evil, and I had meant him to be one. There's nothing more frightening to me than what he started out as, a man who hurts for pleasure, a man who can't be reasoned with, a man so powerful he can take away your will, a man so gorgeous he can take away your breath and will to fight him, a man so strong he could overpower you without needing his powers. I had debated long and hard just how evil I would let him get and where his boundaries were, and even I still didn't know.

The way the light danced in this man's eyes and the casual curve of his smirk screamed cruel power to me. My thoughts were spiraling in every which direction. *Run!* part of me was screaming. I trembled as I heard another part of me demanding, *Bow before him, crawl to him, beg him.*

I shook my head, violently trying to force the thoughts from my brain. What was wrong with me? I'd always been demisexual. I didn't have thoughts like this about strangers, ever. Yes, I was also bisexual, but when I was interested in someone, I preferred women. So what was it about this man? What was wrong with me?

I was being crazy. He was just a normal, exceptionally well dressed, incredibly handsome business man. Just not something I was used to seeing since I didn't spend much time in cities. I fought my legs to stay still, not knowing which way my brain was urging them to go, just knowing they had a strong compulsion to move. Not knowing if I would move toward him. I was drawn to him in a way I couldn't explain, in a way I didn't understand, or if I would turn the other way and move as far from him as I could, like my good sense was telling me to do. But this wasn't one of my stories. I was in a crowded airport in a strange city, so I wouldn't do either of those things. What I was going to do was ignore him and find the girls I was meeting.

When I glanced back in his direction, I blinked in surprise. The man had come closer and his smile had widened into a full out grin. As I tore my eyes from his, I noticed his grin falter.

Out of the corner of my eye, I saw a stunning blonde saunter up to him. I turned back, out of curiosity, I told myself, and watched him. In place of the grin was a full-blown scowl. His eyes didn't leave mine. He tried to step away from her, but she matched his step. He still didn't spare her a glance, continuing to stare at me. I couldn't fathom why when a beautiful woman was right in front of him. It wasn't that I considered myself not to be beautiful. I was in my own right, but I wasn't even remotely interested in that man. Yes, he was handsome and pleasing to look at, like those muscled actors in the superhero movies, but I wasn't even remotely interested in him, and it appeared she was, but he couldn't have been less interested in her, which was a big contrast to the way he had been staring at me.

I couldn't help feeling some amusement at his annoyance. Not that it was his fault his attention had made me so uncomfortable, but I was glad it was over.

I continued to search for the girls, having no idea how I was ever going to find them when I saw a shock of dyed red hair, and then noticed the small homemade poster board in her hands that said, **BGC!** I broke into a grin as I saw a couple of other girls behind her, one of whom was wearing a crown. That was one way to find people. Even as I chuckled to myself, I was relieved they had thought of it. I made my way over to them. The girl with the sign and the mermaid red hair had turned back around and was talking to the others. I had to applaud her forethought. That she not only had the idea to make the sign, but that she actually did it. I knew we were going to get along. I was normally the organized one. My anxiety made it necessary.

I slowed my approach when I was almost at their group. None of them had noticed me, but I was pretty sure I knew the girl in the crown. With her straight black hair and large glasses, it had to be Hanna. That would make the blonde head of curls Sabrina, her best friend. I was only stumped about the redhead. I hadn't gotten a good look at her before she turned around, but no one I had been talking to had red hair, dyed or otherwise. It wasn't Mirabelle with her warm brown skin and dark curls. She had Eve's pale coloring, but Eve was drying her hair dark for the ball. Hanna and Sabrina must have had another friend. I closed the remaining distance between myself and the group and waved over the mermaid hair girl's shoulder to who I was hoping were Hanna and Sabrina.

Hanna saw me first. "Sadie?"

"Hanna?"

We both broke out into grins. She sped past the redhead and, before I could blink, threw her arms around me. I was startled that she was my height. At 5-feet even, I was used to having to look up at people, and she might have had an inch or two on me, but she was right around my eye level. I hugged her back, hoping she could feel how grateful I was at her easy acceptance. My anxiety quieted.

When she let go, she gestured to Sabrina and said, "Sadie, Sabrina, Sabrina, Sadie." She chuckled a moment. "I'm so excited you made it!"

"For real. I can't believe it's finally here!"

I saw the redhead move out of my peripheral vision and turned her way. It took a second, but then it clicked. "Eve?"

"The one and only. Don't look so shocked."

I must have not hidden my surprise. "What happened to your hair?" I blurted out.

She stared at me, confused. I saw the surprised discomfort on Sabrina's face and realized how that sounded. I paled and rushed to clarify. "I love it! I just didn't remember you dying it."

Sabrina's demeanor relaxed, and I heard before I saw Eve chuckle.

"Nice surprise, huh?"

"For sure! Loving the mermaid vibes!"

"I had to. It's a fantasy ball. I thought about cosplaying as a mermaid, but I couldn't get the pieces together in time."

Hanna chimed in, "Wait. The fit didn't come in in time? I thought you ordered it weeks ago?"

"I did! It should've been here in plenty of time. I made sure of it before ordering it, but here we are."

"That sucks, but I'm sure you'll rock whatever else you brought."

"Thanks, guys!"

I glanced around and noticed the baggage claim area was thinning out. "Are we waiting for anyone else?" I asked.

"I think we're the only ones getting in now."

I thought Mirabelle was supposed to be here by now, too, though.

"What about Mira?" I asked.

"She got in a little earlier and was exhausted so she already went to the hotel. She sent her apologies, but we'll see her soon, anyway," Eve explained.

That was true enough, and now I wouldn't have to worry about checking in.

When I found out I was coming, I had gone onto the event group searching for a roommate to help reduce the cost. That's how I found Mira. She was so excited for me as a new ball author and even offered to help me out with setting up shop the day of the convention. I had been a little nervous about getting a roommate in the first place, but she seemed really nice. On the quieter side, but from the little interaction I'd had with her over text, I liked her. I was excited to meet her.

As we headed in the general direction of the ground transportation, I looked around my little group I had stumbled on. Hanna had linked arms with Sabrina and was talking excitedly about the book she had been reading on the plane. I made a mental book to bring it up with them later since I heard them mention Jordan A. Day.

She was one of my favorite authors, an idol of mine, and had been ever since she published her first book as an indie author and took the world by storm. She was an indie author legend; what most indies aspired to be. *A Ripple of Power and Promise* was an incredible story of finding yourself, love, and acceptance. The trio, Ainsley, Dash, and Felix, were all loveable characters flawed in their own way. Their personalities leapt off the page at you in a way that's rare for stories. She had built herself a massive following of people that had fallen in love with her characters, especially Felix. He was a crowd favorite.

I had been dying to meet Jordan, but she hadn't done any events near me. I still couldn't believe there was a rumor floating around that she might be attending. The event was pretty much in her honor, being loosely modeled after the royal balls in Disparya. The event coordinators had been dropping hints and teasing that she might come, but nothing had been confirmed. I hoped beyond hope that she would be there, but I didn't think it was likely.

I noticed Eve had been watching them, too. I smiled over at her and we fell into conversation about Jordan's stories. They had meant something different to all of us, but we were all brought together, all here, because of it. It was crazy that any single story could have that kind of effect over such a big group of people. She had a following that other authors dreamed of replicating. If I could have a quarter of the admiration for my books as Jordan did for hers, I would consider myself incredibly blessed and successful. That was a big part of why I came this weekend, besides the allure of going to a real life ball, and why I wrote my book in the first place. I wanted to put my story out there and give readers a chance to fall in love with my characters as much as I already had.

I couldn't express how excited and grateful I was for Eve when she turned the conversation to my book and asked me about it. I talked poor Eve's ear off the entire way to the hotel, with only a brief intermission to say goodbye for now to Hanna and Sabrina. They were staying around the corner from us, which was an incredibly exciting revelation now that I had met them and knew I enjoyed their company. By the time I said goodbye to Eve and got off the elevator on my floor, I felt even more excited about the weekend. All my earlier nerves were gone, and the excitement had magnified.

I wasn't even nervous anymore about meeting my disappearing roommate, Mira. If she was anything like the other girls, I knew I was going to love her.

THREE

Damien

I had been wandering around aimlessly for the last day without anything answering the tendrils of power I sent out searching for *her*. Everything hinged on me finding her quickly, and I wouldn't fail.

When my spies told me that cursed meddling Fairy was sending the royal guard outside of Zanaria for help, I knew I had to do something. They weren't able to give me a full report, weren't able to get close enough to that damned Fairy to hear more. I debated punishing them for their shortcomings, but decided it wouldn't increase their efficiency. When I snapped at them to leave my presence until they had something useful, one of them added that he had heard mention of a sorceress, one with a power the likes of which had never been seen. I snapped at that. He couldn't possibly mean to suggest she was more powerful than me. I knew there must have been beings outside of the Six Realms whose power matched my own, but to have one of my spies suggest the same was borderline treasonous. If he didn't watch his mouth, I would be forced to punish him.

Fortunately for him, he hit the floor immediately and started groveling. My spies and court had learned long ago the quickest way to defuse my anger was to worship me. They thought I enjoyed it. The truth was, it disgusted me that they had so little backbone. I would have walked all over them anyway, of course, but the fact that they let me without me so much as having to raise a finger or an eyebrow in their direction was disgusting. No wonder the kingdom was a laughingstock. The name of Bancroft should strike fear in the hearts of people, like my name did. Instead, our kingdom was slowly turning into a kingdom of brainless, spineless people who would bow to any power without being forced. There was no loyalty anymore.

It hadn't always been like this, but without Cass, I had gone off the deep end. Each day that passed without him by my side, my heart grew a little darker and my morals a little looser. I was quicker to use my power than I ever had been. That was part of what bothered me so much about my subjects being so willing to follow my every whim. There was no one to use my powers on. With no one to practice on, I was worried I might get rusty. I had thought about forcing people to act out so they could be punished and forced back in line, but so far, I hadn't acted on the thought. I hadn't had thoughts that dark in a long time, since he was first taken.

That first week had been the worst. I had never taken a life until then. I could still feel the blood on my hands, see the bodies as they stacked up. But I couldn't stop myself and wouldn't even if I could have. His screams were ringing in my ears, blocking out any rational part of me. I tried to fight my way to him, but I couldn't harness my power enough to control enough of the army. My powers required concentration and focus, and the only thing I could focus on was the fear in my husband's eyes when they took him. He should have been able to fight them on his own. He was perfectly capable, strong and powerful, in every way my equal. If possible, he might have been stronger than me. So it was still a mystery how they had gotten him in the first place and how they had managed to get that far into our lands before we got word of it.

I saw them inject him with something and saw him writhing and screaming in pain until they carried him off. I was lethal; death incarnate. I slaughtered every soul that came my way, but they kept coming. I wasn't getting any closer and had to watch as he stopped screaming and slumped over. He had to be okay; he had to. I would brutally slaughter anyone who had even glanced at him if he wasn't.

I was struggling to breathe, but redoubled my efforts, feeling more and more frantic the further away they got, but waves and waves of soldiers kept coming. By the time they had stopped, he was out of my sight. I stormed the forest, sending out my power tendrils, searching for any sign of him, but there was none. His power hadn't answered mine. That had never happened before.

I broke, falling to my knees in the middle of the forest, sobbing. I swore that day I would do whatever it took. I would see my husband again and I would get to the bottom of our betrayal if I had to torture and kill everyone in the Six Realms to do it. Since that day I had kept my oath, doing whatever it took to get him back, but I wasn't any closer to finding and saving him than I had been the three long years ago when it happened. I had begged my brother on my knees for his help, only for him to turn me away when I told him it was Altea I was asking him to stand against. Whether he didn't believe me, or didn't care, I couldn't say. What I could say was that he was dead to me. He was no family of mine.

Had the positions been reversed, I would have torn the Realms apart with him to help him get his wife back. I had always admired him, and couldn't believe my older brother would see me that torn apart and not lift a finger to help, but he didn't. Without Cass, I was the sole ruler of Bancroft, and I swore I would have vengeance on him and his kingdom after I had my husband back. He would pay for not helping me. I swore to it. I tried many times to infiltrate Altea to find Cass, but the borders seemed to be fortified against magic. I wasn't able to make myself appear inside, and the moment I crossed the border, the castle was alerted and a contingent of guards was sent, which proved to be more of an annoyance than usual to deal with without my powers. I tried several times before deciding I needed a new tactic. I sent messages to the castle asking their terms, all of which went unanswered. I sent spies, none of which returned.

After one failure after another, I came up with a new plan. I couldn't use my powers there, but I could use them elsewhere. I thought about going back to Somerset and forcing my brother to help, but I thought I might slaughter him on sight. Besides, as formidable as his army was, it was nothing compared to hers. Nothing compared to the power she held.

The power her realm held was indescribable. She was always one step ahead of me and I didn't have the first clue how. Without Cass, Altea was stronger than Bancroft. I needed allies. Miravale wasn't strong enough to be of use and was too vain to help willingly, which left Sherbrooke and the Fairy Queen.

If I could somehow get the Fairy on my side, if we could work together, Altea wouldn't stand a chance. I had tried everything else and nothing had worked, so I turned my full attention to Sherbrooke. I needed a foolproof plan and after the rumors floating around the Six Realms of my brutality toward Altea, conveniently leaving out that she had kidnapped my husband and was doing the gods knew what to him, I doubted anyone would help. My own brother hadn't.

The worst of it was that there was a rumor floating around that I had killed Cass myself in order to gain full control of the kingdom. I had killed the spy who told me that on the spot. I felt a twinge of guilt about that after. It hadn't been his fault, but I had been so blindsided by it, I couldn't control myself. The flames had shot out of my hand and before I noticed, he was alight with green flames, screaming. The piercing screams brought back those of my husband and I couldn't stand it, so I threw a dagger, landing it straight through his heart. I just needed him to shut up so I could think.

By the time I came to my senses, I had a dead spy on my hands and blood and ash all over my throne room floor. I called someone to take care of it and sent condolences in the form of gold to his family. I knew it was a sorry replacement, but it felt too coldhearted to do nothing.

I'd like to think if it had been another one of my men that I would have hesitated more, but he was one of the men stationed in the Altean court and should have known about their plans before they moved to take him.

We should have known before it happened. His failure was the reason I had to sleep alone night after night. The reason I cried myself hoarse every night until finally sleep claimed me, only to wake and do it all over again the next day. It was a miracle really that I had waited so long to end his sorry little life. A blessing to his family that they had gotten a few more months with him. He clearly hadn't been up to the task of handling the Altean Queens, and his failure haunted me every day.

My next move against them wouldn't, couldn't, fail. They had already had him for three years. The gods know what tortures he was subjected to. I didn't even really know if he was still alive, but I had to assume that I would have felt it if he had died. I hoped I would know.

I was still functioning, so he had to be okay. It would have destroyed my soul if he died. I couldn't be fighting for nothing. They had him; they had to have a reason for that. The Queens couldn't have just wanted him dead. If that had been the goal, they wouldn't have taken him. They had to have a motive, a goal, but all my letters went unanswered. It seemed they weren't willing to negotiate. What kind of person took a hostage without making any sort of demands for their release? I had no idea what their plan was, just that I had to get him back before they had time to make things worse. So I turned my eye to Sherbrooke and the Fairy. I focused my spies on finding out how to get a foothold in the queendom.

All the reports told me how suspicious the Fairy was about outsiders, men specifically. She and her wife, the other Queen, kept to themselves. The only promising thing they were able to uncover was that the Queens had a daughter. From the reports, I knew she was twenty-five and surmised they would be looking for suitable matches, ways to improve their realm's status through her.

I didn't relish the idea of a union when my husband was out there somewhere waiting for me, but I felt like he would understand. I would do what was necessary for him. I would stop at nothing to save him. If I had to seduce the Fairy's daughter and charm the whole gods damned queendom to get myself on the throne and get the Fairy's help, I would. Whatever it took.

Only the Fairy's daughter wasn't nearly as easy a target as I had expected. To my amazement, I was able to charm the Queen, but not her. Even the Fairy fell under my spell to some extent, but not the princess.

I resorted to flirting and trying to win her over the old-fashioned way, but she wasn't susceptible to that either. What was so special about her? My magic had never failed me before, neither had my natural charm. What made her impervious to all my advances, I couldn't imagine, but one way or another, I had to have her. I had to have the damned Fairy's help. Having Sherbrooke behind me, I could finally make a move against Altea and their ever-growing army.

Even since they took Cass, it seemed like she had doubled or tripled her army, which was particularly impressive because I had killed my way through a good chunk of it that day. How she continued to be able to replace her soldiers, I didn't know. I didn't care. I knew with Sherbrooke, Bancroft, the Fairy's magic, and my own, she didn't stand a chance. I would level her castle and take back my husband, but I underestimated the princess.

One moment, I was entering her chambers to continue working on her, the next, I woke with a full grown beard and stiff, sore muscles. I used my magic to find her location, because her or that damned Fairy had to be behind this.

When I found her and appeared behind her, I was surprised to see we were in the middle of a battlefield with creatures the likes of which I had never seen before. Seeing her friends were the only ones left standing, I didn't ask questions before grabbing her and transporting her back to my fortress, figuring there would be plenty of time to get answers out of her there.

When I landed back at the fortress, I almost collapsed in the throne room with her in my arms. After her shock wore off a minute later, she started fighting me in earnest. I barely had the strength to contain her. I called for my guards. They came rushing in and grabbed her; it took four of them to secure her well enough to move her from the room. I had them take her to the tower in the East Wing and lock her in. I needed some rest and to replenish my strength before dealing with her.

It took a full week of bed rest for my strength to return.

When it did, I sought her out, searching for answers. I found out from my guards and informants that the whole queendom of Sherbrooke had fallen under a sleeping curse—myself included—and that we had slept for almost a full year. No wonder I was so useless when I woke up. I had wondered why my powers barely worked and why my body felt like it was betraying me.

When I was about to make my way to her chamber, one of my spies rushed in with news of a mist falling over the land and wrecking havoc in its wake. There were reports of it taking memories of those who entered it, but the reports were sparse. Only a select few remembered what happened well enough to talk about it.

Another burst in with news from Sherbrooke that the captain of the guard and the Fairy were cooking up some sort of scheme to get Serena back. He had heard enough of the spell to tell me that the captain had to offer up her most prized possession to make it work. I knew from experience that was strong magic. He said they had found a sorceress that could change their fate but didn't know much else. Good-for-nothing spies couldn't even catch the relevant information.

I went to my study. I should have known I had to do everything myself. I took out my scrying glass. It usually took more power to work than it was worth, so I only used it on rare occasions. This was one of them. I could only hope it would be more helpful this time than it had been when I had continually asked it to show me Cass or where he was, or for any news of him. Nothing ever showed up, but I refused to give up hope. If he was no longer alive, it would have shown me his body. It was almost like he was somewhere else entirely, out of its sight. It didn't matter where he was. I would find him. I would bring him back to me. I needed him.

Through the glass, I was able to see the guard and the Fairy in a magical study very much like my own, but where I liked mine dark and lit by torchlight, she seemed to prefer natural light.

I saw them over her cauldron, and saw the captain hand over an amulet after some hesitation. She didn't want to, but the Fairy said it had to be your most valuable possession. The guard asked if it was worth it. The Fairy said she was sending her somewhere outside of the Realms for help to get Serena back, to reclaim what I had stolen, and to make sure I couldn't hurt them anymore. I couldn't let her succeed, couldn't let her threaten my last remaining plan to get him back. I couldn't let anything stop me. I had to be ruthless. Everything else had failed, and I would not fail again. It had already been too long. I would do whatever it took.

That was what I told myself as I kissed my wedding ring, tears falling down my face as I sacrificed it to the cauldron, to the spell. It was just a piece of jewelry, and I would soon get my husband back. Then I could buy a thousand more rings. If that was what it took, it would be worth it.

That was what I told myself as I traipsed around the strange new world. That was what I told myself, as I was losing faith. I must have done the spell wrong. Maybe the royal guard had already returned successfully, and I wasn't even in the right place. But that couldn't be the case. I had been incredibly careful about wording the spell. I always was. The consequences of not being purposeful were unspeakable. I, of all people, would never forget that.

When I finally felt an answering call to my power, the relief nearly brought me to my knees.

I hailed a servant in a yellow horseless carriage to heed my directions.

FOUR

Damien

We arrived at a large fortress, distinct only from the rest of what these people called a city by the ample machinery driving and flying around the place and the numerous guards. I was prepared to fight my way in, if I must. I would find the sorceress. To my surprise, we weren't stopped. The servant pulled the carriage off to the side with some other carriages. As I exited, I paid the servant a few pieces of gold, enjoying the way his eyes bugged out when he saw them. Apparently, what was a mere trifle back in Zanaria, was a hefty fortune here. When I had gone to find lodging and handed over a pouch of twenty gold pieces, the standard nightly fee at any decent inn, the peasant running the place had told me to stay as long as I liked.

If I hadn't been so miserable waiting for something to answer my power, I would have likely been enjoying myself. It turns out my riches in Bancroft were nothing compared to the riches I held here. I wondered at how impoverished their king must have been compared to me.

Maybe it would pay to stay a little longer. It seemed gold talked around here.

I walked toward the least heavily guarded door, thankful I had donned less conspicuous clothing. When I arrived, I quickly noticed others didn't wear robes or leather. Once I found lodging, I questioned the peasant on where to buy new attire and purchased a few of what they referred to as suits.

Blending in made infiltrating the fortress easier. The guard at the door nodded at me before continuing to scan the area for threats. Did he not qualify me as a threat? This was far too easy. I was starting to wonder if this might be a trap. Could the sorceress know I was coming for her? Could she and the royal guard be holed up in the fortress with an army of guards? The doors were glass, and I couldn't see anyone resembling the royal guard, and there wasn't an army of guards. I would be watchful, but her power was pulling me in, calling to me. It was so like my own; it was staggering.

My power called, and hers sang in answer. I was stunned to feel the pull lead me toward a petite brunette, but then she turned her head and I saw her face. My jaw hit the floor. It couldn't be. She was safely secured in my fortress. This had to be some trick. This sorceress was more powerful than I thought, but as I watched longer, I noticed no telltale signs that an illusion was at work. Even the best left some signs, and I had never missed a sign.

The magic was buzzing all over her, radiating out a good ten feet from her. I would have to be careful. Either she hadn't used any power in a long while or was even more powerful than I had thought. I doubted even my power radiated that far out, but since I couldn't see my own, it was hard to tell for sure. However, I hadn't ever seen anyone whose power was that active and that far out from them, not even that cursed Fairy. Maybe hers would if she ever stopped using it; maybe mine would if I conserved it more.

I hadn't used much power since landing here, instead using gold to get my way. I had been saving my strength for this moment, for her. If she was anything like that cursed Fairy had said, I knew I was going to need all my strength.

As I watched her, her eyes raked over my body. Maybe this would be more fun than I thought. I hadn't been with anyone in a long while, but my husband and I had an open marriage. He would have encouraged anything that brought me any sort of joy right now. He wouldn't have wanted me to be miserable, especially when every waking and sleeping thought was a torment with him gone. If I had to win over the sorceress anyway, he would want me to have some fun with it.

When her eyes met mine, she startled, seeing me studying her. She feigned a look of innocence that had me smirking at her.

She didn't fool me for a second. I was sure she knew who I was and why I was here. She was shorter than I imagined, and a spitting image of my fiancée, Serena. I was still studying her for signs of the illusion when I noticed, really noticed, her face. My jaw dropped. She was blushing.

It had to be some trick of the light. That wasn't possible. Even the best illusionists couldn't make their borrowed faces blush. I studied her closer, but there was still no sign of an illusion. Her power still swam around her, available to her but clearly not in use. This wasn't an illusion. Gods be damned, she was my fiancée's mirror image. How was that even possible? It seemed there was more to this world than met the eye. I would have to be careful with this one, but that didn't mean I couldn't have some fun.

She was beautiful in a way that stole the hearts of most when they saw her, and she was still staring at me, her blush spreading. I cocked an eyebrow when I saw a shiver run up her spine. Did she know who I was? She certainly wasn't acting like it. Most would have run in the other direction by now. I was glad she hadn't. I wondered just what she would look like on her knees in front of me, what she would sound like screaming my name.

Not able or willing to rein myself in, I blasted her with the full force of my power, watching in surprise as only a few tendrils were able to penetrate her makeshift magical shield.

She knew what she was doing, and she did it well. The magic moved to shield her without her even appearing to manipulate it. Even I had a tell when I was using my magic. She had none. If I didn't know better, I would say she wasn't aware of her powers, but you don't get to be that powerful of a sorceress without controlling your powers.

I watched with amusement as her eyes took on a tinge of green. I was more than a bit surprised it had worked. Could it really be this easy? I would be home with this sorceress on a short leash in no time. I would have my husband back, and we would have a new plaything—the perfect welcome home present. He would love to enjoy her, especially since I hadn't planned to keep Serena. There was no need to once I had him back. Serena would be a better ally if I could influence and return her, and that would be much more easily accomplished if she remained unharmed. It was much harder to plant lasting influence in someone that feared you with good reason. I had been struggling to stay away from Serena, and gods be damned, here was my solution. Even if I had had no desire for her, her raw, untapped, untamed power called to me, so like mine, so powerful. I couldn't let that kind of advantage go. I needed her to get him back. She would leave with me.

Seeing my magic take deeper root, I redoubled my strength, throwing everything I had at her, and when I was sure I had her under my control, I sent the thoughts, the images. *Bow to me, crawl to me, beg me.*

I waited for her to drop to her knees. The amount of power I threw at her would have forced her to. Influence or not, the magic would squeeze her tiny will until she bent to mine. Her head would explode in pain if she tried to resist. There was no resistance.

A few seconds passed, and she continued to stare at me. She was more powerful than most. I was shocked she was still standing. I squeezed my power around her a little more, giving her every little bit I had left. It would take a while to recuperate, but it was now or never, and she would be mine. This whole debacle would be over before it could truly begin. She and her power would be mine and she would help me get my husband back, whether she wanted to or not.

Eventually, if she was a good enough girl and begged long and hard enough, we might find a way to send her home, but until then, we would have fun with her.

I watched her shake her head, knowing she was trying to resist and must have been experiencing crippling pain. I knew she must, but I would never know it from her face. She showed no flicker or sign of pain. She was a marvelous creature, with such power. In another life, another world, I would have surely bowed to her, but here and now, she would bow to me.

I watched as she fought her betraying body, fought to not move an inch, and was surprised she was succeeding. No one had ever resisted so long or required so much of my power. Even Serena had seemed more susceptible. I took a few steps closer to her, grinning. She would be mine, and I would enjoy every moment of breaking her strong will.

I watched her eyes flicker to me and then behind her, watched her try to run, but unable to fight how drawn to me she was. When she didn't advance toward me, I faltered for a moment before pasting my grin back on. She would not best me. She would not see me falter.

My resolve almost died when I saw her break her eyes from mine and start looking around, not wildly in panic, but casually, as if I meant nothing and wasn't worth her time.

My blood boiled, my grin faltering, and I took another step toward her. I didn't have long now until my magic faded; I wasn't strong enough in this world to hold the spell indefinitely, so I needed to act fast.

I took another couple of steps toward her, careful not to move too quickly. I didn't have enough magic left to influence any guards if their suspicion was aroused. I would have to be careful.

I caught movement out of the corner of my eye and turned my head, but it wasn't a guard, just a woman. My eyes moved back to the sorceress with my fiancée's face and I took a couple more steps only to bump into the other woman who had stepped in front of me.

I scowled at her, waiting for her to move, but she didn't. She just smiled up at me, batting her eyelashes. If she wouldn't move, I would. I stepped to my right to move past her, but she matched my step. I felt what was left of my powers fading and felt my scowl deepen.

I didn't pay her mind. I only had eyes for the sorceress. Her eyes locked on mine confirmed my fears. The lingering green in her eyes was gone. I had hoped this would be the end of it, but it certainly wouldn't be the last she saw of me. The moment I regained my strength, I would return for her.

For now, I needed to get back to my hideout before anything happened. I was always careful never to completely drain my magic, always to leave a reserve there until I could get somewhere safe, but I had gotten carried away.

A hand on my arm broke my focus. I readied myself for a fight, expecting it was a guard, but it was just the other woman. She was blonde and taller than the sorceress, I was sure others would consider her a beauty, but there wasn't a single trace of power coming from her, only a seductive smile.

"Hi there, handsome." Her eyes roamed over me. "I couldn't help but notice you from across the room."

I huffed at her, regretting I didn't have the power left to make her go away. "And I couldn't help but notice you're in my way." I snarled, turning on my heel and making my way as quickly as I dared to the exit, watching for an ambush from any angle, but, thankfully, none came. As I passed through the glass doors, I glanced back at the sorceress one more time and saw her moving further away from me. I would be back for her. I would do whatever it took.

FIVE

Sadie

I was right. I absolutely loved Mira. She was so easy to talk to. We ended up staying up much later than we should have, getting to know each other and talking about our favorite books.

I was exhausted the next day, but couldn't bring myself to regret it. Thankfully, today was a more relaxing day. We had made plans to meet back up with Sabrina, Hanna, and Eve to explore Portland. None of us had ever been, and we were all looking forward to it. I was mostly excited about having friends to explore it with. People, not friends. I had to correct myself. Happy to have people to explore it with. Happy to not be going alone. They weren't friends of mine. They hardly knew me, and if they really did, I doubted they would like what they saw.

We were all planning to meet up for brunch at a cute place Hanna had found around the corner from our hotels. I, unfortunately, woke early and couldn't fall back asleep, so instead of lying in bed, I got ready and went to explore the hotel. It wasn't a large place, but I had seen a gift shop in the lobby that I wanted to check out. I left our room and headed to the lobby, but the elevator made me do a double take. It was roughly eight in the morning and instead of the soft, calming elevator music I had expected, there was techno music blaring from the speakers at a volume a few notches too high to be considered comfortable. It was the last thing I expected, and I couldn't help but think of the sign I had seen at the airport.

Chuckling to myself, I said under my breath, "Way to keep it weird, Portland."

In the light of day, the lobby and the gift shop were just as weird. The lobby itself was pretty standard with a check-in desk, a valet desk, and a couch. The couch caught my attention, being much bigger than hotels usually had. It was an oversized sectional with twelve pillows arranged on it in a slightly diagonal manner.

I cringed at the thought of anyone sitting there and disturbing the perfectly placed pillows. It was clear someone had gone through some effort to do that. Likely, they were disturbed daily and someone meticulously fixed them after every time they had been moved. But it was a nice touch.

The real odd thing was the oversized desk lamp that hung over the couch. The lamp base itself stood at about 10-feet tall and the lamp head was at least 3-feet wide. It was comically out of place with the nice couch and meticulously arranged pillows.

The gift shop was clearly run by the same person who picked out the lamp. In the middle of the shop was a bicycle, for no apparent reason. It wasn't clear whether it was a statue or functional, but it was clear it wasn't for sale. The gift shop was a hipster's fantasy, selling mainly locally crafted beer, locally made vegan ice cream, dog bandanas, Bigfoot Magnets, Keep Portland Weird bumper stickers, and novelty socks.

The socks caught my attention; I'd always loved weird-patterned socks. I never wore matching socks because it was too hard to pick which pattern or color to wear that day. Why wear one when I could wear two? I had too many socks as it was, but

I kept buying them. I was looking at a pair with French bulldogs in hipster glasses all over them, when I heard someone at the front desk asking where the nearest bookstore was.

I couldn't help but look over. In fact, I was considering going over to let them know that the biggest bookstore in the states, Powell's City of Books, was only a few blocks away, but the words died on my tongue when I saw who it was.

It was Jordan A. Day! I couldn't believe that she was here, and I was standing maybe fifty feet from her! I couldn't believe no one else was around to witness it. I needed to go talk to her, but I needed to pull myself together first.

I was a real author, too. I couldn't make a fool out of myself. I might not feel like a real author most of the time, but I didn't want her to know that. I wanted her to care about meeting me. I didn't want to be just another big fan. I turned back to the socks I had been looking at. I didn't want her first impression of me to be that I was the creep in the lobby who kept staring at her, but I couldn't help it. I took a couple of deep breaths and steeled myself to talk to her. I was ready, but before I could move, I heard the revolving door move.

I turned quickly with a feeling of dread, knowing before I did what I would see. The lobby was empty again. Well, not empty. There was an older woman who seemed vaguely familiar standing over by the couch.

I glanced at my phone and saw that I had twenty more minutes until Mira and Eve should be coming down. I glanced in the woman's direction again, trying to figure out why she looked so familiar. She smiled warmly at me when she caught me studying her. I noticed she was holding a copy of one of Agatha Toller's books. I almost skipped over to her when I saw that. Agatha was a pretty well-known author, but the book the woman was holding, in addition to being Agatha's least known book, was also by far my favorite.

Mira and Eve were going to have to drag me away from this woman to make it to brunch in time. Assuming she was holding the book because she had read it and loved it as much as I did, if it was up to me, I could have been there all day talking about it. I never understood why the story was so underrated. It was about a travelling renaissance fair that held more mystery, wonder, and magic than met the eye. The story's premise was incredible, but the mythical creatures and characters really made the story. The characters were lovably flawed and perfectly written. Their personalities sprung off the page, but my favorite thing about her stories were the representation.

Her stories held a special place in my heart as being the first sapphic books I consumed. As a long-closeted woman, it was revolutionary to see myself represented in her stories. She helped me to learn to accept myself and be okay with who I was and her story inspired me to come out myself.

Now I wrote exclusively LGBTQ literature. That's not to say the female main characters never end up with men, just that the majority of the characters in my stories aren't strictly straight. I enjoy writing queer characters and it's been a nice niche that I have formed for myself. Besides, they tell you to write what you know, so I do. While my characters are usually all queer, they sometimes end up in straight passing relationships, like my main character Serena and her love interest Tristan. They embody the character tropes of the bisexual girl and her gamer boy/golden retriever boyfriend. Serena resents people thinking she might be straight and is quick to set the record straight whenever someone makes that incorrect assumption.

My writing, in addition to being inspired by the goddess who just left the hotel, was largely inspired by Agatha's work. The woman was still smiling when I approached her.

I didn't know how to start, so I simply pointed at the book and said, "I've read it a million times and am absolutely obsessed with it. I've been dying to talk to someone who's read it. Tell me you've read it? What's your favorite part?"

She let out a warm laugh. My smile brightened at the sound. "Well, dear, it's so hard to play favorites."

"But you've read it?" I pressed.

"More than any person probably should have or would ever want to."

"I might have your record beat. It's one of my top comfort reads, right up there with Pride and Prejudice and Jordan A. Day's stories. My copy got so worn out I had to buy two others. I've been trying to get my hands on a signed copy but haven't had any luck."

With a twinkle in her eye, she said, "Well, dear, this is your lucky day."

"What?"

"I can get you a signed copy."

I stared at her in disbelief. I gestured at her hands. "You can't mean that copy is signed?" I didn't add what else I was thinking, but I'm sure she read the implied, "And you can't really mean you would give it to me," in my eyes.

"Not yet, it isn't, but yes, I mean to give it to you. I have more of these than I know what to do with."

She was such a sweet woman. I couldn't help but smile at her generosity. "That's too kind of you, but I really couldn't take that from you. Besides," I added sheepishly, "I have a few copies already, but if you get your hands on a signed copy you're trying to get rid of, I'm your girl."

She tilted her head to the side and stared at me for a moment. I couldn't understand her reaction. When she spoke again, she spoke slower. "I think you misunderstand me. I have every intention of giving you this book, signed, personalized even if you would like."

Now it was my turn to be confused. "I thought it wasn't signed?"

"It isn't."

"But it's going to be?"

"Yes. I will make sure it is before I give it to you."

I took a breath before asking, "You can't mean you know Agatha? That she's here?"

She burst out into laughter. If this was her idea of a joke, it was a cruel, weird one. It took her a while for her to catch her breath. I tried to hide my annoyance, but I wasn't sure I succeeded.

She smiled apologetically at me. "I'm sorry, dearie, I thought you knew. I knew I was getting older, but I thought I might still be recognizable."

She flipped the book over and held it up to her face. I still didn't get it. I scanned the blurb and the about the author section until my eyes halted on the author photo. I squinted at it. There were fewer wrinkles, and the face was more youthful, but the eyes were the same striking blue and the nose was the same. But it couldn't be. I looked back and forth between the woman standing in front of me and the photo. It couldn't be, but maybe...

"You don't mean you're..."

"Agatha, yes; it's me. Pleased to meet you, my dear."

I couldn't decide whether to be more excited or embarrassed. A deep blush stole over my face as I shook the hand she offered.

"Sadie Hawthorne, a newbie author and your biggest fan."

She smiled again. "I suspect besides myself, you're probably the person who knows this particular story the best in the world."

"I am so, so sorry, Mrs. Toller. I can't believe I didn't know you were you. I'm so, so sorry."

She waved off my apology. "It's Agatha, dear, and don't worry another minute about it. I should have known I'm not quite as recognizable as I used to be. But here, I was going to give this to a friend of mine I was meeting for coffee, but she'll understand. Even if she loved it, it wouldn't mean nearly as much to her as it would to you. Just let me get a pen." She rifled through her purse. I hoped with everything in me that she had one. I would beg, borrow, and steal to get a signed copy of this book. I had never dared to dream I might have the honor of meeting her and getting a signed copy. This, by far, made up for my blunder with Jordan earlier. Although I would be lying if I said I still didn't hope to meet her. She pulled her hand out of her bag with a triumphant grin. "I knew it was in there!"

I still couldn't believe this was happening.

She opened the book and touched the crisp page. It was a brand-new copy. I hadn't seen a new copy of the book in years. "Can I write what I want, or did you have something in mind?"

Something in mind? I had never dared to even dream it might be possible for this to have been happening.

"Please, just write whatever you would like. I'm just thrilled to have met you. The book is icing on the cake."

She smiled knowingly at me, and I knew she saw right through me. Yes, it was amazing to meet her, but the real prize was the signed book that was now going to be one of, if not my most prized possession.

She had propped the book up against the wall and was signing it there.

"You don't want to sit down while you're doing that?" I gestured to the sofa.

She considered a moment, her expression unreadable. "Do I look that old that I shouldn't be standing?" I felt my palms go sweaty and my heart race as I rushed to find something to say, but a second later, she winked at me. A relieved laugh came out of me. "I'm sorry, dearie. I can't help it sometimes. But no, I took one look at those pillows and knew I didn't want to wreck them."

That's it; she was my new favorite author. She might even have become my new favorite person. I highly doubted many other people would have noticed the pillow arrangements and felt any sort of guilt about messing them up by using the couch as it was intended to be used.

A minute later, she finished with a flourish and handed it to me. I was dying to see what was written inside, but it felt rude somehow to read it in front of her, so I kept it closed and held it close to my chest.

"Thank you so, so much. You have no idea how much this means to me."

"Always happy to meet a fan, especially a colleague. Do you have a card or something so I can find your book later?"

I couldn't believe how nice she was. I quickly found one of my business cards in my purse and handed it to her sheepishly. "You don't have to. Just you being nice to me was enough to make my year."

She laughed at that, and I watched her eyes move over my card that described my series. "This sounds wonderful! Take care not to sell yourself short, my dear. Plenty of people will do that for you already. It's okay to take up room and to be proud of your work."

I started to tear up and couldn't find words. Before I knew it, I had launched myself at her and folded her into a hug.

She let out a startled gasp, quickly followed by a chuckle as she wrapped her arms around me, returning the hug.

When I pulled away from her, she asked, "This story of yours, I think my granddaughter would like it; is it spicy?"

I blushed. She wrote clean fantasy, and I had wanted to impress her. I hated having to tell her it was spicy. I didn't want her to think less of me or my story, but I wouldn't lie to her. I couldn't imagine her horror if she gave her granddaughter my books, only to find out they were too spicy for her.

"They do have some heat, relatively low heat, but probably only recommended for ages 16 and up."

"Well, probably best not to get them for her then. No one wants spicy book recs from their grandmother."

The mental image of my dear sweet grandmother reading or gifting or recommending a spicy book to me was enough to bring tears to my eyes.

When she caught her breath, she added, "Better not do that. I'll just have to keep this one to myself then." She slipped the card into her purse. "Hopefully, I'll see you again so I can get a signed copy."

"I'm actually in town for a convention and have some copies on me if-"

"Books Gowns and Crowns?"

"Yes! You've heard of it?"

"Heard of it? I'll be there, too."

"What?! There's no way! I would've seen you on their posters or announcements. I definitely wouldn't have forgotten that."

"I was supposed to be out of town, but it turns out I was around this weekend and the founder was more than happy to squeeze me in."

"I'm so excited you'll be there!"

"Me, too, dearie. I'll get a book from you there, if you have extras!"

"I'll make sure I do. You can have all of them if you want them."

She laughed at that. "Don't go to any trouble for me, dear, but I'm happy this won't be our last encounter." She glanced at her watch, and said reluctantly, "I must be going, but if I don't see you before, I will see you at the signing."

"See you then! Have a great time with your friend!"

"You, too, dearie!"

She hurried out of the lobby, through the revolving doors. I watched as the doors finished their spinning and settled. I glanced at the couch, wondering if I should suck it up and take a seat, when I heard the elevators open behind me and saw Eve's bright red hair and Mira's dark curls. Eve was concentrating on her phone, but Mira gave me a small wave. A few moments later, when Eve saw me, she broke into a grin.

"I knew I liked you! Hope you weren't waiting long. I thought being downstairs five minutes early would make me the first one here. I was surprised to meet Mira on my way."

"And I didn't know where you were, so I figured we'd be waiting a while," Mira chimed in.

"Same! There was no way you were already up and out before me. I'm always the first one to everything, but you're gonna make me step up my game, aren't you?" Eve asked, grinning.

I broke into a matching grin. "What can I say, if I'm not early, I'm-"

"Late," Eve finished for me.

I laughed hard at that, Eve and Mira joining in, too. After a second, when I caught my breath, I added, "I was actually going to say anxious, but that works, too."

"Do either of you know where we're going? We should probably head out pretty soon."

"Not a clue," I said with a shrug. None of us had ever been to Portland, so that wasn't surprising. If they knew me better, they wouldn't have bothered asking me. Most days, I couldn't find my way around the city I practically grew up in.

Eve held up her phone. "Don't worry, I got us. It's only a few blocks away."

"Perfect! Are we meeting them there?"

"I don't think we decided," said Mira.

"Well, I don't see them yet, so I'll let them know we're heading over and to meet us there," I said.

I pulled out my phone and quickly typed out the message. Before sending it in the group, I checked with Eve. "You're sure it's super close?" It was an unfamiliar city, after all. The last thing I wanted was someone getting lost in the city. Sabrina and Hanna were together, so at least neither would be walking alone, but still.

I had grown up in a small town right outside of what was technically a city as far as New England goes, but it was a small city. I was, by nature, not a city girl. There were too many people in the cities. It was too crowded, too busy, too wild and unpredictable. You never knew who was watching you and who could be following you. You never knew who or what could be waiting for you around the next corner. Some people liked that feeling, thought it was exciting and loved the unpredictability; I wasn't one of them.

But Eve was sure they'd be fine. It was only a few blocks. From what I'd seen so far, she would have taken gold if being prepared was an Olympic sport, so I bowed to her expertise and sent the text.

SIX

Sadie

Unsurprisingly, Eve was right and they made it there without incident. Brunch passed by in a flash, leaving me with a feeling of warmth I was grateful for. No one wanted the fun to end yet, so we decided to keep the party going and head over to Powell's City of Books.

On the way there, we got sidetracked by a witchy, new age crystal shop. I didn't know enough about crystals to be excited about the store, but Hanna and Eve wanted to stop, so we did.

I was looking at the beautiful amethyst, the only crystal I knew by name, when an olive, mossy green crystal caught my eye. I felt drawn to it. I picked it up and ran my fingers over the coarse edges and for some reason I couldn't explain, knew I had to have it.

Before I could think too much about it, I went to the cashier and held it out to her. She took the crystal and inspected it a moment before saying, "Need change, huh?"

"I'm sorry? I was planning to pay with card. I can't help with getting you change."

She laughed at that, explaining, "No, no, sweetie. I meant the moldavite."

"Is that what it's called?" I asked.

Her eyes widened. "Oh no. Now there, I don't think I should be selling you this if you don't know what it does."

Well, that was a little rude. Just because I didn't know all the crystals names didn't mean my money wasn't just as good. "I'm not normally a crystal person, but this was calling to me. I feel like I need it."

She looked surprised before nodding. "Moldavite has a way of finding you when you need it most." I reached out for the rock again, but she pulled it back closer to her. "But I can't in good conscience sell this to you without a warning. Moldavite is a powerful devil. I want you to know what you're signing up for. Moldavite brings positive change, but drastically. If the universe thinks you need a new job, the moldavite could get you fired. A new boyfriend, the moldavite could get you dumped. At first, the changes seem terrible, but they have a way of ending up being for the best."

She couldn't be serious. A rock had ways of getting someone fired? I barely kept myself from rolling my eyes. "Well, no job or boyfriend here, so no worries, right?" I joked before adding, "But I'll take it."

She nodded, ringing it up and handing it back to me. "I really hope you know what you're getting yourself into."

I thanked her before walking away with the crystal in my pocket, wondering why I had even bought it in the first place.

SEVEN

I was in awe of the store, not able to tear my eyes from the shelves. The many rows of bookshelves stretched up to the ceiling, aisle after aisle, room after room; the store and the books just kept going. How anyone could figure out where to start, how anyone could even find anything in the store, was beyond me. Luckily, I didn't have to figure it out. Luckily for me, and everyone else in our group, we had Eve.

I hadn't even noticed the maps on the way in, but somehow, she had. Not only did she already have a map, but she had already mapped out the ideal strategic way to tackle the bookstore and hit all the sections we wanted to. At her direction, we started for the Rose Room which housed the Young Adult section. It was the furthest away of the sections we wanted to browse, so Eve figured it made the most sense to start there and work our way backward. I was growing more and more grateful for her presence and her guiding hand, letting me take a more passive role and simply enjoy myself. It was a luxury I wasn't used to.

It wasn't that I made an inordinate amount of decisions, or took the lead more than the average person, although it certainly seemed it to me. It was that I agonized over every decision, worried that I would make the wrong one and that there would be consequences. It didn't matter how big or small the decision was; the anxiety was always there. Although, sometimes, it was worse than others. I had noticed that it was worst when I was deciding for others. Once I made a single decision for a person or group of people, I felt responsible for every consequence and result of that decision.

When we first entered Powells, besides the awe I felt, my anxiety had surfaced. It was such a big place and there were so many places to start. Technically, we had time since we didn't have much of a plan for the day besides dinner, but I knew there were a lot of consequences to making any decision.

What if I were to have decided to start in the Blue Room for the classics, and Jordan was actually still here in the Red Room and we missed her? What if one of the girls was destined to be in the Coffee Room at a certain time to meet their soulmate, and I messed that up for them? What if, while we were browsing the Rose Room, someone was buying the only remaining copy of a book one of the girls wanted desperately?

I knew I was overthinking, but the knowledge didn't help quiet the worry. I knew I was exaggerating my own importance. They might not even ask me to choose, but the possibility was there, and that possibility was torturous.

I knew no one else assigned the same responsibility or blame to someone like I did to myself. Hell, I didn't even assign the same responsibility to others. If any of the girls picked a room to start in and it had unforeseen consequences for me, I wouldn't blame them. I would blame myself, and I suspected they felt the same, but I couldn't open myself up to that. I couldn't be the one to decide and potentially ruin everyone's day. They would hate me, even if they were starting to like me. They would never forgive me if I ruined what was supposed to be our perfect getaway.

I knew I was spiraling, but I couldn't stop. I felt my throat constrict, felt as breathing got harder, felt my breath come in pants, and then I heard Eve announce where we were going and saw her with the map. Eve was my own personal angel of organization. All it took was just her gentle direction and I could breathe again. I wondered if she had any idea what she had just done for me, but I doubted it.

Relief washed over me. How the rest of the day went didn't matter. I wouldn't have to be in charge. That was such a freeing feeling that I felt sure even if everything went wrong for the rest of the day, I would still feel it had been a wonderful day.

We were excitedly discussing what books we might buy, when we heard someone loudly say, "BGC!" from somewhere in the stacks. We all glanced at one another for a moment before all taking off in different directions, searching for the voice. I turned a corner and barely had time to register the blur of a person flying at me and the, "SADIE!!" they had said before they had their arms wrapped around me. From the split second I saw of her, I knew it had to be Naomi. I had been talking to her for a while and she was ecstatic for me when I was accepted to Books Gowns and Crowns. I had been thrilled, too, especially that I was going to get to meet her. It almost didn't feel real. I hugged her back fiercely until a few moments later when she let go.

I took a step back to get a better look at her. She and I had video chatted so often that it felt so surreal seeing her in real life. She was all curves and curls, practically bouncing in excitement. She was wearing a yellow dress that popped against her dark skin. She was on the shorter side, too, but she had a larger-than-life presence that made you pay attention to her. It didn't take a genius to figure out she was the one yelling, "BGC!" throughout the store.

"I can't believe I'm finally meeting you!"

"I can't believe how cute and little you are!"

I couldn't help but laugh at that. I had long since grown used to my short stature, but she was maybe a few inches taller than me.

"You know you're not that much taller, but you're definitely just as cute."

We both laughed, but Naomi's quickly turned into a joyful squeal. I turned around and saw Hanna rushing toward us with Sabrina in tow.

While Naomi and Hanna shared an enthusiastic hug, I saw Eve and Mira coming from the other end of the aisle. When my eyes drifted around me, I noticed A Ripple of Power and Promise, Jordan's first book, the very one that brought us all together in the first place, and we were all standing right under the shelf full of the series. Feeling a little teary-eyed, I was startled when I saw Mira watching me with an understanding smile. I had felt a little embarrassed until then. Her smile told me she understood; it was a magical experience, and it was okay to be emotional about it.

I bought myself another copy. I couldn't help it. It was the very thing that brought me here in the first place. I was considering asking them all to sign it, like a yearbook, but decided that would be too cheesy and they would probably laugh at me for it.

They liked me so far for some reason, and I wasn't trying to ruin that. But I couldn't bring myself to leave without the book. I tucked it under my arm for safe keeping when we left the Rose Room and moved back toward the front of the store to do more shopping.

We spent hours in the store, but it still felt like we had barely scratched the surface of what they had to offer. Knowing we would come back was the only thing that got us all to leave on time. We parted ways with Naomi, agreeing to meet up for dinner.

EIGHT

When Eve had said she made us a dinner reservation at an old school building, I hadn't the slightest idea what to expect, but it wasn't this.

This was a proper old boarding school. The dated brick building was huge, much bigger than I imagined. It even had rooms you could stay the night in. As we pulled open the large doors, I gasped. I had expected they would have redone the inside, only keeping the bare bones, but it was like walking into a time capsule. The interior appeared to be left largely preserved.

While it was cool to get to explore an old school building of the past, I hadn't expected the building to feel as eerie as it did. I couldn't pinpoint why, but the feeling only grew stronger as we started down the long hallway to what used to be the dining hall and was now a restaurant. I hoped it wasn't much further and that Naomi wouldn't have to wait long for us. A few steps later, I noticed the paintings and came to a full stop so abruptly that Hanna collided with my back.

"I'm so sorry, but someone else needs to look at this. Am I going crazy or are their eyes following us?"

Eve had been leading the group with Mira, but they both turned around. Hanna and Sabrina peered at the painting, too.

The painting shouldn't have been remarkable, but the longer you stared at it, the weirder it became. The couple posed in front had seemed normal until I noticed their eyes moved with you. From the way they were positioned in the foreground, they were likely the founders of the school. Behind them was a group of school children, all girls, in white dresses. They were gathered around a May Day pole and had ribbons in their hands, but they were just standing there with blank expressions staring out of the painting. The more I studied it, the more the painting gave me the chills. Everything about it was creepy. The only non-creepy thing in the painting was weird enough that it was almost creepy. Off to the left, for no apparent reason, was a parade of cows. The cows weren't there for any rhyme or reason, and neither the couple nor the children were looking at them. The couple and the children were all staring directly out of the painting at us, watching us.

Sabrina stepped in front of me, standing at the center of the painting, and leaned slowly all the way to the right and then all the way to the left.

"Well, it's not just you."

"That's so cool!" Hanna exclaimed.

"Yeah..." I said doubtfully. "Cool, sure."

She laughed. "It's not too often you see an artist get the look just right, so it actually follows you. So, yes, Sades, it's quite cool."

I would have continued our debate about her radar for cool things, but the "Sades" stopped me. I couldn't remember the last time anyone had cared enough to give me a nickname. Well, to be honest, I could still remember, but I had been trying to put that and her out of my mind. Usually people only gave nicknames to their friends. Could Hanna really already think of me as her friend? My heart leapt for a moment, before I gave myself a much-needed reality check. I was probably overthinking it. It probably just slipped out, or maybe she didn't attach the same importance to nicknames that I did. I doubted very much that anyone besides me did.

Mira hadn't stopped staring at the painting since we stopped. Her eyes were fixed on the woman's. Eve lightly touched her shoulder to get her attention. Mira startled slightly, jumping, before seeing it was Eve. Mira shuddered and took a step back, glancing anywhere but at the painting, before settling on Hanna.

"I don't care how much work the artist put into it, it's still creepy," she said with another shudder.

I definitely agreed with her.

Eve rested her hand on Mira's shoulder as I linked my arm through Mira's other arm. Hanna and Sabrina took up the rear and followed more closely behind now as we continued down the hallway. I didn't think it was possible, but the paintings continued to get creepier the further we went. Mira hadn't stopped studying her shoes since the painting. Thankfully, Eve continued to shepherd us to the dining hall.

About halfway down the hallway, the hairs on the back of my neck stood up, and I suppressed a shudder. I felt like there were eyes on me. Rationally, I knew Hanna and Sabrina, who were just a few steps behind me, had their eyes on me, but this felt different. It felt more sinister somehow. I pushed Eve and Mira to go faster. I thought about glancing over my shoulder, but couldn't face the idea of what I might see. Knowing they would all think I was overreacting, hoping I was overreacting, I pushed them a little faster. We were almost running down the hall now. When we finally reached the end and turned the corner, we had entered the dining hall. When I sighed in relief, Mira smiled at me and leaned closer.

"Thank you," she whispered.

I knew she meant for getting us out of there quickly and probably for not laughing at her fears. Had she seen my face a few seconds ago, she wouldn't have been thanking me. She would have been questioning me.

I knew I was being crazy, but I had learned early on that no matter how crazy it seemed sometimes, I needed to trust my gut. It was better I look crazy than let something terrible happen to me or someone I cared about because I was too worried about seeming crazy.

We were safe now, though, from whatever might have been there. Realistically, I knew I had probably been overreacting, but I felt relieved to be in the safety of the dining hall with the other people. We could already hear the loud chatter and scrapping of forks and knives on dinner plates. There was safety in numbers. That we hadn't encountered a single other person on our way here was unnerving, to say the least. We must have taken a back route to the dining hall, a back route we most definitely weren't taking back. I didn't care if we had to walk around the entire outside of the building in the dark. I would sooner do that, and would feel safer doing that, than to walk back through that never-ending hallway of creepiness. I was so glad we weren't spending the night there.

As we approached the hostess stand, Mira unlinked her arm from mine and fell back into step with Hanna and Sabrina. When she did, I glanced over at Eve to see if she was going to take the lead on talking to the hostess, but the words died on my lips when I saw she was just as shaken as I was. As much as I wanted it to have been all in my head, as badly as I wanted to think I was crazy, if I was, so was she. Whatever bad vibes I had been feeling, she had felt them, too.

I wanted to ask her about it, but one glance toward Hanna, Mira, and Sabrina told me now wasn't the time. I turned back to Eve, but she was already heading toward the hostess to explain we were meeting the rest of our party here.

It was then that my other nerves hit me. I had been so distracted by the hallway I had forgotten about our huge dinner tonight. I couldn't believe how little I had thought about it all day. We were meeting up with Naomi, who was bringing some friends of hers, and we were meeting up with some friends of Hanna's. It was going to be a full house for sure, and the pressure was on big time. Not only was I the only author that would be at the dinner, but I was one of the two queer authors in attendance. I usually felt like I was under a microscope, but this weekend I actually was. The last thing I wanted to do was offend or upset someone and have it reflect badly on me, my book, and the whole LGBTQ community. Not that I didn't worry about that in my daily life, but I was even more on display here. I took a deep breath as we entered the room.

The space was bigger than I imagined and had enough plants hanging from the ceiling that it felt like a greenhouse. With the ceilings as tall as they were, the greenery was a welcome touch, making the place feel less industrial than it would have otherwise. We snaked our way through the occupied tables, following the hostess to the far corner of the giant room. Once we got closer, I noticed it had been roped off and was marked reserved. I wondered who we'd be sitting near. Maybe one of the authors was having a group dinner here. I couldn't wait to see who it was. It wasn't until she approached the rope and moved it for us that it computed that it was us getting the VIP treatment.

Once we got past the rope, I noticed there was a girl already sitting in the booth off to the side. When I saw her hair, I had to wonder how I had missed her. Her hair was a light brown until about halfway down, then it turned into a gorgeous soft emerald color. I was immediately drawn to her. Something about a girl with unnaturally colored hair just told me we were going to be friends.

I smiled at her, wondering whose friend she was and how to introduce myself. She returned my slightly unsure smile, but then saw Hanna and her smile widened. That answered that question. She hopped up and hugged Hanna. Now that she was standing, I could see her long flowing skirt she had somehow matched exactly to the shade of her hair. I knew it was probably a coincidence, but the thought that she might have dyed her hair to perfectly match her skirt made me happy.

Hanna introduced her as Jade. As we filed into the booth with her, I debated what to ask her first. A million questions came to my mind about her taste in books, her life, and her style, but before I could say anything, a couple more people arrived. I looked at Hanna, but she didn't seem to recognize them, so they must have been Naomi's friends. I smiled and waved.

They both smiled back as they took a seat in an adjacent booth in the area that had been blocked off for us. The man had purple streaks in his hair and an eyebrow piercing. Those things alone told me he was my kind of person. He either listened to pop punk music like I did, or was somewhere on the LGBTQ spectrum; either way, I wanted to be his friend.

The girl seemed incredibly familiar, but I couldn't figure out why. She was stunningly gorgeous. She stood at probably five-and-a-half-feet, and had the shiniest hair I had ever seen. She was a redhead with blue eyes I could have stared into for hours. I was torn between whether they were closer to the sky or the ocean. The thought that I knew her from somewhere was nagging at me, but I knew there was no way I could have known her and forgotten about her. It must just have been that I wanted to know her.

I was surprised by the amount of people I felt an instant connection with so far this weekend. That rarely ever happened to me, but this was a special circumstance. The event was bound to attract a lot of people similar to me, but I hadn't given much thought to that. Now that I was here, it seemed silly I hadn't thought of it before. I was growing increasingly nervous and increasingly hopeful.

I might actually make some new friends here.

I mean, things were going well with Mira, Hanna, and Sabrina, and, hell, Eve and I were essentially the same person. Maybe I would get more out of this weekend than just a few book sales. Maybe, or maybe I was getting ahead of myself. I was kicking myself for not having introduced myself to the new guy and girl, but something about leaving the table right now was unappealing. I could introduce myself later. For now, I was enjoying being with the others. Even having just met Jade, I already felt pretty comfortable around her, which was quite a rarity for me. I loved her vibes. She gave off a friendly but mysterious vibe, like you couldn't tell what she was going to do next, but knew for sure it would be something fun. You couldn't tell what she was thinking, but didn't have to worry if she liked you. I wondered if the mysterious vibes would fade the more I got to know her, but as she ordered a drink I had never heard of from the waitress, I highly doubted it.

After the waitress took our drink orders, she made her way to the booth with our other group. As she did, another small group showed up with Naomi leading the way. I smiled and waved to her. She returned the smile with an enthusiastic wave and moved over to the waitress. The other table had spotted Naomi and was excited to see her. I watched as she scooted past the waitress into the booth.

I watched Hanna jump up from the booth to go greet the others. One of the three girls immediately caught my attention. She was around my height with the most beautiful short turquoise hair. It was wavy and had different shades of blue throughout the waves. Even if she hadn't had such beautiful hair, I probably would have noticed her first, since her energy level matched Hanna's, which was an impressive feat.

Hanna led the group over to us, briefly introducing them. The turquoise haired girl was Skylar. With Skylar was a tall brunette named Erin and a friendly, freckled girl name Courtney. After introductions, Hanna led them over to sit with Naomi and the others.

When I turned back to the others, they were talking about tropes. After a moment, Jade asked, "What's your favorite, Sadie?"

I didn't have an answer ready. "Umm… let me think. I love a good enemies-to-lovers, and fake dating or forced proximity. No. You know what? I think my absolute favorite is childhood friends to enemies to lovers with forced proximity in there. I know that's a mouthful."

Jade just smiled and asked, "Okay, but why? Out of all the tropes, why that one?"

That's a damn good question. I thought about it for a second before answering, "So, I love the enemies-to-lovers trope on its own, but sometimes, if it isn't done right, it's too much. Sometimes their differences and reasons for being enemies are too irreconcilable for me to root for, or even imagine them being able to fall in love and maintain a healthy relationship. With the childhood friends sprinkled in there, it softens the enemies part. They were friends at one point. They had enough in common and no big fundamental differences that stopped them from being friends as kids. So there was probably a big falling out or some incident that happened that they haven't been able to move past, but that they would be able to in the future. Since they were friends before, it's been shown they can have a positive, healthy relationship; they just need to be able to get past the event or issue. That's where the forced proximity comes in. I don't want them to want to work out their issues. They aren't real enemies if they want to, so the forced proximity forces them to spend time together, start to see eye to eye, and then realize they love each other. That's definitely my favorite; watching them unwillingly fall in love with someone who you know will be a good match for them."

When I finished talking, everyone was staring at me. "What?"

"Girl, that's adorable! I was expecting more like a 'I like friends-to-lovers' or enemies-to-lovers, or fated mates, or something like that. I wasn't expecting a dissertation." I blushed. I knew I shouldn't have said as much as I did. She must have seen my face change, because she quickly added, "Not that I minded! I just didn't expect such a thought-out answer when I put you on the spot like that."

Eve chuckled next to me, which surprised me, until she said to Jade, "If you haven't figured it out already, Sadie's the resident author of the group."

I couldn't help but laugh at the "aha" moment written all over Jade's face. "That makes so much more sense. I'll make sure to ask you first next time so I have time to come up with a better answer than enemies-to-lovers or forbidden love."

Hanna drifted back and asked what we were talking about. Jade explained and asked her her favorite trope.

"Personally, I love fated mates, or soul mates. There's just something about two people being destined to find each other that gets me every time."

She was right. There was something terrifying about the universe in that sense. I didn't quite know what I believed, but the universe certainly seemed chaotic and unplanned at times. The thought that you could make the wrong choice and miss out on the life you might have had was terrifying to me. I hated the idea that with any given decision I might have been ruining my own future and have no idea. To know beyond a shadow of a doubt that there was someone out there destined for and waiting for you was a huge comfort in the face of a universe so chaotic. I could definitely see the allure of the trope.

I noticed Mira had been quiet and was curious about her thoughts, so I asked her, "Not to put you on the spot, but what about you, Mira?"

She thought about it for a moment before saying, "It might be the unpopular opinion but friends-to-lovers is my favorite."

"Friends-to-lovers can definitely be good if it's done right," Sabrina said.

"For real, as long as the friend who falls first isn't creepy about it and doesn't act like they deserve their friend's love because they're nice to them, it for sure is a good read," I added.

That got me a few nods and a couple of confused blinks in my direction, and semi-concerned stares from Eve and Mira. *Oops, I guess my trauma was showing. My bad.* I had always been an over-sharer. I learned early on to be an open book, to not build walls, because no one would take the time to break them down. Kay taught me the moment people got to know the real me, they left. It was inevitable. Being an open book just expedited the process.

I didn't know what to say, but, thankfully, Naomi wandered over, and asked, "What are you guys talking about?"

"Favorite tropes," said Sabrina. "And...go!"

Naomi chuckled. "To be honest, I'm pretty sick of tropes at the moment, pretty burnt out from reading in general, so I don't really have an opinion."

Hanna giggled. "I'm sure that'll pass. Watch, you're gonna text us all in a couple of months with a list of your favorite tropes,"

"You're probably not wrong."

I turned to Eve, saying, "Last but not least. No pressure, Eve." I laughed at that before continuing, "What's your favorite?"

"Easy, fated mates, but there has to be the 'who did this to you' trope in there."

There was a chorus of 'oohs' and general agreement, but it was Naomi that added, "Ditto. That's mine, too."

We all, Naomi included, laughed at that.

NINE

When more people arrived, I turned to Hanna and Naomi expectantly, but they both shrugged. Neither of them recognized the newcomers. I was surprised when Jade jumped up and made her way over to them.

Out of the corner of my eye, I saw more movement from the other booth. It was the redhead. She had shrunk down a couple of inches in the booth, not enough that I would have noticed if I hadn't been paying attention to her earlier. The man with the purple hair put his arm around her, protectively, and drew her in to him, glaring daggers at the back of Jade's head.

I glanced around to see if anyone had caught that and saw Eve watching them, too. Seeing the newcomers had everyone else's attention, I leaned over and whispered to Eve, "Any idea what that's about?"

She stared at me, surprised. "You don't know? I thought everyone knew."

"I'm pretty new to the online book scene."

"Even still," she playfully shouldered me, "you must live under a rock to have missed that drama." I thought she was gonna make me ask, but, thankfully, she continued, "Well, I know you noticed the redhead over there."

She wiggled her eyebrows at me, and I tried to quiet the giggle that burst out of me. "I mean, how could I not? You've seen her. She's stunning."

"Fair point, but did you recognize her?"

"I mean, maybe? I thought she seemed familiar, but I figured it was wishful thinking."

"Thank goodness. If you said you hadn't even an inkling of recognizing her, I wouldn't have known what to do with you." We both laughed for a second before she continued, "So, the redhead is Gwen Pendragon."

"Gwen Pendragon, the famous cosplayer Gwen?" I asked in disbelief.

I pulled my phone out, needing to check for myself. I had been following her account for at least the last year, since the first time she had shown up on my feed. What could I say? She was gorgeous. I couldn't believe I hadn't put two and two together, but, really, why would I? If that was Gwen, she had at least 450 thousand followers, and she was at dinner with us? I wouldn't have believed it even if I had thought harder about it. To put that in perspective, I had just broken 1.5 thousand followers, so she had 448.5 thousand more than me. The idea that the Queen of Cosplay herself—people had started calling her that after she adopted the name Gwen Pendragon—was at dinner with us was crazy to me. I pulled up her page while Eve watched over my shoulder, and sure enough, Eve was right. It was undeniable. It was her.

I knew my jaw was on the floor, but I couldn't hide the shock if I tried. "What the hell is she doing at a dinner with us?" Half a second later, I realized that might've sounded offensive, but, thankfully, Eve laughed.

"Hell if I know, but we're definitely talking to her at some point."

"Speak for yourself. I don't know that I could form a coherent sentence in front of her."

She gave me a 'come on now' look and said, "Girl, you're an author; one of only twenty-five here. That's a huge deal. Hell, she might even have read your story."

I stared at her incredulously, expecting her to laugh, but she was serious. She just shrugged. "You never know."

"I mean, I guess. I just can't believe she's here with us. I had heard she was coming, but didn't think I would ever be this close to her. I can't believe she's here." After a moment, it occurred to me to ask, "Do we know what her actual name is?" The last thing I wanted was to call her Gwen if her real name was public knowledge. Although I highly doubted I would have missed that if other people knew her actual name.

Again, Eve shrugged, "Beats me. I've never heard of anyone calling her anything except Gwen and the characters she cosplays as, of course, but most people call her Gwen. There's a good chance that's her actual name."

"Is she okay? Before I knew it was Gwen, I was tempted to go over and make sure she's okay."

"And you're not now?"

"I'm even more tempted, but I don't think I will. The last thing I want is her thinking I'm looking for gossip." Eve gave me a pointed look. I held up my hands in defense and chuckled. "Okay, okay, good point. I am curious, but more just hoping that she's okay."

"Okay, well, now that you know it's her, I'm sure you remember all the drama with her ex, right?"

"Arty? A little, but probably not nearly as much as you know."

"Well, you knew about her ex before Arty, right? The piece of human trash who put his hands on her?"

"The piece of what who did what?!"

Eve shushed me, but no one else seemed to hear, thankfully.

"Her ex before Arty was an abusive asshole, so when her and Arty started showing up in each other's videos together after she ended things and got away from him, people were so happy for the two of them. It was largely speculated they were together, and the chemistry was undeniable. They did a few cosplays together, and, damn girl, the heat could have melted an igloo. There was a hot debate going around about whether he would be the King to her Queen. Most people were completely for it. Personally, so was I. I mean how could you not be, seeing how happy they were together? But the lovers of King Arthur lore were adamantly against them getting together. They said them being named Gwen and Arthur was a terrible omen for the both of them."

"But that's ridiculous. Who even knows if those are their actual names? Besides, the story ended pretty well for Gwen."

"In some of the versions."

"Fair point. Those are the ones I choose to read."

"Same here. They're one of the first historical pairs I consider soulmates."

"And without a doubt, Lance is a 'who did this to you' sort of man."

"Oh, definitely. I won't accept any criticism on that."

"Cause he essentially politely said screw the kingdom, screw my best friend, Gwen deserves happiness and for some reason she wants me. Come hell or high water, he wouldn't have let anyone separate them."

"For real! Goals right there. But, yeah, so you may or may not recognize the purple-haired man. That's Gwen's best friend Ollie. He might be familiar. He's been in a ton of her videos."

"Oh yeah! That is him! Geez, I'm so glad you're here. No idea what I would do without you. I for sure would have put my foot in my mouth with them. But I still don't get it. Why's he so pissed at Jade?"

She glanced at the blonde for a minute before saying, "He's not pissed at Jade. Not really anyway. If you look at the other group that just came in, you should see at least one familiar face."

I glanced over, as discreetly as I could manage, but no one really looked familiar. "No one seems familiar, except maybe the tall person in the black coat with the half-shaved head."

"That's Arty's best friend; went by Ash back then. The three of them were inseparable. There are at least a hundred videos of the three of them together. Now she goes by Morgana; changed it right after the breakup. In case there was any doubt where her loyalties would lie, there wasn't then."

"So, does she still go by Morgana?"

"As far as I know. I don't know if Ash is her actual name or not, but I doubt it."

"Why?"

"It just doesn't seem to suit her. I mean, really does she look like an Ash to you?"

I studied her for a moment. "I guess not. I wonder what her actual name is."

"Don't we all, but, yeah, so now you're caught up. By Gwen's and Ollie's reactions, I would guess they didn't expect to see her here. They must have heard she was coming to this weekend. It wasn't a secret, but they probably didn't expect her to be here tonight."

Eve and I breathed a sigh of relief together as Morgana and her friends took their seats at the table closer to our booth. It felt like a catastrophe had been avoided. Until a moment later, when Morgana laid eyes on Gwen. It was impossible to miss the tension in the air. Gwen didn't see Morgana notice her, since she was cuddled up with Ollie, trying to make herself as small as possible. I was happy he was comforting her, but was worried about how things would play out. I saw Morgana go through confusion and disbelief and land on anger. She glared daggers at Gwen and Ollie. Ollie tightened his hold on Gwen and returned Morgana's glare.

That really pissed her off. I saw her considering whether to go over there. I jumped up and moved past Eve instinctively. Before I knew where I was headed, I was standing in front of the other booth, with no plan and no idea what to say, just that I had to block Morgana's path over here. She was on a warpath and I hoped my blocking Gwen from view would break whatever spell she seemed to be under.

Everyone in the booth just watched me expectantly. *Crap, I hadn't thought this through. What the hell am I supposed to say now that I'm standing here?*

"Hi."

They all just stared at me. Gwen freed herself from Ollie's hold and peered up at me through her long eyelashes. Her eyes were arresting, but even more startling was seeing that they were watery. She continued to watch me with her big blue eyes. I felt like I was drowning in them. The movement of her lips broke the spell her eyes had over me.

"Hi," she said with a small, sad, smile.

My heart broke for her right then and there. There wasn't anything I wouldn't do for her to make that smile genuine. I couldn't think of anything that would stop me from taking the sadness from her eyes.

To everyone else, I turned and said, "Hi, guys. I just wanted to come over, say hi, and introduce myself. Since I've already said hi, I should probably get to the introducing." I laughed at my joke. I was surprised that Gwen laughed lightly, too. "I'm Sadie Hawthorne, one of the authors for the event. You may or may not have heard of me, probably not to be honest, but I wrote a queer feminist Sleeping Beauty retelling and a queer feminist Beauty and the Beast retelling. If any of you have read them yet, I'm sorry for the ending and I promise the next one is coming soon."

They smiled at that and asked me a bit more about the story that I answered and then they started talking about retellings in general. I took the opportunity to scoot in next to Gwen and Ollie. Ollie seemed a little wary but didn't say anything. I leaned over and motioned for Gwen to come closer; she leaned across Ollie's lap to move closer to me. I leaned to her ear and whispered loud enough so only she and Ollie would hear.

"I'm so sorry. I know you don't know me. I just wanted to make sure you knew Morgana seems like she's on a war path. I came over here to try to divert her attention from you." I glanced up and saw what I was dreading. She was heading over. "But I guess it didn't work. I'm so sorry, but I promise you I'm not moving and you know Ollie isn't either."

I settled in, trying to appear as casually comfortable as possible. Anyone with eyes could see how tense we were, but that didn't stop Morgana from stomping over. She stood imposingly at the end of the table, towering over us. I was increasingly glad I was there to form more of a human shield between Gwen and Morgana. I felt Ollie tense next to me. I didn't want to imagine what might have happened if there was nothing between Ollie, Morgana, and Gwen, but I knew it wouldn't have been good. I just hoped I could handle whatever happened next.

"Pendragon. Lancelot. Didn't expect to see you here. I didn't know you'd taken things so public." She gestured at them.

After getting over the shock of hearing her call Ollie Lancelot, I noticed what it was she was referring to. I hadn't really noticed before, or thought to question, that Gwen was practically in Ollie's lap. *Fair point. That doesn't exactly look innocent.*

Ollie gave Gwen a chance to speak up, but when it was clear she wasn't going to, he said, "Morgana, is it? At least I think that's what you're going by these days. Fitting since she was a nasty, conniving sorceress who didn't give a damn about anyone except her precious, perfect, could-do-no-wrong Arthur."

"Leave Arty out of it," Gwen interjected quietly, but not quietly enough for Morgana not to hear.

Morgana turned a shade of red I didn't think was possible. In that moment, I wouldn't have been surprised to see steam coming out of her ears. "You don't *get* to call him Arty. You lost that privilege the second you became a cheating hoe and left him."

"I know you're not talking about Gwen like that," Ollie said.

But Gwen again cut in and said, "It's okay, Ollie. I'm not guilty in the way she thinks, but I know I hurt Arty and I get why she's angry."

I could see Gwen was having a calming effect on Morgana. Morgana was shocked into silence at Gwen. I don't know what she expected. Gwen was sitting over here practically crying over Morgana having showed up. Did she really expect a fight from Gwen? She seemed about to leave, but couldn't help throwing one last parting remark.

"That's right, homewrecker. Listen to your-"

She didn't get to finish. She was cut off by Gwen leaping across Ollie and colliding with me. I almost tumbled out of the booth, but kept my footing. There was no way in hell I was moving, no way I was removing the last barrier between them. Gwen didn't push any further but stared down Morgana without flinching. Morgana had a good six inches on her, but even at her height, with the way Gwen was staring her down, I was surprised she didn't cower.

Gwen spoke low and slow, enunciating each word. "Listen, Morgana, I don't care how you talk to me. I know I hurt you when I hurt Art- Arthur, and you are too bullheaded to move past any sort of action you view as personal, but you will leave Oliver out of it. He didn't do a damn thing wrong except be there for me when no one else dared to. He is the only one that cares about me, so you will leave his damn name out of your mouth."

"Or what, Pendragon? You're sure talking a big game there. Ready to back it up?"

"Anytime, anywhere."

"If there's one thing I actually like about you, it's how easy it is to rile you up. It's cute you think you could handle me."

"Any. Time. Any. Where. I tried so fucking hard with you. I was fucking terrified to end things, terrified I would lose you. I wasn't your enemy until you made me be. You keep pushing and pushing and pushing. It's a wonder you haven't pushed Arthur away, too."

"As if, Pendragon. No one and nothing could come between us."

"There was a time I thought that about us. I hate how wrong I was."

"That makes two of us. It sucks finding out your best friend's girlfriend was a no-good cheating whore."

Gwen's face told me her bravado was fading. Ollie turned to her, and I turned to Morgana.

"That's enough. I know you don't know me, but my friends over there…" I pointed to my booth and saw everyone quickly glance in different directions and try to appear casual, but of course they had been listening. Morgana hadn't exactly been quiet. "They organized a nice get-to-know-each-other dinner for us all. I won't let anyone ruin that. I understand you and Gwen have issues," Morgana went to speak, but I continued, "but I don't care about that. What I do care about is that everyone is able to eat their dinner in peace without crying or without murdering someone. You probably are quite a nice person usually, so I am asking you to go take a seat and back off of Gwen."

"Well, you certainly won't find me crying." Her eyes met Gwen's. "What? Can't fight your own battles, Pendragon?" Gwen didn't respond, which I was grateful for. Ollie might've, but Gwen was in his arms again and I heard a distinctive 'humph' from him that had to mean Gwen had elbowed the response out of him.

"Morgana, I think that's what you go by? If you have something else you'd prefer to be called, you can tell me and I'll use that, but for now, do you want to take a walk with me or go back to your seat?"

She startled at my question and stared at me again, taking me in for the first time. "And who are you?"

"I'm Sadie Hawthorne. Under other circumstances, I'm sure it would be lovely to meet you. Why don't you introduce me to your friends over there?" I gestured to the table she had come from.

She rolled her eyes and scoffed in disgust seeing that Gwen was still in Ollie's arms. "Fine, but don't think this means you won or that we're friends or anything like that."

"Of course not, but I'd love to meet your actual friends."

I walked over with her, shooting a last glance over my shoulder, and saw Ollie give me a nod of thanks and approval. At least it seemed like I might have made two friends. I stood there awkwardly while Morgana took her seat. Her friends were silently watching us both, waiting for an explanation, trying to make some sense of the interaction. I still was, too, if I was being honest. I wasn't normally outspoken, so I was a little surprised by my own boldness.

I waited a moment, but Morgana was lost in thought and seemed to have forgotten she was supposed to introduce me. "Hi, guys. I'm Sadie Hawthorne. I'm an attending author this weekend and just wanted to say hi. I already met Morgana here, but I'd love to meet you all, too."

They went around the table, somewhat robotically saying their names while still staring at me. I almost asked why they were staring at me like that, when the last person said, "I'm Eli. Great to meet you. Why don't you introduce me to your friends?"

"Of course!" Finally, someone was acting normal. "I'd love to. Come on over!"

Eli and I walked away from the table, and quietly he said, "I'm sorry about my friends, and about Morgana. You probably won't believe me, but she's never like that. We've been friends for years and I've never seen her like that. Although, to be fair, no one's seen her around Gwen since 'the incident' with Arty. If we had any idea she was gonna be here tonight, we would have steered clear. Honestly, I feel bad for Gwen, but if you tell anyone, I'll deny it. I know she didn't mean to hurt Arty, but she didn't seem to get it wasn't just Arty she was hurting. And I have no idea what she's doing flaunting her thing with Oliver in front of Morgana. She should really know better." He must have sensed I was about to protest because he quickly added, "Not that that's at all an excuse for Morgana's behavior. She was out of line, I know that. I'll do what I can to keep Gwen out of her crosshairs. I owe Gwen that much. Arty, too. I know you don't know him, so you'll have to take my word for it, but this is the last thing he would want Morgana doing."

I didn't know what to say, or even really why he had told me all this, so I just said, "Thank you. I appreciate that, and I know Gwen and Ollie do, too."

A frown crossed his face before he said, "Trust me, I'm not doing it for Oliver. He deserves all of Morgana's wrath, but Gwen doesn't, and Arty wouldn't like it, so I'll do what I can."

I was dying to know what was up with him and Ollie, but knew better than to ask, so I just thanked him again, and he headed back to their table.

I went to head back to my seat but thought better of it. I needed some fresh air. I thought about asking Mira or Eve to join me, but I wouldn't be long.

The moment I left the dining hall, I realized my error. Somehow, in the chaos, I had forgotten both how creepy the school was and how little I knew of the layout. I had no idea how to get anywhere from here. I thought about turning back and getting someone to come with me, but they didn't know the place any better than I did, and I didn't want to be a burden.

Besides, I knew it was all in my head. There wasn't anything inherently eerie about the school, if you didn't look too closely at the walls. I just needed to double back the way I came. Surely that would bring me to the entrance we used.

TEN

As I went down the hallway, I was kicking myself for not just going out onto the dining hall's patio. But more than I needed air, I needed space. I needed a moment alone to process. Being around so many people was overwhelming, especially with the conflict I witnessed.

I had instinctually ruled out the patio after seeing how crowded it was out there. Plus, I knew without question that Eve or Mira would have been worried about me if I just wandered outside.

I was going to wander outside for a few minutes, but at least this way I had an alibi, since I was heading in the direction of the bathroom. Not that I thought anyone would question me, but I felt bad keeping things from them. I didn't want anyone to think I had a problem being around them. I didn't. It was just that there were a lot of new people around. A lot of new names and faces, and a lot of pressure on me to perform well.

Well, a lot of pressure I put on myself to represent myself positively as an author and as a member of the LGBTQ community. I knew it was all in my head, but knowing that didn't make it any easier. I had grown more comfortable around Eve, Mira, Hanna, and Sabrina after having known them for a little while and having been talking to them. Even Naomi I felt pretty comfortable around even though I had barely spent any time with her so far, but meeting so many other new people at once was a lot for me.

I was scared if I had to explain that to someone that they might take it personally, when that wasn't at all true, so I continued down the hall on my own. I thought I had backtracked, but the hallway was shorter than I remembered before I came to an intersection. I had my eyes glued to the floor, but since the area didn't look familiar anymore, I was forced to look up.

I glanced around quickly, trying to decide which way to go. I felt a shiver run up my spine and fought the urge to glance behind me. There wasn't anything there, I knew that. I had just come from that way.

When my eyes landed on a framed photo on the wall, I had to suppress the urge to turn and run back to where I came from. It was a seemingly innocent black-and-white photo in a thin black frame. The photo appeared to be of some of the school's old students in front of the school building. They were all young girls dressed in white and staring at the camera. There was a big pole in the middle of them with ribbons running down to each girl. They seemed to be in the middle of some sort of May Day celebration. I couldn't figure out why the picture made the hairs on my neck stand up and why my blood ran cold until I realized it was incredibly similar to the painting we had found so creepy earlier.

I couldn't believe I was letting a silly picture frighten me like that for absolutely no reason. I forced myself to take a step closer, wanting to understand what it was that felt so wrong about it. I studied it before realizing it was the lack of motion that was unsettling.

I had a very basic understanding of what cameras were like back then, enough to know you would have had to stay still for a long period of time for the camera to work, but it was unnatural. The girls were all standing there with blank expressions staring at the camera, holding their ribbons. The stillness was unnerving.

Had the girls been in motion when the picture was captured, it would have made a much worse picture, but would have been far less creepy. Even if the girls were smiling, it might have been better. I pictured the same photo with the girls smiling and shuddered. That wouldn't have been better at all. That actually might have made it creepier if all the unmoving girls were just standing there smiling.

I pulled my eyes from the picture and found what I was searching for. There was a signpost that listed the different places in the school. I don't know how, but I must have found a different hallway, because there was no way we passed that on the way in.

The sign showed the front desk was up ahead. That sounded promising. The front desk would have to be near the entrance. The restrooms were also in that direction if anyone came searching for me. There was also something called the Boiler Room and the Detention Bar off to the right. I glanced down the hallway to see if I could see anything in that direction, but there was nothing to see. The lack of other people in every hallway I had been in so far was entirely unnerving. I hoped if I came back later with some of the girls that it wouldn't feel as creepy if I wasn't alone. Hopefully, because I wanted to see the Detention Bar and was thinking maybe we could check it out later. I headed down the hall toward the front desk and restrooms, but didn't get far before I was forced to glance up again when I heard a rattling noise.

The moment I looked up, it stopped. I glanced around, trying to find the source of the noise, but I couldn't find anything. It had vanished. I surveyed the area, but I was still very much alone, and the hall was quiet again.

Feeling unnerved, I thought about just turning around, or even calling one of the girls to join me. I felt like I was being crazy. I really should just turn around. I had no idea where I was going, anyway. Before I could change my mind again, I turned on my heel and went back the way I came.

When I got to the intersection with the sign, I paused and stepped closer. I could have sworn I had come from straight across the way, but the sign showed the restaurant was off to my left. Maybe it was a shortcut, I reasoned. It was highly likely I had gone the long way around, especially since there hadn't been a soul in sight in the hallway I had taken.

I shrugged and took a left, hurrying down the hall. I was about halfway down when I heard a noise that sounded like it was coming from behind me. I glanced hopefully at the end of the hallway, trying to gauge if I could get to the end quicker than whatever was behind me, but I was too far away. *Well, there goes flight. Fight it is.* I whirled around, putting my hands up in front of me, finished my turn, and dropped my weight into my heels, ready to tackle whatever danger was behind me, or at least I hoped I was, but the hallway was still empty.

I took a deep breath, trying to calm my nerves, but my heart wouldn't stop racing. In that moment, I was glad no one else had come with me to witness how crazy I looked.

I went to turn back where I was heading, but stopped when I noticed another painting. There was a row of children in a classroom. They sat at individual desks facing a teacher standing at the front of the class. It would've been normal enough, except the tops of the children's heads were all opened up as if on hinges. Their teacher was spewing blackened words that were filling each of their heads. An unnerving way to illustrate teaching; it felt more like it was showing mind control.

I shuddered. "Well, that's unnerving."

"Really? I quite like it."

I gasped and whirled around to face the voice, ready to scold them for sneaking up on me, but when I saw who it was, the words died on my lips and I froze.

He seemed to revel in my fear. He licked his lips while he watched me with a smirk on his face.

"It's you," was all I could utter after a moment. I couldn't believe it, but he was a dead ringer for Damien Bancroft. He moved a little closer, and then my senses came back to me.

This wasn't Damien, and if it was, I should have been running. This was just a stranger who happened to look like him. A stranger that I had seen in the airport. I was almost positive it was him. Maybe I should run anyway.

I took a small step backward and noticed the anger flash over his face for a brief second before the smirk reappeared.

"Yes, darling, it's me. No need to be afraid."

That sparked indignation and confusion in me more than fear. "I'm sorry, do I know you?"

Again, the anger crossed his face, and he rushed forward, closing the gap between us too quickly for me to move back. Before I could think, he had grabbed my arm. Instinctually, I wanted to pull back, but this stranger was clearly dangerous. Better to play along and buy some time until someone else happened across us. Someone had to come sometime soon, right? Yes, the halls had been completely empty before, but someone had to happen across us at some point.

As I was trying to come up with some sort of plan, he was staring at me. He hadn't let go of my arm yet, either. With his free hand, he traced a single finger down my face to my chin and tilted my chin up so I couldn't avoid his eyes.

"You must recognize me, my dear. Power recognizes power. You must feel the thrumming in your bones, your heart racing, the tingling sensation of my touch."

He slid his finger down my throat lightly and back up to my chin. He was right. I couldn't stop thinking about his lips, about how good they would feel pressed against mine, about how good other things would feel pressed against me. I somehow instinctually knew that he could have been mine. All I had to do was submit to him... submit...submit...submit.

No! What the hell was I thinking? I was being manhandled in a hallway by a stranger who may or may not have stalked me all the way from the airport. How the hell was I thinking for a second about enjoying this? I shook my head to clear my thoughts. I couldn't deny he was right about the sensations I was having, though.

I hated that he was right. How could he possibly know how I was feeling right now? But he was still wrong; whatever the hell he was implying was wrong.

My heart was racing, yes, but with fear and anxiety. I tried to take a step back, but he pivoted and backed me into the wall. I felt the painting digging into my shoulders. So much for buying time. Whatever he wanted from me, I knew it was no good. I tried to move past him, but he moved both his hands to my shoulders and pushed me roughly back against the wall and held me there.

"Look into my eyes. You can't dare tell me you don't feel something, that you aren't feeling the need to be close to me."

The need to be close to him? The nerve of this man! I could feel some of what he was describing, but that wasn't me. This situation was wild and my mind didn't know how to think about this. I was trying to survive and my brain was doing mental gymnastics to make sure I could think straight, to make sure I wasn't scared out of my wits. That was all that was happening here. I hadn't even been in the hallway with him for more than a few minutes, but here I was already fawning over my captor. I could only be grateful none of that came out of my mouth.

"I can tell you what I need," I said with a drawl.

"Tell me, darling. I'm sure I can make it happen."

"I need…" I drawled out, drawing out the word in suspense. "You…"

He said, "Say no more," but I interrupted before he could finish.

"…to get the hell away from me."

At that moment, I brought my knee straight up to his groin with as much force as I could muster. It was a direct hit; he crumpled to the floor. I pulled away and started off down the hallway quickly. Before turning down another corridor, I couldn't help but glance back. I had to make sure he was still there. I breathed out a sigh of relief that he was. I don't know what I had been expecting, but he had appeared so suddenly behind me the first time, I had to make sure he was still there.

He sensed me watching him and glared at me. He was still crumpled on the ground, groaning in pain, but even from that distance, the anger on his face was unmistakable. Seeing he still wasn't moving, I couldn't help myself.

"I don't know who the hell you think you are, but if you don't stay the hell away from me, I can guarantee you'll be in much more pain than you are now."

I took off around the corner, not wanting to wait to see what he might do or say. I didn't know where the hell this badass had come from, but I was incredibly lucky that I had found that in myself. I shuddered to think what might have happened if I hadn't.

ELEVEN

I wheeled around another corner and ran headfirst into another person. I almost screamed before I noticed the height difference. They were taller than me, almost everyone was, but they were a good deal shorter than my stalker.

I took a deep breath, my hands on my knees, taking a moment to calm my racing heart before seeing it was Sabrina.

"Sadie! There you are! We've been looking all over for you and Naomi! When Eve noticed you were gone and Hanna noticed Naomi was missing, we figured you guys were in the bathroom. Hanna and I had to use the bathroom anyway, so we went, but you guys weren't there, so we were getting worried. Not that there was a real reason to be, but it's a big place, so we figured you guys might've gotten lost." She took a breath and seemed to notice for the first time I was alone. "Wait, where's Naomi?"

"I have no idea. I haven't seen her, but I did just get attacked on my way through the hallway."

"Attacked?! What do you mean attacked?" she asked in a panic, only relaxing minutely when after studying me, she didn't seem to find any visible injuries.

"I'll explain as we head back. I don't want to linger here."

I checked over my shoulder, making sure we were still alone. We were, but who knows for how long? I was worried he would come for me again, and I didn't want to be caught alone in the hallway with Sabrina.

She followed my gaze and nodded. She led the way as I talked.

"I was taking a little walk," I said sheepishly. "I wanted to clear my head. Confrontation takes a lot of me and so does socializing." I paused to gauge her response. I was worried she might take offense to that, but she gave me an understanding smile. "Good for you. With all those people in there, I was dying to do that myself, but couldn't bring myself to brave the hallways alone."

"Definitely better you didn't. I shouldn't have either, really. But I did, and I got a little lost. I thought I was going back the way we came in, but I must not have, since I had no idea where I was. I was too focused on getting through the hallway to the restaurant on the way there that I probably didn't pay enough attention. I stopped a few times, trying to find my way to the exit and then decided I had better head back since I couldn't find it. I was getting a bad feeling from wandering the halls by myself. It felt even eerier than when we came in. I was hurrying back, but I think I got turned around again. These damn hallways are worse than a labyrinth. I ended up stopping for a second to glance at a painting and, all of a sudden, this man, who I swear hadn't been there a moment before, was behind me."

I paused at the horrified expression on Sabrina's face. "I'm fine. I promise I'm fine, but it was terrifying. I had surveyed the hallway since I thought I heard a noise, but there wasn't anyone there. So when I heard his voice, I freaked out, especially when I recognized him."

"Wait, you knew him?!"

"I mean, kind of, sort of, I think."

At the confused expression on her face, I rushed on to clarify, "So I don't know him, not really anyway, but I saw him at the airport near baggage claim."

"Really? That's so creepy! Don't be offended, but are you sure it was the same guy?"

"Positive. There was something unnerving about him at the airport, too, so I remembered him. I know it's going to sound crazy, but I had a bad feeling right before he showed up. Like I know this place is creepy, but it was more than that. It felt like I was being watched."

I couldn't bring myself to mention the even stranger part that he looked just like Damien, my made-up villain. I didn't know Sabrina all that well, but I was sure she would think I was crazy if I brought that up.

"He was a total creep here, too! Showing up like he was the answer to my dreams and like he expected me to bow down to him and worship the ground he walked on. I have no idea what he expected or wanted from me, but I got away before he could try much, thankfully."

"Thank goodness! I'm so sorry no one was with you!"

"I'm not! Who knows what he would've done then? Besides, it's my own fault no one else was there. I easily could've had someone come with me, but I didn't want to be a burden."

The look she gave me stated the obvious, but she said it anyway. "Quit being dramatic. You're definitely not a burden. I would've happily come with you. You're not the only one who found that big group overwhelming."

"Thank you."

"Of course, but yeah, I'm glad we found you. Now we just have to find Naomi."

I glanced behind me, but the hallway was still thankfully empty. "And quickly."

"Do you think maybe you should call someone?"

"And say what?"

"That the creep followed you from the airport? And assaulted you?!"

"I don't really have proof he followed me. It could just be a coincidence."

She looked at me doubtfully before adding, "I mean fine, maybe, but he assaulted you!"

I blushed. "Well, not exactly."

"What do you mean, not exactly?"

"Well, he grabbed my arm and he touched my face. I think I told him to stop. I'm pretty sure I did, at least."

"You don't remember?"

"Not really. I was in full on panic mode. I somehow remember he smelled like smoke and old books, but I can't remember what I did or didn't say to him. Tell me how the hell that makes sense."

"I still think you should tell someone."

"I told you."

"I mean someone important."

"You're important to me."

She rolled her eyes. "Quit playing around. You knew what I meant. What if he comes after you again?"

I shuddered at the thought. "You think he would?"

"He might!"

I frowned, but she had a point. "If he shows up again, proof or no proof, I'll call someone. But I'm not calling anyone yet."

"But what if it's worse the next time?"

"It probably would be. Whatever he wanted before, he's for sure not my biggest fan now."

"Why? I thought you just ran away?"

"I might have kneed him in the groin."

"Damn! You go, girl!"

"So, yeah, I don't really think it would be a great idea to call the police and tell them that this man who may or may not have followed me from the airport, assaulted me, especially when he only grabbed my arm and said some weird things, and I can't even remember if I told him to stop before kneeing him in the groin. They would think I was crazy! And it's just my word against his. He could even probably press charges. After all, I did technically assault him. I know I'm not the crazy one. I know what I did was justified, but I don't trust law enforcement to see it that way."

"That's a good point, but promise you'll call and tell someone if he shows up again."

I reluctantly agreed, hoping I wouldn't have to follow through on that.

"So, where do we think Naomi might have gone? She wouldn't have left the school, would she?"

"Before dinner? Not a chance. Plus, Hanna checked her phone. She's still in the building."

"They have her phone?"

"No. They have her phone location. They shared their locations with each other earlier to meet up more easily. Thank goodness for that, but it isn't exact enough that we can tell where in the building she is. We tried calling her, too, but it went straight to voicemail."

"Crap. She probably doesn't have service."

I pulled out my phone and saw that I only had one bar. "It must be this old building. I can't get much signal either. We should probably get back quickly before anyone worries about us."

"Yeah. Hopefully Naomi showed up while we were gone. We just have to get Hanna from the bathroom, and then we're heading right back. We're almost there now. I didn't want to leave her, but I heard some sort of commotion and had to check it out. I thought it might have been you and Naomi. I started in that direction and found you. I was half right, but still no Naomi. We'll head back right after. I don't want anyone thinking we're missing now either, and we might want to warn the others about your mysterious stalker."

We turned another corner and spotted the bathrooms. Hanna was just exiting, and was relieved to see us. "Thank goodness we found you, Sadie! We were worried!" A moment later, she realized it was just the two of us and asked, "Where's Naomi?"

"We were just talking about that. She wasn't with me."

"Crap."

"Yeah, that's what we said," agreed Sabrina.

"We should probably head back to the restaurant. Odds are she is already back by now," I said, hoping it was true.

They both agreed, and Sabrina added, "That's probably the best plan. Besides, we know your stalker was with you when she was missing anyway, so she shouldn't be in any danger."

Hanna's shocked gasp reminded us both that she hadn't been filled in yet.

"It's a long story," I said.

She didn't hesitate. "Well, it's a long way back. You have to fill me in. You can't just throw something like that out there and not expect me to ask questions."

Sabrina gave me a pointed look at Hanna's reaction. They both clearly thought I was underreacting to the situation. But I couldn't help it. Now that I was with Sabrina and Hanna, it felt like it had been a bizarre dream. It didn't feel real.

Things like that didn't just happen … well, maybe they did, but they didn't just happen to me. As we walked back to the restaurant, I explained to Hanna what happened. Sabrina continued to shoot me 'I told you so' looks. It had been a weird, scary situation, but there was no way anything like that would happen again. He had to have gotten my very clear message to leave me alone.

TWELVE

When we got back to the restaurant, Naomi still wasn't there. Hanna tried calling her again, but her phone didn't ring.

Without any way of knowing where she might have gone, we sat down and waited a little longer. After five minutes, we thought we would give her five more. After a full ten minutes had passed, though, we were getting more concerned. We tried Naomi's phone again, but still no ring or answer.

Crap. Where the hell was Naomi?

I thought back to the sign I had seen and mentally went through the list of places in my head. We knew she wasn't in the bathrooms, the hotel rooms, or, clearly, the restaurant. That ruled out a lot of possibilities, really only leaving only a couple of places she was likely to have gone.

"Guys, maybe we should check the bars?"

A few of the girls stared at me, and a couple of others laughed.

"We're at a restaurant that serves alcohol. You really think she would have gone to the bar?" Jade asked.

"Fair point, but she doesn't seem to be anywhere else, and we know for sure she's still in the building. How about Hanna, Sabrina, Skye, and Erin check the Detention Bar, Mira, Eve, and I can check the Boiler Room, and you guys stay here in case she comes back?"

They all nodded in agreement. "Hopefully, we find her quick," said Skye, "because I'm getting really hungry."

There were a couple of laughs and a couple of grumbles of agreement.

Mira, Eve, and I set off toward the Boiler Room. Thankfully, Eve had a better handle on the hallways than I did. In record time, we found a sign pointing to both the Boiler Room and the Detention bar. I wondered if the other group had fared as well. From what we figured, the school's hallways were all interconnected, so we had split up to cover more ground. With our luck, Naomi would probably find a way back to the restaurant or a different part of the school that didn't cross paths with us. But that was a chance we had to take.

There was a good chance she wouldn't be in either place and would be waiting for us back at the restaurant, but the bars were the last places we had to check, so it wouldn't hurt to have a look.

As we walked, I filled them in as quickly as I could about what happened with my stalker. Both of them were horrified and worried. Their reactions made me feel guilty I had gotten myself into trouble in the first place, but they assured me they were just glad I was okay. I was, now that I was with them. It was hard to feel as worried now that I had them with me.

I hoped my stalker had already left, but at least I wasn't alone anymore. The threat already didn't feel as real as it had earlier. Even the hallways had much less of an effect on me now that I had a purpose. We were going to find Naomi.

A few minutes later, we found the door into the Boiler Room. The room had an industrial feel with pipes lining the huge ceiling and coming out of the walls. We went down the stairs, searching the crowd for Naomi. There were a few pool tables that had a crowd around them, but none of the people were Naomi.

We descended another set of stairs to the bar itself. There were even more people there, but still no Naomi.

"Now what?" asked Eve.

"We could head back, or we could go meet up with the other group at the Detention Bar." I figured it would kill two birds with one stone—I would get to see the Detention Bar and we would see if Naomi was over there. The sooner we found her, the better. Who knows what kind of trouble she might be in?

Thankfully, the Detention Bar and the Boiler Room weren't far from each other and, impressively, for me anyway, we managed to not get lost on our way there. As we turned the corner and found the bar, I simultaneously noticed two things; the first being that the bar was a little bigger than a walk-in closet and was completely packed. It wouldn't have been surprising to find the bar packed, except there were only five people there, and in the middle of the other four, was Naomi.

I was so relieved they had found her. We stood at the door and waved when they spotted us. There wasn't enough room for us to squeeze in.

The bartender nodded to us. He was the tall, dark, and handsome sort, with tattoos all over his chiseled forearms. He was wiping down the bar and was none too pleased about the crowd not buying anything.

As soon as I was able, I got Sabrina's attention and signaled that we should go. Thankfully, she was able to round up the rest of our friends and we headed back to the restaurant. I heard snippets of Sabrina's and Naomi's conversation, but it was clear I had missed some of the important details. I was hoping Sabrina would fill me in later, but the gist that I picked up was that she had wanted to get a drink and explore the place. She had planned to come back shortly, but she had run into an extremely handsome, tall, dark-haired man with a chiseled jaw in a three-piece suit.

My blood ran cold when I heard that, but it had to be a coincidence. Even as I told myself that, I wasn't sure I believed it. He couldn't be the same guy, he just couldn't. But as we re-entered the restaurant, I couldn't help but scan the place, checking for him. Thankfully, I didn't see him. But as I took in the other patrons of the restaurant, the odds it was probably the same man increased, since no one else was dressed even remotely as formally as he had been.

With a sinking feeling, I pulled Naomi to the side and told her about what had happened. She was horrified for me and gave me a giant hug, before telling me, "I don't know if it was the same man or not, but he was nice enough to me. A little weird, but he was handsome enough to get away with it."

"Okay," I said doubtfully. "Just promise me you'll be careful if you see him again."

"Girl, he'll have to be careful of me," she said with a wink before laughing, "But, yes, I'll be careful. Geez," she said with a grumble, "I can handle myself. I know what I'm doing."

"I know you can," I said quickly, hoping she wasn't offended. "We were just worried about you when we couldn't find you, that's all."

"I know. I'm sorry. I honestly didn't think anyone would notice. I was just gonna be gone for a few minutes."

I wanted to tell her to be more careful next time, to not run off by herself like that without telling anyone. I wanted to say all of that, but the words died in my throat before I could say them. I wasn't a hypocrite, and hadn't I done exactly that a few minutes ago? The only difference being that I had been in actual trouble and no one knew where to find me. Naomi had been fine. We really both needed to be more careful. But I was so used to doing things on my own, it hadn't felt right to ask for anyone's company and I hadn't known how to explain myself or where I was going. I hadn't even known where I planned to go.

Not knowing what else to say to her and understanding more than she knew how she must have been feeling, I just nodded. "I know. I get it. Just promise to be more careful next time."

She frowned. "There won't be a next time." She took in the concern on my face and her eyes softened a bit, and the frown faded a little. "But I will, I swear."

I smiled and gave her a quick hug before releasing her to let her head back to her table. As I watched her make her way there, I caught Gwen's gaze. She gave me a small smile that I returned. A quick glance showed Morgana was in her seat still and that she hadn't burned the place down in our absence.

The others went to take their seats, and I followed them to our table, sliding back into my seat, happy everything turned out okay. As I sat there, I realized with wonder that I was feeling more safe and comfortable in any group of people than I had in a long time.

The rest of dinner, thank goodness, was much less eventful. Most of the group made their way over to the Boiler Room for drinks and pool after, but I was pretty exhausted and emotionally drained from the day. I was thrilled when Eve and Mira voiced they wanted to go back, too.

We took the trip together, and as we took the elevator up, Eve checked her phone before saying, "You know it still is pretty early."

"Early? Dude, I'm exhausted," I said.

Mira nodded in agreement. "Same here."

"Dang, no worries. I was thinking we could do a movie night."

I perked up a little at that. It wasn't too late in the evening and it did sound like that could be fun.

"What movie?"

"A daring tale of a farm boy, a princess, and a mercenary."

"You mean the Princess Bride? Because I'm so in if you did," Mira asked excitedly.

Eve shrugged, a gleam in her eye. "Well, I was talking about Star Wars, but I guess we could watch Princess Bride instead."

I laughed hard at that. "I'd actually be down for either, but Princess Bride goes more with the vibe of this trip."

"Glad you would've been in for Star Wars, too, though."

"Absolutely!"

"I'll change into my PJs, grab some snacks, and be back in 10."

"Perfect!" I said.

"Great!" said Mira at the same time.

A couple of hours and a lot of laughs later, the end credits were rolling. We were all exhausted, and I was struggling to keep my eyes open. I kept them open long enough to set an alarm for the morning and then fell asleep.

THIRTEEN

Damien

The gods damned witch had attacked me physically. I hadn't expected that; I had been prepared for and shielded against a magical assault. I hadn't expected her to have the guts to attack a man so much larger than her. I had underestimated her. That was what I got for trying another attack when I wasn't at full strength, but sensing the royal guard getting closer to the witch's part of the city, I knew I was running out of time. It wasn't that I couldn't take the sorceress and the guard, but taking her before the guard interfered, before the sorceress was more prepared, would be easier.

I had thought at our first meeting that she didn't recognize me because we hadn't spoken, but now I couldn't deny she just didn't recognize me. It angered me that she didn't. With all that power, it was clear she was as great a sorceress as they said. She would have to be to resist my powers as well as she did. So either she didn't think I could possibly be myself, didn't believe I would've really come for her, or she didn't think I was a threat to her. Either way, it pissed me off. How could she not feel how her power called to mine? How was she not bending to my will? The same power had cowed armies and whole realms. How was she possibly resisting?

I hadn't expected complete submission, not after her first display, but then I had slammed her with power. This time, I had tried to be more tactful. I had to be, since I hadn't given myself time to regain my full power. I was hardly at half strength, but I hadn't been willing to sit around resting longer. I had to find her before the royal guard did and made my job harder.

Now that I knew that even on her own, she wasn't going to be an easy target, I knew I was going to have to try harder tomorrow. I couldn't keep waiting. I hadn't drained the entirety of my power like yesterday, but between trying to influence her and the pain in my groin, I wasn't in the best shape. I slowly walked through the halls. This was a drinking establishment. Surely some ale or something stronger would dull the aching.

I found a liquor room a little bigger than a closet and sat on the stool, groaning as I did. The bartender took one look at me before saying, "Rough night? You'll want the strong stuff."

I nodded. At least some of the peasants knew how to serve around here.

A few moments later, he placed a small glass of something strong smelling in front of me. I took a gulp. It burned going down. Just what I needed. I thanked him with five gold pieces and he disappeared to the back. The bar and the stools in front of it took up the whole of the closet. The door behind the bar must have been where they stored the rest of what they served.

I didn't care. I was grateful to be away from prying eyes while I nursed my bruised ego. I shouldn't have let her get the upper hand. I still don't know how she was so easily resistant to me, but, clearly, I wasn't trying hard enough. The next time, I would be ready.

I took another sip, savoring the burn in my throat when I heard a woman's voice ask tentatively, "Mind some company?"

I glanced over, ready to order her away, but I saw a few wisps of purple power trailing off her, the same that had been on the sorceress. She had marked this woman. Maybe some company would be nice indeed.

I smiled at her, and moved the next stool over, making room for her. "Not at all. Can I get you something to drink?"

She grinned at that. "I was hoping you'd ask. When the bartender comes back, I'll have whatever you're having."

I was a little surprised. Surely, she would prefer something less strong. "It's quite strong."

"Just how I like it," she said, grinning. "So, what brings you to Portland?"

I wasn't sure if Portland was this establishment, the world we were in, or this part of the world, but it didn't matter. The answer was the same. "A woman," I said, opting for the truth.

Her eyes assessed me again before saying, "But it didn't go well, I take it?"

I blinked at her, surprised. Was there more to her than I thought? No. I studied her a moment and was sure the power was the sorceress's, not hers. She couldn't be a seer, just observant.

I cocked an eyebrow at her. "What makes you say that?"

"Two things. I can smell the drink from over here, and you're here alone, drowning your sorrows. I was returning to my friends, but you seemed lonely."

I wanted to scowl at that, but she wasn't wrong. I missed my husband dearly. The hole in my heart, the ache in my chest, never dulled. I missed him more than life itself, and it was torture not knowing where he was or how he was doing, torture knowing he could have been suffering right now and there was nothing I could do about it. I hoped he knew I was doing everything I could to get him back, but with any luck, I would have him back soon. This would have to work. I would do whatever it took to make the sorceress return him to me. I couldn't keep going on without him.

I must have been quiet for longer than I thought since she put her hand on my arm.

It was startling. It had been a long while since anyone had dared to touch me like that. A part of me, the weakest part, didn't mind it and I hated that. I took another swig of my drink, willing myself not to move my arm. I turned to her again and saw an understanding expression on her face.

"I just got out of something myself. I know what it's like to be lonely," she said, with a far off look in her eye.

The bartender returned, and I ordered her the same as I was having. He had it in front of her a few moments later and then excused himself again.

She took a long drink and when she finished, I asked, "What brings you here?" I was hoping she might mention the sorceress. Any information I was able to collect might end up being valuable.

"I came to the city to meet some new friends, and we're all going to a ball in a few days."

I smiled at her. Now I was getting somewhere. The sorceress had to be one of her friends. "I'd love to hear more about your friends."

She obliged and started talking about them. It didn't take me long to deduce that the short one she kept calling a firecracker was the sorceress. I learned her name was Sadie, and that she was always writing something. What I wouldn't do to be able to see her spell book with all those spells she must have been constantly jotting down.

A few minutes later, I thanked her for her company and took my leave. I had considered for a moment following her back to her friends, but it was too risky. I was nowhere near full strength and would need to rest up if I hoped to take on Sadie the sorceress. The sooner I had her in my control, the better. The gods knew I needed to be getting home. There was too much hanging in the balance back home. I had a kidnapped princess to attend to and a captive husband to free, and I wouldn't dream of keeping him waiting any longer.

FOURTEEN

Sadie

When I woke up to the blaring alarm, it took me a minute to figure out where I was, especially when I saw the shock of red hair lying next to me. Then our slumber party movie night came back to me. Mira and Eve were both somehow still asleep. I shut off the alarm, trying to remember why I had set one when it suddenly hit me.

Crap! Today was the day of the book sale. Not only was I probably already behind schedule, but I hadn't prepared any of the things I had planned to prep last night.

I was panicking, but took a few deep breaths, hoping it would help calm me. It didn't.

I thought maybe if I hopped in the shower and got myself ready first, the rest would seem easier. Mira had already agreed to help me with the setup, so, hopefully, with that extra set of hands, things would go a lot quicker. Although even with Mira's help, I wasn't sure there would be enough time.

With that ever so helpful thought, I hopped in the shower. As the hot water flowed over me, I tried to let the negative thoughts go with it, let them flow through me and down the drain with the water. It was easier said than done, but I found the more I practiced, the easier it became.

Some days it was harder than others, like today, but even today I found some moments of peace. When the thoughts came, I caught them before letting my thoughts spiral, acknowledged them, and let them flow over me without giving them more thought than I already had. By the time I stepped out of the shower a little while later, I felt raw from the heat, but fresh and ready to hopefully tackle the task at hand. I quickly toweled off and threw a tank top and shorts on. When I eased the door open, the light was on, and Eve and Mira were talking. I heard rustling noises coming from where they were, too.

"Good morning-" I don't know what else I was going to say, because my brain nearly short-circuited at the sight in front of me. Mira and Eve were both out of bed and hard at work packing up everything I would need for today.

They both turned and grinned up at me, basking in my speechlessness. "You guys didn't have to do that!"

"Nonsense. We're here to help," said Mira.

"More than happy to help, but why didn't you tell me last night you left early to get this done? I wouldn't have made you guys stay up with me if I knew," added Eve.

I shrugged. "I had a good time last night, and I hoped I would have time to get everything ready in the morning."

Eve rolled her eyes at that. "It really shouldn't surprise me you weren't going to ask for help. When Mira and I woke up a little while ago, she filled me in on how early you have to be there today and how much you still had to get done. There's no way you would've been able to have all this ready in time."

Mira shot her a fake offended look, so Eve amended, "Well, I'm sure Mira would've helped, but I'm here, too, and I kept you up late last night, so of course I'm helping."

I felt like I should protest. I wanted to protest; they were both doing too much for me, being too good to me. But, rationally, I knew I would never get this accomplished on time without their help.

"I literally can't thank you enough."

"Neither of us needs compensation, but since I'm sure that'll offend your need to repay us, I could go for a coffee," said Eve with a grin.

"Coffee actually sounds good," Mira agreed.

"Done, but you guys are really too much. I can't thank you enough."

They both protested, so I added, "So I won't, but I hope you both know how much this means to me. You have both single-handedly, double-handedly, whatever the right way to say that would be... You both will be the only reason I stay sane today and I love you both for it."

I sank down to the floor with them and got to work. With two extra sets of hands, the prep work flew by way quicker than I could have imagined. We had an hour to spare before we could start setting up at the convention, which was a perfect amount of time to grab coffee. Eve and Mira even begrudgingly let me buy them their breakfast pastries, but from knowing them as well as I did now, I could guess that Eve would force another act of kindness on me as repayment and Mira would find a subtle way of her own to repay me. These two would keep me on my toes.

When we finished up breakfast and called an Uber, I expected Eve to say goodbye and head back up to her room, but she didn't. She wouldn't be able to come inside the convention area for another hour. I had named Mira as my "personal assistant" for the day to make sure she could come in early with me and to ensure someone was there to help me set up, but I couldn't bring Eve as well.

I was panicking that that had somehow gotten miscommunicated when she told me, "I'm tagging along, and before you insist I don't, because I'll just be outside waiting for a while, don't waste your breath. I'm doing it, anyway. I want to be there if you or Mira need anything."

Contrary to her warning, I was going to argue that she was being too nice and should stay and get a bit of rest when our Uber driver pulled up. She slyly nudged me to the passenger seat, quickly gesturing Mira to get in and scoot over. Before I could say anything else, she and Mira were in securely with the door shut before I could protest further.

The drive was relatively quick, especially since the driver surprisingly asked a lot of questions about my book when he found out that was why we were in town.

When he pulled up to the venue, there were already plenty of cars and trucks parked and unloading books and other things for other attending authors and vendors. He pulled right up in front of the building and asked, "Is this the place?"

"I think so," I said, staring at the mass of people already there. My throat was suddenly dry, and I wasn't able to focus on what he asked next.

"Any idea where I should park?" he asked, surveying the chaos.

Eve answered for me. "Anywhere, really. Just pull over and pop the trunk. We can take it from there."

He pushed the car into park. "Here's as good a place as any. After all, we have the author in the car."

I blushed at that; I hadn't meant to imply that I was the only author and that all of this was for me. I went to correct him but before I could, Eve said, "Absolutely!" and jumped out of the car.

I opened the door and followed her around to the trunk. To our surprise, the driver also came around and joined us at the trunk.

He popped the trunk and said with a smile, "I can't let the author of the hour be seen lifting her own bags out of the car now, can I?" he said with a wink.

My blush deepened at that, and both Eve and Mira giggled. All I could say was, "You're too kind. Thank you so much."

He unloaded all the bags on the curb and got back into the car. With a wave and a, "Good luck today!" he was gone.

I turned to Eve and Mira to explain I didn't ask for any of that and hadn't told him that this whole thing was for me, but they were both already smiling at me.

"Well, miss fancy author, now that we're here, where do you want your bags?" Eve asked.

I burst into laughter at that, and they both followed suit.

When I caught my breath, I said, "You guys know I didn't ask for any of that."

"You know it's okay to celebrate your own accomplishments and let others celebrate them, too, every once in a while, right?" said Mira.

"Seriously, this is a huge accomplishment. You're one of twenty-five authors here. It's a big deal!" said Eve.

"I mean, I guess," I said doubtfully, as I continued to take in the amount of people that were here for the setup alone.

When I had agreed to this, I hadn't given much thought to the six-hundred people that would be here. Even when I was ordering books and merchandise for my table, I hadn't given much thought at all to the sheer volume of people I would have to talk to today. I was glad I hadn't, because now that I was seeing the scope of the event, I was panicking again.

"Deep breaths," said Eve. "You two go ahead. I'll be out here if you need anything at all. There's a store around the corner if you need me to make a run for anything, but other than that, I'll be here."

I felt so guilty and unbelievably grateful that she was willing to sit out here for the next hour, just in case I needed something.

"You really are the best." I looked over at Mira and added, "Both of you."

Mira checked the time and said, "We really should go in, but, Eve, if we have extra time or need anything, I'll come let you know. We'll see you in a bit!"

"Bye for now, and thank you both so, so, so much!" I added quickly before picking up a couple of the bags and heading in. I didn't need to glance behind me to know that Mira had done the same and was following me.

When we entered, there were only a couple of other authors already there setting up. The rest of the people were volunteers finishing their preparations before the first wave of people started coming in in an hour.

The floor was full of 6-foot-long tables set up in rows, and most of the tables were empty. I surveyed the space for any familiar faces, but didn't see any. The tables weren't labeled, so I wasn't sure where to go. Thankfully, a woman dressed in black jeans with a walkie talkie attached to her belt stopped and asked us if we needed any help.

"Are the tables assigned?"

"No, honey. Just pick whatever table you want and start getting set up." She glanced at her watch and added, "Might want to be quick about it. We have T-minus 55 minutes until launch."

I almost laughed at the way she said that, but held it in. I glanced at Mira and saw her also holding back laughter. I thanked the woman, and we headed a little further into the venue.

"Where to, boss?" Mira asked, grinning.

I glared at her for half a moment before laughing and saying with a shrug, "I vote you should pick."

She didn't entertain that. "Not a chance. It's your day. You pick the table and just tell me what to do."

I surveyed the area, thought about it for a second, and surprised myself with making an easy decision.

I went to the second row, took a left, and followed it all the way to the end, to the table facing inward at the end of the row.

"Good choice. That way people will have to see you when they come down the row."

I hadn't actually thought about that, but she was right. It was definitely a good vantage point.

I didn't actually know why I picked that table, but the choice felt right. I had tried not to put too much thought into it, since the last thing I needed right now was to be paralyzed by indecision. I had enough going on and was scared enough about the event and all the people I was going to have to talk to. The last thing I needed was to have a panic attack over choosing a table.

I was realistic and knew I wasn't going to be anyone's favorite author here, especially not with the likes of Jordan A. Day and Agatha Toller coming.

Realistically, my choice in table mattered a lot, especially since I wasn't that well known, but also since I was an alternate. I hadn't had nearly as much time as some of the other authors to market my books to the ticket-holders and let them know I would be there.

There was a lot of pressure on me today, and I had quite low expectations, but I was happy at least that I had survived the first big decision without letting my thoughts drown me. I was even happier that Mira also saw the merits of the table and that it was chosen so we could hurry and set up. We opened the bags and began taking out the books. I had brought about fifty of the first book in the series and twenty of the second. The last in the trilogy had been underway for a while, and I had finally decided on an ending, but it was still a ways from being published.

I hoped the first book would reel people in and get them to want the second book and to be excited for the third and final installment.

After the third book, I couldn't decide what would come next. I was entertaining the idea of doing a spinoff about the love interest's sister, but I couldn't decide what my plan was for her, especially with how I decided the trilogy would end. When I first had that idea, my concept for the end of the trilogy was much different, so now I was struggling to imagine how a spinoff for his sister would play out. I would probably have to scrap the idea, or at the very least, make a lot of extreme changes to her character and what I had planned for her. I was just grateful I knew how the series was going to end now. With that in mind and fully written, I could tell readers with more confidence than I had before that the ending was coming.

We ended up stacking the first book into a pyramid on one side of the table. We left the middle open for now, and on the right side of the table, started lining up the two book bundle packages. They were put into gift bags that held both books, a bookmark, a couple of character art prints, and a candle that smelled like either Tristan, Damien, or Serena, depending on the reader's preference.

I hoped people would love them and hoped they would sell well. I had spent a decent amount of money on them and needed them to sell well to justify that cost. I knew I wasn't going to make my money back by any stretch of the imagination, but I hoped I would make enough that it would seem worth it.

With the packages and books stacked, we moved on to figuring out what to put in the middle. I would be sitting in the middle, so I didn't want anything too tall or in the way. I was pretty short and didn't want anything obstructing my vision, or the readers from seeing me. I decided to put out a copy of each of the books, each on their own little display stand, and laid out some bookmarks and character art. I was hoping the bookmarks and character art would help catch people's eye.

I had a few different character art prints to choose from and ended up displaying one of a beautiful rendering of Serena's dragon form and another of Serena and Tristan together. I was on the fence about whether to put out the other prints I had. They were of Inez and Serena sparring together and a print of Serena and Damien. I didn't want to spoil too much of the story, and wasn't sure if these would. Mira decided they wouldn't, so I put those out, too.

When I checked the time again, I realized we had somehow finished setting up in only twenty minutes. It felt like it had taken forever, but we still had forty minutes. New authors were still straggling in. The tables on my left and right were still empty.

When I saw Agatha come in with a couple of heavy looking bags, I immediately rushed over to her and offered to take one.

"I know I'm not as young as I used to be, but do I look like I'm struggling that badly that you had to run over here?"

I blushed before she laughed and handed me the bag. "We just finished setting up, so I figured I could give you a hand. Besides, now I can steer you to the table next to me, so really I did this for me." We both laughed at that.

I pointed out my table to her and then the table to its left. "If you don't tell me otherwise, that's where I'm bringing your bag."

She looked around the room, before nodding and walking over to the table I had pointed out. "Great job, dearie! Most people know that in events like these, the most important thing is location, location, location, but everyone usually wants to be in the first row, or right next to the aisle. Personally, I like the end of the row facing in tables the best. Then people have to look at you the whole time they're coming down the aisle. It gives you a lot more face time than if you're in the aisle itself. Trade secret so don't tell your friends. I don't want to have to fight them off for my favorite tables," she said with a wink.

I was too busy being thrilled that I had chosen right, according to someone as experienced as Agatha, that I didn't know how to respond. She thumped her bag down on the table and I lifted mine up and did the same.

Unsure whether I should offer to help, I glanced back at Mira. She was sitting behind my table tidying up the packaging I had used to protect the books on the way here, but besides that, everything was done. I caught Mira's eye a half of a second later and waved her over.

She headed over, and I introduced her to Agatha. "Mira, this is Agatha, author extraordinaire, who somehow crafts worlds and characters so realistic that they seem to leap off the page at you."

There was a twinkle in her eye when she said, "You'd be surprised at how real some of those characters are."

She held out her hand to Mira, and I added, "Agatha, this is Mira, my new…" I hesitated for a moment, unsure what word to use. I felt like this was maybe the beginning of a friendship, but I didn't want to jinx anything. After a moment of awkward silence with them both watching me expectantly, I

113

finished. "…assistant." I saw Mira's face fall a fraction of an inch and rushed to add, "Well, assistant for the day. She's my roommate for the trip and was nice enough to help me out. She's been a lifesaver."

She smiled a bit at that and shook Agatha's hand. "It's wonderful to meet you! I've heard such good things about your stories."

Agatha smiled at her and said, "And it's wonderful to meet such a good friend of Sadie's."

Mira's smile widened, as did my own. I was thrilled she was happy about being referred to as my friend. She certainly deserved the title after how big of a help she'd been, but I had no idea what I had done to deserve her friendship.

Mira and I both simultaneously offered to help Agatha set up her table, and between the three of us, we made quick work of it.

When we finished and went back to my table, Mira went to go check in with Eve, so for the first time, I was alone at my table. Well, not really alone if Agatha being at the table right next to me counted. I was more grateful than ever that she had agreed to set up right next to me.

She caught me watching her, and said, "Deep breaths, dearie. We're getting company soon."

I followed her gaze and could see through the fence that the line to get in was long enough I couldn't see the end.

My face paled, and Agatha's smile was gone. She stood and walked over to me, carefully weaving through the maze of boxes that needed to be broken down and suitcases that had held my things to sell. When she made it to my side a moment later, she had a concerned expression on her face.

"Dear, I'm guessing this must be one of your first times?"

I nodded. "The actual first."

She let out a whistle. "Dang, honey, you don't mess around. Normally, people start out slow. My first event, maybe fifty people came."

"I kept putting off doing events, especially with COVID," I said with a shrug. "There kept being excuses not to, and then when I was invited here, I figured if I had to rip off the bandaid at some point, it might as well be here. Go big or go home, am I right?"

She laughed at that, but I could still see the awe in her eyes. "That's one way to do it. You definitely have guts. My younger self never would have started in a place like this." She saw I was getting paler and backtracked, "But just because I wouldn't have had the guts, doesn't mean it isn't a great idea. This is such a good way to market your stories to new readers who might not have found them otherwise. Just be yourself and they'll love you. It took you all of a minute to win me over. Just be yourself and you'll sell out your books in no time."

I was doubtful, but feeling a little better, if only because I knew she was there for me and that in and of itself was so insane I was having trouble thinking of much else. I was being comforted by Agatha Toller. I wouldn't have imagined that in my wildest dreams.

A moment later, a woman in a bright pink power suit approached us both, asking if we needed anything. She had dyed red hair and had a walkie-talkie strapped to her hip. I was about to shake my head and thank her when she introduced herself as Kodie. *The* Kodie, the extraordinary woman responsible for making so many people's dreams come true.

I shook my head. "I'm all set, but I did want to say thank you, from all of us, really. This is such a dream come true."

Her eyes brightened at that and her smile widened. She was about to say something when her walkie-talkie rang. The volunteers needed her.

"Well, that's me! But thank you, truly. I can't wait for everyone to see the ball, because this was nothing. The ball is going to blow everyone away." With that, she hurried up front, and a few moments later, the gates opened.

FIFTEEN

My heart raced until I saw everyone was being funneled through a well-organized check-in station and we wouldn't be descended upon all at once. I took a few more deep breaths and relaxed a little after seeing that. It also helped that Eve and Mira, who was now with her, were at the very front of the line.

The moment they were both past check-in, they headed directly over to me and made sure I was doing okay and asked if I needed any help or needed anything. I assured them I was fine and to go explore. I wanted them to enjoy themselves, too; it was their trip, too.

Eve headed off on a mission, with Mira in tow. I didn't have to ask to know who she was searching for. Jordan would be the first person most people went to see, especially since it was rumored she was doing an early access launch for one of her books here. Even as one of the attending authors, I didn't know how true that was, but we were all excited and hopeful.

Eve had said she would try to get me a copy of the book if she could if it was there. I was hoping she would be able to. I wasn't sure if I would have time later to go over and introduce myself, since the book sale was only four hours and there were six-hundred people expected to attend. I was grateful she was willing to try to grab one for me. I hadn't seen Jordan during setup, so I hoped they had better luck finding her than I did.

The first people trickled in and a couple people actually came over to my table and asked me about my book. They had heard I was one of the LGBTQ authors at the event and wanted to hear about my stories. It was crazy to me, since I had just recently come out, that something that I used to be so scared of people finding out about was now a source of pride for me.

I was ecstatic to be writing stories that featured bisexual people and to be out of the closet while doing it. It was incredibly important to me personally to help combat the bi-erasure that happened all the time in the culture and in mainstream media. Whenever anyone came out as bisexual, their past and present dating history was essentially examined to judge the validity of their claim, and then when they ended up in a committed relationship, the gender of that person was used against them.

People loved to pigeon-hole bisexual people into the normal boxes of gay or straight, but sexuality and life weren't that simple. Society loved to make things black and white, and ignore the gray, but life didn't work that way.

My stories had always and would always feature bisexual characters for the mere fact that most stories didn't. I wanted to show the nuisances of being bisexual, and from a plot and romance standpoint, having bisexual characters made for a more chaotic, messy story where you could make readers think that anyone was a possible love interest, and as an author who enjoyed misleading her readers, that was definitely a big bonus.

It seemed my mission resonated with other people as well, even more so than I could have hoped or imagined. A couple of hours into the convention, I had talked to countless people and had sold fifty-five of my seventy books!

I had thought I might sell twenty if I was lucky. I was ecstatic. I was pretty close to selling out, and the event was only halfway through! Mira and Eve had been checking in on me throughout the event, thank goodness, because I hadn't assembled nearly enough bundles for the amount of sales I was making.

The influx of orders had caught me off-guard, and I was stressing over how I was possibly going to finish assembling everything while still making sales and talking to readers, but before I could start searching for them, Eve and Mira showed up. I shouldn't have been surprised. Since I had met them, they had been continuing to prove they would be there when I needed them. Rationally, I knew that when most people said they would be there for you, they meant it, but Kay never was. I was always there when she needed, but she seldom returned the favor. Seeing them so willing to drop everything to help me, without me even having to ask, had me holding back tears.

Hanna, Sabrina, Naomi, and the new girls we met at dinner had all come over to my table, gushing about what an honor it was to meet me. I blushed as red as a tomato, but it worked. The people mulling about were more interested. Especially since Hanna and Skye both asked for pictures with me. I couldn't believe it.

The convention was going better than I could have ever imagined. With only a couple of hours and twenty copies left, I was letting myself dare to dream I might actually sell out.

SIXTEEN

My heart stuttered when I saw her. She looked just like I imagined. Yes, there was fan art and character art, but this was different. I hadn't truly pictured her, what she would look like living and breathing, until just now.

And it was unreal.

I couldn't stop myself from gawking at her, but it was like she had stepped directly out of my imagination.

Whoever she was, she had gotten the details just right, down to the queendom's crest on their leather arm guards. I couldn't believe it.

I quickly scanned the room, searching for Mira or Eve. They needed to see her. Someone else needed to see how perfect her cosplay was.

I was floored anyone would go to that length, especially to be Inez. That was the most shocking part. I hadn't dared to dream there would be any cosplayers here for my story. But if I had given it any thought, I would have assumed someone would have chosen to be Serena, not Inez. I was surprised anyone liked Inez enough to go through the trouble.

Lately, I was struggling myself to like Inez. Honestly, I had been toying with the idea of killing her off, so I didn't have to deal with the reminders of who she was modeled after, but I hadn't yet had the heart to do it. She may have started in the likeness of Kay, but she was my character and Serena's best friend. Serena had been through so much already. I couldn't imagine making the selfish decision to punish her by taking away her best friend just because I couldn't come to terms with my feelings. So Inez had stayed safe so far, but it was still surprising someone wanted to cosplay as her.

When the first book had hit the market, I had hardly expected to sell more than a couple of copies, so anyone knowing the story was still a shock. As I stared at her, I tried to guess how long it might have taken her to make and put together her outfit, but the shear thought of the time and effort that must have gone into the project nearly brought me to tears.

In fact, I could feel my eyes watering. I couldn't help it; it honestly still didn't feel real that I was published at all, never mind that someone would go to that effort for my book. The idea that someone loved my characters as much as I did was crazy to me.

As I watched, she started to make her way to my table. There were a couple of people milling about, checking out my book, but I paid them little attention. I only had eyes for her.

I pleaded with the universe that she was headed my way. She must have been with the outfit she was wearing. There was no way she wouldn't stop over.

I hoped she would ask for a picture. I couldn't let her leave in an outfit like that without a picture, but I didn't want to have to ask. I would if it came down to it, though. I needed proof.

I quickly glanced around, not wanting to take my eyes from her for long, worried she would disappear if I did. I was desperately hoping to find Mira, Eve, or anyone from my group, but I didn't see anyone I recognized. Of course I would be the only one to see this. I wished someone was around to be freaking out about it with me.

She continued in my general direction, and I tried to think of what I would say to her, tried to decide what was and wasn't safe to mention. I always struggled the most with that, remembering what parts of the story were published and what parts were still a work in progress. I figured as long as I didn't mention wanting to kill off Inez, I was probably fine. But I always worried about making a bad impression on my fans. I hoped she would be easier to please than the real Inez would be.

I gulped when her eyes drifted up to mine. She was a dead ringer for Inez. I was going to have to talk to her, but my mouth was so dry I didn't know if I would be able to form words. I swallowed, hoping it would help. It didn't.

She continued to watch me with interest. I desperately wanted to impress her and hoped I would somehow live up to whatever high expectations I was sure she had of me. You don't go to all that effort to cosplay a character without having high expectations of the author.

It was fans like her that made me love writing. I had put so much into those books, thrown every piece of myself into them. Knowing that she must have loved the story and my characters as much as I did was insane.

As I watched, she was stopped by a group of cosplayers. I just barely stopped myself in time from making an audible groan. I wished she would hurry up and get over here. Dragging out the interaction wasn't helping my nerves. I noticed Morgana and Eli were a part of the group, and was surprised to notice Eli was cosplaying Jordan A. Day's A Ripple of Power and Promise's Felix damn near flawlessly.

I had glimpsed the silver hair earlier and knew it had to be Felix, but hadn't guessed it was Eli. Eli was standing with an Ainsley and a Dash; the whole trio was here.

I saw Eli notice me and waved to him. He gave me a trademark Felix wink, which had me laughing. He was really in character.

Movement from her had me turning my eye back to Inez. I knew without being within earshot that they had to be asking her who she was cosplaying. I wasn't delusional enough to think most people here would know about my book. I just hoped she wasn't embarrassed having to continually explain her outfit.

As I watched, her face hardened to impatience. Her acting was incredible; she even had Inez's mannerisms down pat. She would have that same expression on her face now. In fact, she probably wouldn't have lasted as long as they had before getting annoyed. Inez would have been pissed at any sort of distraction or delay in her mission, and would have been annoyed at being asked stupid questions.

She sidestepped the group and continued on her way. My heart sped up the closer she got. As she strode closer, I audibly gasped. She even had Inez's tattoo, the mark of the royal guard. I squinted, trying to get a better view to see if maybe it was a coincidence, but I spotted the crown held by the dragon's tail. There was no mistaking it. It was the mark of the royal guard. The dragon's tail wrapped around her bicep before meeting with the body and head, the wings spread wide as the dragon roared.

I stopped trying to hide my staring. She stopped a few hundred yards away from my table and I watched as she pulled something out of her pocket. I squinted, trying to get a better look, but I couldn't tell what it was. As I watched, she did an about face.

I panicked for a moment, wondering if I should go over there. *If she left now, would I ever see her again?* She had to be coming to see me, with that outfit and even the tattoo. She had to be coming to see me. I wasn't able to tear my eyes from the tattoo. I expected it to be drawn on, but it seemed real. But there was no way. There was no way my book mattered enough to anyone to get a symbol of mine tattooed on their body. It had to be drawn, which was also incredibly impressive.

I breathed a sigh of relief as she turned back around. She glanced at the object in her hands before glancing up directly at me. I was startled that she caught me staring, but offered what I hoped was a welcoming smile. I didn't want to scare her off.

She sauntered over to me, stopping in front of me and glancing back down. Now that she was closer, I could see that she was holding a compass. It struck me as an odd choice. Sure, Inez probably used a similar instrument on her journeys, but I had never explicitly written in a compass.

As I took in the rest of her outfit, I noticed that her trademark amulet was missing. That surprised me. With all the other details she had added, even getting the tattoo just right, it was odd to me she didn't choose to add the amulet, too.

Besides the amulet missing, I couldn't fault her perfect cosplay. Hell, she looked exactly like the character art I was selling, even down to her skin tone and hair, if it wasn't a wig. Inez was the fantasy equivalent of Latina, with her bronze skin tone and long, dark, wavy hair that she often complained about being an inconvenience but secretly loved. She frequently talked of chopping it off, but never would.

When she glanced up at me, I was mesmerized by her mocha eyes, until I saw her frown.

My anxiety spiked the moment her face showed her displeasure. I hadn't even spoken. How could I have possibly already disappointed her?

Her eyes moved past me. I glanced over my shoulder as well, but there was nothing and no one there.

She glanced back down at the compass, still frowning. I followed her eyes, and was startled to see that though she shook it somewhat violently and the needle moved a little with the shaking, it was pointed directly at me.

"Stupid Altean compass!" she muttered under her breath, giving it a thump on the bottom. I flinched at the unexpectedly loud noise. "Gods damned stupid magic...it should still work..."

I peeled my eyes from her, looking at the compass in her hand and saw that no matter how she angled the compass, it was still stubbornly pointed at me. I was just thinking I must have been facing north when she stepped around my booth behind me.

A low groan came out of her mouth. "This can't be right," she said under her breath.

I tried to reason that she was clearly upset about something else. She hadn't even spoken to me. She couldn't possibly be mad at me or disappointed in me, but my thoughts were spiraling. Without even trying, this fake Inez was making me feel as inferior and insignificant as her real-life counterpart had. Why I had ever thought Kay was a good friend, or included her in my story, I couldn't for the life of me figure out.

I took a deep breath. There was no way the cosplayer meant to make me feel like that. They were just doing a phenomenal job of being Inez. I took another deep breath, willing myself to be calm and not snap at them or betray any of the other emotions they were making me feel.

"Can I help you?"

She spun around on her heel and was staring directly at me. She was probably half a foot taller than me, but she seemed to tower over me. She checked the compass. I did, too. To my shock, it was still pointed at me.

That didn't make any sense. It couldn't be pointed at me now that she was standing behind me. It should've been pointed behind her.

She gestured at the compass. "Well, according to this stupid thing, you can."

I gulped. I felt like shrinking. I had thought I could handle her undivided attention, but, clearly, I was wrong. I had no idea what to say to her, or how to answer her accusation or question, whatever it was.

The thought frustrated me. I had written Inez; she was my character, but whoever was cosplaying her was going off script. There was a reason Kay and I weren't friends, and I didn't know how to handle this very real reminder of her. If anything, this was worse, because here was a diehard fan that I was apparently already disappointing.

She continued to stare at me, waiting. I stammered out, "I-I'm not sure what the c-compass has to do with anything, but I'd like to help, if I can."

She shook her head again and said, "It can't be you."

Now I was getting a little annoyed. I wrote Inez and her story. I was the author who was picked to appear at the convention, albeit as an alternate, but still. She had crafted an entire outfit just to come see me. I knew Inez could be a bitch, but come on, the fan in her should have broken character by now to actually talk to me.

My annoyance seeped into my voice, but I didn't care anymore. "Listen, 'Inez', I appreciate your dedication to the act, but I think you'd be better suited acting yourself. I'd love to sign a book for you if you'd like. I still have a few copies-"

She cut me off before I could finish. "You know me?" she asked in disbelief.

I fought not to roll my eyes. Her dedication was admirable, and would have been harmless if she had picked any other character, but being face to face with Inez was almost too much for me.

"Of course I do. You're Inez Cyneward from the queendom of Sherbrooke."

Her face softened a little, and she studied me, the appearance of awe on her face. "Maybe you are the one I've been seeking."

I chuckled at that. Maybe playing along wouldn't kill me. "I should hope so. I assume you've been searching for Serena's story?"

Her eyes lit up at that. "Yes! She told me I would find you, but I was starting to doubt her." She scrutinized me before adding, "Please forgive me, but I didn't expect the all-powerful sorceress to be quite so... short."

"Sorceress?" I asked.

"Yes; the one who can control our fate and change our destinies."

Ah, I was wondering how cosplayers addressed their authors while in cosplay. I had to admire her commitment and quick wit. It was a smart workaround, and to be honest, I didn't hate being called a sorceress.

She bowed slightly, putting her at eye level with me. She quirked an eyebrow at me and added, "Forgive me, lady. Celeste talked only of your power, nothing of your appearance. I hardly expected the all-powerful sorceress to be so..." She seemed to catch herself, stopping short before whatever likely insulting thing she had been about to say, and instead said, "But that doesn't matter. You're here and I found you. Now that I found you, I need your help."

"What can I do for you?"

She took a step closer to me and lowered her voice to just above a whisper. "As much as I hate to admit it, I can't fix things on my own. I need you to fix it. Change things. Quickly.

Before he hurts Serena, or worse." She shuddered at the thought. "I just need you to fix it. You seem to know me and how important Serena is to me. I would go to the ends of the world for her." She gestured around her, continuing, "I literally went to the ends of the world for her. I lost her once, and then I lost her again. I can't keep doing this. First to him and now to the Murderous King of Bancroft. I need her to be okay. I was closer than I'd ever been to finding my true love, to getting answers about why the Gods didn't see fit to bless me with Serena. I was so close. I was okay, I really was, or I was getting there. It didn't physically pain me to see Serena with him anymore. I only ever wanted her to be happy, and it took some time, but seeing her happy with Tristan, I was learning to live with it. When I saw his amulet, I knew what it meant, whether or not she did, but from the fact that she hadn't kissed him yet, I knew she suspected, or hoped. My heart shattered into a million gods damned pieces, but I was learning to be okay. I was going to be alone forever, and I was okay with that. My amulet probably didn't even work, since it had never lit up. Every day and night, I had prayed that it would, that one day it would light up for Serena. It was the only thing I had ever kept hidden from her, but it never did. And just when I had grown to accept that was how things would be, Serena and Tristan happy together and me alone, the stupid amulet lit up. It hadn't so much as flickered before, but it had the nerve to light up then. And before I had a chance to think about what that meant, we were thrown into a battle that we narrowly escaped with our lives. Serena was almost killed, and I couldn't get to her in time. Tristan saved her and almost died himself. I truly forgave him then. Anyone willing to die for Serena was alright by me.

"Just when I thought we were out of the woods, Serena messed up big time. She kissed him. When they pulled apart, I watched the realization of what she had done dawn on her, but it was too late. There wasn't a single thing anyone could do. The King grabbed her and whisked her off, and now he has her and is doing the gods know what to her. Things have been changing, people have been changing, and don't even get me started on the mist. Please, you have to help me."

I was standing staring wide eyed at her. She really was taking this whole cosplaying thing to the next level, and, clearly, she had done her homework. Everything except whatever she was saying about mist was true to my writing. She was so distressed that I didn't know what to say. Without having a better plan, I continued to play along.

"I'm sorry things have been so tough for you. It can't have been an easy journey here from Sherbrooke, either."

She gaped at me. "How did you know I came from Sherbrooke? That was supposed to be a secret. Everyone was supposed to think I was still in Altea." She stared at me for another minute before shaking her head. "But of course we can't hide anything from you, the Sorceress Sadie of Hawthorne."

I couldn't help laughing at that. She scowled at me. "It's not a laughing matter. It was a harrowing journey from Sherbrooke. You don't, or actually you probably do, know what it cost me to be here. I had to give up my amulet to make the spell work. That amulet hadn't worked my whole life and now, all of a sudden, it works and I have to give it away. Of course. I shouldn't have been surprised. It was just my luck. I should've just let Tristan come, but I couldn't do that. With Serena still there, he needed to be, too. I couldn't have kept her as safe as he could. I couldn't protect her or break spells on her like he could. I knew that, so I came. Serena might not forgive me for doing it, but someone had to come. Believe me, if there had been any other way, one that didn't involve leaving her and Bella on their own, I would have, but there wasn't another choice. Now she's waiting, counting on me. They all are, if they even remember me. Who even knows with that mist." Her frown deepened before her eyes met mine again and she brightened. "But everything's changed now. I found you and you can fix it all." She smiled hopefully at me.

Well, I was glad she was smiling, but I had no idea what she was talking about or how to respond. In my story, Inez had her amulet. That explained the omission from the cosplay, though. My published works ended with Serena being kidnapped. The last book wasn't published yet and I had kept changing the ending. I finally decided how the series would end and finished it a couple of weeks ago. I had wanted to give it a happy ending, I really did. I had grown to love Serena and wanted her to be happy, but it didn't make sense for the story.

When I started the series a few years ago, I was younger and more idealistic, more naïve. I had believed there was no problem that couldn't be solved when you loved someone, no problem too big for good communication to fix.

I wholeheartedly believed that no obstacle was too big or untamable as long as two people were willing to work together, but Kay shattered that for me. Seven years. I had put seven years of my life into her, shared seven years of tears and triumphs with her just for her to go silent on me. Absolute silence for the better part of a year. It was coming up on the anniversary of our big fight. I felt like such a fraud. How could I possibly write about a found family when my own best friend didn't want anything to do with me? When my own best friend turned her back on me because it was easier than fighting.

She didn't care enough to fight for us; I wasn't worth fighting for. I can't say I blame her. I don't know that I would have fought for me either, but I had believed with everything in me that she was like a sister to me. She was the family I got to choose, only for her to abandon me.

I had cried over her for days. I had tried to fix things, but there was nothing but silence from her. I had been trying; I hadn't actually given up until my birthday passed without a single word from her.

I wouldn't say I was a shallow person, but my birthday meant a lot to me. As a recovering people pleaser, I very rarely let myself be the center of attention, so I always placed high hopes on my birthday. Which almost always led to disappointment.

This year for my birthday, I caught COVID and didn't hear a word from her. That was when it hit me how truly over it was. I was sitting there, nearly dying, and didn't hear a word from her. To be honest, I had a very mild case and was mostly better in a week, but as I was lying in bed with a fever crying on my birthday, it hit me how over things were between us. She used to be the one I called for everything. She had seen me through everything, but now, suddenly, she was gone. I said one thing she didn't like and all of a sudden she was gone. So much for sisterhood and communication.

After my birthday, I turned back to Serena's story. Feeling more jaded, I took one look at my outline and I knew it wouldn't work. Serena's friends were supposed to band together and rescue her, and then they would all fight and save the Realms together. But they would never stick together in the real world, not in the face of such power. They would fall apart the moment Damien came for them. The moment Serena was taken, they would abandon her.

They were supposed to go after her, but they wouldn't. They didn't stand a chance, and they knew that. Going after her wasn't brave; it was foolish and foolhardy. They were lucky to have made it out alive in the first place.

They wouldn't rush back against all odds into the face of danger to save her, especially Inez. The moment Serena didn't give Inez what she wanted, Inez wouldn't come. Inez wouldn't be able to put aside her own feelings of rejection to try to rescue her friend. The friendship would die, and Serena might die, but Inez wouldn't rush into danger for her. None of them would. Well, Tristan would, and he would be a fool for it. He would die before he could rescue her on his own. Isabella would want to, but Draco wouldn't let her until they had a better plan. He knew Damien and how he operated. He would never let Bella rush into that kind of danger without a plan, whether or not her sister was in danger. The moment Inez saw the odds, she would abandon Serena, and the rest of the group would fall apart, and Tristan would die. I didn't even want to imagine what would happen to Serena, but it was a necessary evil. She didn't deserve it, but sometimes bad things happened to good people. That was life. Things weren't always fair. Sometimes the villain won.

Even if by some miracle, Inez didn't abandon them, which I was sure she would, and they all stuck together, they wouldn't be equipped to deal with what was coming for them. It was wishful thinking to think my little ragtag band of misfits would have been able to fight off everything Damien was going to throw at them. There was only one way their story would end, and it wouldn't be pretty. The readers were going to hate it and I didn't particularly like it myself, but there was only one possible way for it to go. It was going to be emotionally devastating, but life was like that. Life didn't have perfect happy endings, and the best fiction mimicked life. I wouldn't pander to my readers and give them an easy ending; I would give them a real one. Sometimes love wasn't enough, and sometimes people who claimed to be your family abandoned you.

If Kay couldn't be bothered to communicate with me through a simple disagreement, what hope was there for Inez to stick around and fight a losing battle for Serena? I so badly had wanted Serena to get her happy ending. She deserved it. She didn't deserve the hell that was waiting for her at the end of her story, but that was how things went sometimes.

But there was no way for this Inez cosplayer to possibly know any of this. Maybe they were just theorizing about what they thought might happen? Still, I had no idea what this mist they were talking about was, and they had Inez all wrong. She had been noble and caring until Serena unknowingly rejected her.

She had never spoken her feelings for Serena aloud, but when Serena chose Tristan, she felt rejected anyway. She wasn't able to see past her own feelings to enjoy her friend's happiness. She only cared that Serena didn't pick her. Never mind that she wasn't Serena's true love, Serena picked him instead. It had always been them against the world, and now it was just Inez. When Serena was taken, a part of Inez felt like she deserved it. Serena was kidnapped after kissing Tristan; it felt poetic. Inez didn't love the idea of Serena in Damien's control, but there was nothing to be done. His fortress was impenetrable, and she wouldn't die trying to save the girl that broke her heart. Besides, even if she managed to rescue Serena, it would have been just for her to run back into Tristan's arms. She wouldn't risk her life for that.

But I couldn't blame this Inez for not knowing that. So far, I had tried to only show Inez in her best light, but that all changed when Serena rejected her. *She* changed when Serena rejected her. I paled to think about what this person would think about Inez after reading how the story really ended. But they didn't want the truth of where my story was going. I could let them keep their hope a little longer.

"Tell me how you would see things fixed and I'll do my best."

The hope in her eyes grew. "To be honest, I don't care. As long as Serena's safe, I don't care. I wanted her to be mine, but now I only care that she's happy and safe. You know what Damien is capable of, and without her shifting, Serena's more vulnerable than ever. I would see her rescued."

The emotion in her voice was startling, as were her feelings about Serena. "And would you do the rescuing?"

She didn't hesitate. "In a heartbeat, if that's what it took, but as long as she is safe, I don't care. I want her safe and want whoever rescues her to be safe as well. I would say send Tristan, but if anything happens to him, it would kill whatever is left of her." She shuddered at that. "Can you turn back time? And stop all of this?"

I supposed I could; they were my stories after all. "If I could, what would you have me change?"

She thought about it for a moment. "I would have things go back to before Serena and Tristan kissed."

"Not earlier?"

"You could do earlier?"

"Darling, I'm the all-powerful sorceress. I can do whatever I like," I joked, but she didn't laugh.

She considered for a long moment, before she asked carefully, "Can you change inherent truths in our land?"

I saw where she was going with that from a mile away. Many people that had read my story had wanted Inez to get her girl in the end and hadn't been anymore thrilled than Inez was about Tristan. People had grown to like Tristan, but there were still a lot of people that thought Inez and Serena should end up together.

"Like the true love bond?" I asked.

Her eyes were on the floor, and she wouldn't meet my gaze, but nodded.

"If I could, would you have me do it?"

Her eyes widened. "You can?" she whispered. Her eyes fell to her hands and said softly to herself, "Serena could belong with me," with wonder in her voice. She really was in character. She met my eyes again. "What would become of Tristan? And the woman actually out there for me? Can you tell me who she is? Although I don't know how anyone could compare to Serena."

When I had written the part about Inez's true love, I had still expected the story to continue. I had planned for her to have a future and her own love story, but now, with the new ending, that didn't seem possible.

I shook my head sadly. "I can't tell you who."

She didn't seem surprised. "Of course," she said thoughtfully. "Can I have some time to think about it?"

That surprised me. The Inez I had written, at least the Inez in the last book, wouldn't have hesitated. I nodded solemnly, still playing along. "Take all the time you need."

"But when I decide, you can send me back and it will be like no time has passed?"

"Send you back where?"

"To Sherbrooke," she said matter of factly.

Geez, she really is in character. I wondered if there was anything that would make her break character. I had seen a lot of cosplayers today, but none of them were as dedicated as 'Inez'. Whenever one of them came over to my table, they had talked to me as themselves. I had even briefly talked with Gwen, who was cosplaying Ivy, a princess from a popular series I hadn't read yet. The shocking part came a little later when I saw Morgana. She nodded in acknowledgment of me, but that wasn't the shocking part; the shocking part was that she was dressed as Cassandra, Ivy's enemy turned lover. The irony was too much for me. I wondered if either of them knew. I had half a mind to find Gwen again, or Ollie and let him know, but I couldn't find either of them and couldn't leave my table.

Gwen was dedicated to her character, but even she broke character to talk to me. 'Inez' refused to, and while I had to admire it, she wasn't the easiest to talk to.

"Look, I'm sorry. It's not that this hasn't been fun, but I'm pretty new to the convention scene and to cosplayers. This is the first time I've had someone cosplaying one of my characters, so I'm not really sure how I'm supposed to act."

She tilted her head at me before saying, "Forgive me, Sorceress Sadie of Hawthorne-"

"You can just call me Sadie," I injected.

"Okay, Sadie of Hawthorne-"

I tried again. "No. Just Sadie; no Sorceress, no of Hawthorne. Just Sadie."

"Okay, sure thing, Just Sadie."

I didn't know whether to laugh or hit my head against the wall. Whoever this was, was sure getting a kick out of messing with me.

"Just Sadie, or should I call you Sadie the Just? I hope that proves to be an earned name. I have to level with you. I'm unfamiliar with the customs here in Hawthorne, so please tell me, what is this 'cosplaying' you keep accusing me of?"

I didn't know where to start with that, so I latched onto the first thing I could think of. "This isn't Hawthorne, this is Portland."

She cocked her head at me, confused. "Are we not in your homeland?"

I shook my head. "I travelled a long way to be here, too."

She nodded. "Well, it seems good fortune is on my side that I found you. Now tell me of cosplaying."

136

I was getting annoyed, but took a deep breath and tried to rein in my feelings. I should have been grateful they cared enough to be going overboard.

With a sigh, I tried, "Cosplaying is when someone, like yourself, dresses up as and acts like a character from a book, TV show, or movie."

"You mean like the travelling actors in the theaters?"

She was working overtime to stay in character. "Yes, like that, except in this case you're obviously cosplaying as Inez. What's your name? I'd love to sign something for you."

"I'm not following."

"What's your actual name?"

"Inez, but as the all-powerful Just Sadie, you know that already."

I groaned. I couldn't help it. "I'm sorry, 'Inez'." *Gosh, I was terrible interacting with cosplayers, terrible at doing this whole author thing. I actually put air quotes around Inez. Even I hated myself a little right now, but I couldn't make myself stop.* "But I really don't have time for this. I have a line of people waiting to buy books from me." It was sort of true. There were a few people milling about who were interested, but I could have easily kept talking with 'Inez'. I was just worried I was going to say something else I would regret. Inez was too much like Kay, and this cosplayer was doing too good a job at being Inez. I couldn't deal with it.

"So much for being Sadie the Just. Celeste said you would help me. Maybe you're not the one I was searching for after all."

She took up her compass again and turned to go, but she glanced at my table and stopped in her tracks. I followed her gaze and saw she had seen the character art, and was staring at the one of Inez and Serena.

She grabbed it and whipped around to me. "How did you get this?"

I barely stopped myself from rolling my eyes. "I'm the author. I had them made for most of my characters." I grabbed the others of Damien and of Tristan and held them up to show her. "See? I have Damien and Tristan, too."

"So it is you. I knew it!"

"Yes, I'm Sadie Hawthorne, the author."

"Sadie the Just, you have to help me."

I rolled my eyes and turned to a reader who had been patiently waiting with a book in hand to purchase.

"Look, whoever you are, I'm sorry, but I have a customer to help."

She stared at me for a moment before hurriedly saying, "I'm so sorry, Just Sadie. I didn't mean to offend you. I'm not used to the Hawthornian customs, but whatever I can do to make amends, I will. I desperately need your help."

"You don't understand. I don't even know who you are. How can I help you?"

"Of course you know me." She held up the character art of Inez and pointed back and forth between it and her own face. "I'm Inez Cyneward, captain of the royal guard of Sherbrooke." She gestured to her tattoo. From closer up, I could see it was definitely real. I gawked at it.

"How long have you had that?"

"Years, since I was appointed to be Serena's personal guard, since she wouldn't have anyone else." Her chest puffed up with pride when she said that. "After all, I'm quite good at what I do."

"You sure are, and I admire your dedication. You really make a great Inez."

"I ought to. I am Inez."

"You really have her down to a tee."

"Are you saying you believe me to be some sort of imposter?"

"Here in 'Hawthorne', we call it cosplaying, but yes."

Her eyebrows scrunched together, and she asked indignantly, "You don't believe me to be me? How can I prove it? There must be a way."

"I'm sorry, but I really don't have time for your games. I have others waiting."

Again, I gestured to the one or two people milling around my booth.

She crossed her arms. "Fine. If you won't help me, I'll find some other way." She threw her compass in her pocket and stalked off toward the entrance.

If all cosplayers were as intense as her, maybe I was lucky I didn't have any others for my story yet.

My eyes turned in Agatha's direction to see if she had caught the interaction only to see her watching me with concern. I shrugged and did my best to smile, but the concerned expression stayed on her face as she watched Inez stalk off.

A few minutes later, Eve and Mira wandered over. Of course they showed up a few minutes after she left. When I told them about the weird encounter, they both shrugged it off, agreeing with me she had taken things a little too far, but that was pretty normal for a cosplayer.

I glanced over to Agatha's table, to see what she thought, but she wasn't there anymore. I must have missed her leaving. I surveyed the area to see if 'Inez' was still around to point her out to them, but she wasn't anywhere to be found. With the chaos that was 'Inez', I had completely forgotten to get her picture. If it wasn't for the missing character art of Serena, I might've convinced myself I imagined her.

SEVENTEEN

A few hours later, the five of us met up to tour the Rose Gardens. Naomi was spending time with her other friends, but the rest of our little group were all there.

Eve and Mira already knew my news, but I was elated to tell the others that I sold out of my books! Not only had I sold out, but with an hour and a half to spare. I had actually cried sitting there at my booth. I just couldn't believe it. I was so ridiculously grateful that anyone had cared enough to buy my stories.

The moment I saw Hanna, I bounced over to her and hugged her, barely restraining myself from jumping up and down. Sabrina quirked an eyebrow at me over Hanna's shoulder. My grin broadened. I broke away from Hanna and actually started jumping up and down. Hanna seemed as excited as me without even knowing why.

"Guys, guys, guys!" I was still bouncing, unable to contain my excitement.

Sabrina laughed. "Come on, out with it. Don't keep us waiting."

"You'll never guess how many books I sold!"

Hanna jumped in. "Well, how many did you bring?"

"70."

"Geez, no wonder you were so slow going through the airport," Sabrina joked.

"For real; they were ridiculously heavy, even in a rolling suitcase, but oh my gosh, you guys, you won't believe it!"

"Come on, tell us!" Hanna said.

"I sold.... drum roll, please," without having to be asked twice, Sabrina rhythmically started slapping a drumbeat on her thighs, "EVERY. SINGLE. BOOK I brought!" I shrieked loud enough it scared a couple of birds that had been resting near the roses into flight. It also gained me a couple of dirty looks from nearby flower enthusiasts, but I couldn't bring myself to care.

Hanna rushed over and pulled me into a hug that quickly expanded into a group hug as Sabrina, Eve, and Mira joined in. When I stopped squealing and pulled away, Sabrina was the first to say, "Dude, that's freaking awesome!"

"For real! It's insane!"

"We never doubted you!" said Hanna with a grin.

I laughed at that. "Trust me, I doubted me enough for all of us."

Eve surprised me by saying, "Well, now that you're a fancy sold out author, you might just have to believe in yourself a little more."

I looked around at everyone and said, "I'm so excited and so happy I got to share this little triumph with you guys, and I'm ridiculously happy I met you all."

There was a chorus of "awwws" and "me toos!" before Sabrina said, "Okay, okay, that's enough sap. Let's go see some plants."

As we walked over to the Rose Garden, she fell into step with me and pulled me into a side hug., "Glad to have met you, too."

I couldn't help but think I didn't know when the last time was I had felt so appreciated and cared about by a group of people that could still be considered strangers given that I had only actually met them a few days ago. I couldn't help but feel like I had known them much longer.

EIGHTEEN

The Rose Gardens looked beautiful, but, while I enjoyed nature, I wasn't much of a flower person. I didn't mind them; I just didn't care for them as much as others tended to. I wasn't crazy about getting flowers as a gift. The concept was strange to me that someone was giving you a gift of fleeting beauty. To pluck the flowers and give them to someone as a sign of love, knowing they wouldn't last, never made sense to me. It seemed like a bad omen.

I craned my neck to see how far the gardens extended, but couldn't see the end. They seemed to go on forever.

There were a couple of paths before us, one of which was open, airy, and lined with pink and white roses. I could smell them from where we were standing a good fifty feet away. The other path was lined with hedges about my height, not a flower in sight. The path was more closed off and private; I was wondering where it would lead to, but Hanna set off immediately to the path on the right. All of us could smell the roses, and she didn't waste any time moving toward them.

I saw Sabrina had been staring down the same path I was, and half chuckled when Hanna picked the other one, smiling before following her.

Eve and Mira hung back with me. Eve was watching me, but Mira's eyes were locked on the other path. She took a half step forward before stopping. She noticed for the first time that the others had already started down the other path. When she turned to me, Eve was watching me, too.

After a moment, Eve said to the both of us, "If you want to go that way, we can."

I glanced over at Hanna and Sabrina, slowly making their way down the path and further away from us. I didn't want to leave them, but I was struggling to fight my curiosity. There was something about the hedge path that made me want to see where it led. But I was reluctant to leave the others.

"Are you sure?"

"Definitely," said Mira.

Eve added, "It can't be that long of a path, and it probably meets up with the other path further down. I'm sure we'll find them later in the garden, and we all have our phones. They can call if they get worried. I'll shoot Hanna a text and let her know."

I smiled at them and started down the path. The hedges were taller than I thought, and I couldn't see a thing over them. One glance back at Eve and Mira, who both were taller than me, showed that they couldn't either. The sun was beating down on us, but the hedges thankfully offered a little shade if you pressed up against them. I was thankful for the little bit of refuge from the sun's rays. The hedge path continued around a bend before coming to another fork. We studied both paths for any sort of context clues for where each led, but the two paths were indistinguishable.

"Right or left?" asked Mira.

"Left," said Eve.

"Right," I said at the same time.

"Why right?" Eve asked.

I shrugged. "Because it's the right choice?" I said with a grin. "Seemed as good a direction as any."

She quirked an eyebrow at me, seeming to sense there was more to it than that. After a moment of silence, I felt compelled to explain, "When I was younger, I travelled a lot with my family and I loved going to new shopping malls. I loved shopping in general, but whenever we went to a new, big place like that, I would get a little overwhelmed. I would worry we were going to miss some places I would like to go into or that we would get lost. My parents never seemed worried about that, so I followed their lead. After a while, I noticed my dad always stuck to the right, so I asked him why. He made the same stupid joke I did about it being the right choice, and then explained to me that if you just pick and commit to one direction, you can't get lost because you'll end up back where you started, eventually. Of course, we'd rather come through to the other side, but worst case, if we pick and stick with one direction, if we don't find a way through, at least we can make our way back to the beginning and head back the way they went."

Eve chuckled for a moment before saying, "I picked left for pretty much the same reason, but I figured going left would probably lead us to intersect with their path. From the outside, it didn't seem like these paths went too far to the right, so I thought right would be a dead end," she said, thoughtfully examining the righthand path. "But we can try that way if you want."

I laughed and shook my head. "Nope. I'm directionally challenged, and that's pretty sound logic. We'll go your way."

"But we can keep making lefts," added Mira, smiling at me.

Eve nodded. "Fine with me, unless the other path is clearly the better choice."

145

I laughed at that, but Mira and I both agreed, and we set off to the left.

A few more left turns later and we still didn't have any clue where we were going or if it was the right way. I had been examining the dirt for our tracks, but it was too well trod. It wasn't possible to pick out if we'd walked this way before.

We came to another turn and had to debate whether taking another left was a good idea. Another left should have taken us back to the starting point, but the hedges thinned toward the right.

"I think we should go right," Eve said. She must have noticed the hedges thinned there, too.

"Are you sure? Another left would probably take us back," said Mira.

"But I have a good feeling that the right will lead us right to their path."

I nodded, agreeing with Eve. Mira shrugged and fell in line behind me and Eve as we took the right path. As we got closer, the path thinned, but didn't get any shorter. I had hoped maybe it would and we would be able to see over it, but we had no such luck. I was confused by hearing running water and hastened down the path.

The hedges continued to thin, but across the way, instead of the rose garden paths, there were just more hedges. It seemed like there was a clearing up ahead. I quickened my pace and rushed into the opening. A quick glance around showed me that it was a clearing with five other paths also converging into it. In the dead center was a large fountain with water coming out of it. The water cascaded down the tiered pools to the large pool at the bottom of the fountain. It was made of stone and had flowers carved into it. A step closer told me they were roses.

Half a moment later, the hairs on the back of my neck stood up, and a chill brushed over me. *RUN!* shot through my brain without rhyme or reason. I tried to tell myself I was perfectly safe, but my brain wouldn't see reason. I couldn't figure out why until a second later when I heard what sounded like someone clearing their throat on the other side of the fountain.

I couldn't see over it to the other side, so I followed my instincts that wanted to flee and took a step back. As I did, I collided with Eve, who had come up behind me. I jumped about a foot in the air and leapt to my right, sweeping my right foot behind me and dropping my weight on it to anchor me. I pulled my hands up in front of my face and leaned back a little.

A second later, I registered it was Eve and felt a little silly. Until I heard the noise again from the other side of the fountain.

I rushed around it and had to laugh when the only living creature in sight was a frog resting on the stone edge of the fountain. It must have been the frog's croak I had heard, but the feeling still lingered. I reasoned it was leftover adrenaline and took a couple of deep breaths. I stooped down to the frog's level. "Why, hello there, mister. You gave me quite a fright-"

"Shame on him. That's what I'm here for."

The familiarity of the voice brought back my fear in full force. I jumped up, and tried to adopt the same position as before, but I hadn't accounted for the fountain being right behind me. I wasn't able to move my leg back and knew he was too close for me to move away. He would grab me the second I tried to move, so I braced myself as well as I could against the fountain, put my hands in front of me, and resolved to wait for any opening.

I had no idea how I possibly had missed him earlier, but from where he was standing, he had probably come out of one of the less visible paths. He was practically looming over me by the time I had noticed him. If I wasn't so scared, I would have been embarrassed that I had been that easily snuck up on.

As I stared at him now, I saw he was wearing another dark three-piece suit. Even I had to admit he had style. His dark hair was ruffled in a neater version of bedhead, controlled chaos. He was better suited to be modeling menswear at a fashion show or photoshoot than to be following me through gardens. The thought was almost laughable.

I risked a quick glance behind me, trying to see if Eve and Mira were visible from here. It was a small consolation that they weren't, but he took advantage of my distraction and moved closer. When I turned back to him, he was within half an arm's length of me. But it had been worth it to make sure Eve and Mira weren't visible. I didn't think he knew they were there, but if I didn't say something quickly, they might wander over here. That was the last thing I wanted or needed.

I wanted them far away from here as soon as humanly possible. Where they were right now, they could easily get away, and it was all the better if he didn't notice them before they escaped. The last thing I needed was him knowing that I had friends with me. The absolute last thing I wanted my creepy stalker to know was that I cared about them and their safety. They needed to get away, quickly, and hopefully come back with help, but as long as they made their way out, I was much less worried. After all, I handled him the first time, I probably could again. My resolve wavered when I met his eyes. They needed to run, *quickly*. I fought my panic, trying to think of what to say to alert them to his presence but keep him in the dark.

I was running out of time to think, so I settled for loudly asking, "Did you follow me here, too? I'd say I was flattered if you were more handsome," I said nonchalantly, both enjoying and being a little terrified of the way his anger lit up his eyes.

"But there's nothing special about me. I don't know why you've been following me since I got to the city, but I can assure you stalking me won't win my favor, especially when I don't even know your name."

My self-defense lessons from high school were kicking in. Get him talking, keep him talking. The longer I dragged this out, the more chance there was for Eve and Mira to get away, and then for me to get away. I hoped they would come back with help, but I didn't plan to wait. I would have to incapacitate him and get away like last time. I knew Eve and Mira would come back with help as soon as they were able, but with us being in the middle of what had essentially turned out to be a maze, who knew how long it would take them to come across anyone who could help.

He had just smirked at me before saying, "Darling, you know you know me. The most notable, powerful ruler in Zanaria, you must know who I am, but if you must hear it, I'm Damien Bancroft, King of Bancroft, soon to be ruler of Sherbrooke, and then all of Zanaria."

Great, another whack job. I laughed before I could think better of it. "What it is with people insisting they're from Zanaria today? You're no more Damien Bancroft than I am Serena Sherbrooke."

"My life certainly would be much easier if you were, though, since she's already in my power and under my spell. I hadn't expected you to be as easy a target, of course, but sooner or later everyone succumbs to my charms, everyone submits to me eventually. You've lasted longer than most, but you're certainly no different."

His eyes were hard to look away from. Somewhere in the back of my mind, my brain registered the sounds of footsteps retreating. Eve and Mira had gotten away. I was grateful for that. Now to find any sort of opening to get away myself. But I struggled to tear my gaze from him, not wanting to drop my focus from him for a moment for fear of what he might do.

I could only thank the universe he wasn't actually Damien. Even knowing of Damien's powers wasn't enough to resist him and fight his control. Very few had ever been able to. Most were lost in his eyes before they even knew what was happening. Before they could think to resist, he was already in their head with thoughts about how resistance was futile and obeying would bring them such pleasure and would please him. They wanted to please him.

I wanted to please him.

A moment later, I shook my head, trying to clear my thoughts. I pulled my hands away from his and tried to take a step back, but my balance was thrown off and I fell backward. Before I hit the water, his arms were around me. I hated that it didn't feel unpleasant. He grabbed me and righted me back on my feet before spinning me around, pressing my body to his tightly, lacing his arms under mine and gripping me tightly by my shoulders. I squirmed and tried to move away from him, but only succeeded in rubbing my body against his own. The sickening thought that he might have been enjoying that made me stop my escape attempts. *Think smarter, be patient, wait for an opening.* There would be one. He would slip up eventually and I would escape, probably not before hurting him, though. Thankfully, he deserved it.

His lips brushed up against my ear as he whispered in a husky tone, "Here's what's going to happen, love. You're going to come with me, without complaint, or-"

"Or what?" I asked.

I had to keep him talking. Keep him talking and it would slow him down. I had to get him to stay here long enough for me to escape or for help to come. I couldn't let him get me to wherever he wanted to move me. That was the first thing they taught you in self-defense; don't let yourself get moved to a second location. If your attacker is trying to quickly move you to a second location, it's because they think there's a chance they're going to get caught where they are, a chance that help would come. The chance of escaping that second location was slim to none. I had to keep him talking, delay our moving, otherwise who knows what might happen? If I left with him, I didn't know how my friends would find me. An errant thought ran through my head that I didn't know when I started referring to them as my friends, but I brushed off the thought. It clearly wasn't the time for introspection.

Louder now, he said, "Or we can do things the fun way, with you bound and gagged." I felt him shrug his shoulders behind me. "It really doesn't matter to me. I quite like the thought of you silent, compliant, and completely in my power, but as we'll soon be working closely together," he pressed me back against him even closer and I felt the heat of his breath on my ear, "very, very closely, might I add," he breathed into my ear, before adding louder again, "I figured I would be a gentleman and offer you the choice. So what will it be, sorceress? The easy way or the fun way?"

His lack of concern about his volume and his relaxed manner scared me more than his words. He didn't seem worried we would get caught, and despite my escape in Kennedy's, didn't seem worried I would get away this time either. As he waited for my response, my eyes darted around for any means of escape, but found none. I glanced at my feet and noticed his were within reach of mine. *Perfect*. A moment later, not giving him time to react, I shifted my weight to my left foot, picked up my right foot, and with as much strength as I could, slammed it down on his right foot.

He groaned in pain and instinctually looked down at his foot, putting him within reach of my waiting elbow. I elbowed him hard in the nose with my right arm. That did the trick. He released me in an instant and grabbed hold of his nose. In the split second I watched him, I could see his eyes were watering as he groaned. *Good.* I didn't wait a second longer before sprinting down the path he had come from. It had to lead somewhere.

I heard him scream in frustration and glanced back for just a moment, worried he was coming after me, but he hadn't advanced. He held his left hand over his face, but his right hand was now extended toward me. Thankfully, I was well out of his reach. I felt triumphant for half a moment before I felt my foot catch on something. I went tumbling forward, meeting the ground. Not a moment later, something green rushed over me. I felt an impossible heat and lifted my head.

I couldn't believe my eyes. The hedges in front of me were disintegrating in a wash of green flame. The flames had made a hole in three or four hedges and through them I could see roses. I didn't have time to process my shock or fear. I just hurtled myself through the first hedge. I was halfway through the second before I saw Agatha's face come into view in the opening in the last hedge. My eyes widened in disbelief, but I had no time to pause.

I was through the second hedge, two more to go, before she cried, "Sadie! Thank goodness! Hurry!"

She didn't have to say that again. I was through the third hedge before her face disappeared, making room for me just in time to go sailing through the last one. I collapsed on the other side, but was quickly pulled to my feet. Agatha's strength surprised me. I heard her ask someone what they needed to do now.

"Get her to safety, quickly." A moment later, the familiar voice said, "Gods be damned, there's no time. Find the others and hide, well. Make sure I can't see you, but more importantly, make sure he can't see her."

Agatha didn't waste time on words. She took my hand and ran. I didn't hesitate to follow. She led us around a few bends, up and down pathways of roses, but these weren't nearly as high as the hedges, so I could see our destination before we got there. I wanted to call out to them, since I don't think they saw us yet, but wasn't sure if that would be smart. We were supposed to stay hidden.

A few more moments later, we came crashing into the clearing our friends were at. They were standing around arguing while Eve stood on a bench with her phone held above her head. When they noticed us, they all fell into relief.

Eve jumped down from the bench and there was a chorus of, "Sadie! Thank goodness! We were so worried!"

Eve was the first to pull me into a crushing hug. A moment later, she let go of me and I saw the conflicting emotion on her face before she said, "Sadie, I swear to god if you ever pull something like that again, I will kill you myself."

I was confused, and it must have shown on my face because she clarified, "I was so freaking worried about you. I should have stayed, I knew I should have, but when we heard your warning, we took two seconds to realize we didn't know which way we were supposed to go to get out. I was terrified to leave you, but we had to get help. The two of us split up and took separate paths, hoping one of us at least would get out quickly and get help. I was trying to call the cops, but I didn't have enough service. We were just debating what we should do next. I wanted to go try to rescue you ourselves, but we couldn't agree on a plan."

I was shocked to see how worried she had been. Even more shocked when I saw they all had similar expressions on their faces. I hadn't expected them to have been nearly as worried as they were. I didn't know what to say, but, thankfully, didn't have to.

Agatha piped up, "I'm so glad I found her, but we're not out of the woods yet. We have to get out of here before something worse happens."

Not a second later, we heard a loud noise coming from behind us. Agatha cursed under her breath, before saying, "We don't have time. We have to hide. Get down, make sure he doesn't see you."

Everyone, myself included, looked at Agatha with surprise, but we all did what she said. A few moments later, we saw him come crashing into the rose garden, but he wasn't alone. He was locked in a fierce battle with none other than my Inez cosplayer, except now it was dawning on me as I watched the green sparks he was emitting and her casual grace with her sword, that there was only one explanation for what I was seeing.

Only one way for this to possibly be explainable, but it wasn't possible. It wasn't rational, but I could think of no other explanation unless this was some elaborate prank, but even then, the green flames I was seeing couldn't be a trick of the eye.

As they fought, I racked my brain for any other explanation or conclusion and, coming up empty, had to admit that there really was only one possibility. No matter how impossible it seemed, it was the only thing that made sense.

They were real.

And I was terrified.

NINETEEN

They were locked in battle, and I was scared for Inez. I knew Damien better than anyone and knew he wasn't nearly as fierce as my readers thought, but he wouldn't let anything get in his way of getting what he wanted. He couldn't. There was too much at stake for him. And for some reason, it appeared he wanted me. And, somehow, Inez was here, and even though I hadn't believed her and had been dismissive of her, she was here, fighting for me and trying to protect me. I couldn't believe it. The Inez I had planned for the last story would never put herself in danger for a stranger. She wouldn't have even put herself in danger for Serena, her best friend, after Serena rejected her. So why was she protecting me? And why did she think I could help her?

I needed answers and hoped she would be alive to give them.

I gulped as Damien pressed Inez back. She had put herself between us and him, as if she instinctively knew where we were hiding and her yielding even an inch told me how dire the situation was. I signaled everyone to get ready to run. Inez wouldn't have surrendered an inch of ground if it could have been avoided. She would want us to run at the first sign that things were going south. I knew her well enough to know that.

I was just about to give the signal to run when I heard a pained cry I recognized. It came from Damien and sounded even worse than the sounds I had made him make.

I risked a glance over my shoulder and was amazed at what I saw. Clenched tightly onto Damien's right hand was a black cat. The cat had latched onto him by its teeth. I couldn't believe it. He tried to shake the cat off violently, but the cat held for a few moments. When the cat let go, they landed gracefully on their feet.

Damien's hand was bleeding.

He took one look at his bleeding hand before glancing around, searching for something. I wasn't quick enough to duck before he saw me. His eyes locked on mine and I froze. I watched him assess the distance between us, Inez in front of him, his injury, and the likelihood he would get past her and make it away with me. There was fire in his eyes, but he turned and retreated into the hedge maze.

A moment later, an older man dressed head to toe in biker leather came running toward us through the gardens.

We stood up, and when he saw us, his eyes widened and he looked around quickly searching for something. Noticing our fright, he must have thought he was the cause, because he slowed a little, but his eyes continued to dart around us to the ground.

"Pardon me, ladies, but have any of you seen Mo?"

"Mo?" Hanna asked.

He met Hanna's eye with a small, pained chuckle. "Sorry. Mo, my black cat. He got loose, and I can't find him."

A moment later, Inez came strolling into the clearing, cradling the black cat—Mo, apparently. He had taken a liking to her. He was purring loudly.

The man let out a relieved chuckle. "There you are! I should have known." Ol' Mo's always been a ladies' man," he explained with a grin.

He approached Inez and held out his hands for Mo.

She peered at him appraisingly before asking, "He's yours?"

The man started to answer, "Yes. That's-"

Inez glared at him for a moment before saying, "I was asking him," looking down at Mo.

Mo purred louder as she scratched behind his ear and then leapt out of her hands to the ground and sauntered over to the man.

The man stopped staring at Inez and immediately scooped up Mo. He perched Mo on his shoulder and Mo seemed settled. He gave Mo's chin a little scratch. "Thank you, ladies. Little Mo here gets into trouble a lot of the time. I'm glad he had you all looking out for him." He grinned, turned to Mo, and said, "Let's roll, Mo," and with that, they were off.

Not wanting to test our luck, we left the gardens immediately. We called for a ride, wanting to be anywhere but here. We settled on a bar Sabrina had heard of called Church. I was grateful, but surprised when Agatha agreed to come with us.

Inez, Mira, and I rode in the back row of the minivan. Inez had some trouble getting her sheathed sword into the car, but she managed. As we sat in silence, I knew I should thank her or say something to her, but it wasn't the time yet. The driver was an unusually chatty one, and I figured our conversation was one that shouldn't be overheard. Inez either understood or was content to be in silence, since she didn't press me.

The others were just as silent. Even Hanna was uncharacteristically quiet. Thankfully, Agatha had sat in front with the driver and was amiable enough to them for the rest of us. When she told the driver we were going to church, they put on a radio station of church hymns. Even with how preoccupied my thoughts were, I couldn't help but find it hilarious that they thought we were going to an actual church, with Inez in her battle leathers and sword.

The other girls were trying not to laugh, too. Thankfully, the ride was a short one.

# TWENTY

Damien

I had been so close. I almost had her. She had been in my grip; I had her. I had half expected us to disappear together when I had grabbed her, but since we were still here, there was something more that needed to be done.

I planned to bring her back to my rooms with me, willingly or not. I thought perhaps she could help figure out how to get us back, but if not, I would keep her captive as long as it took. I just needed a little longer to work out how to get us home, but I had had the sorceress, so I felt sure it wouldn't be much longer.

It continued to surprise me how easy she was to get alone and how much easier still she was to capture. Yes, she had gotten away every time, but she was easy to locate and capture. I couldn't fathom why she wasn't using her power to fight me off. I was expecting a magical attack, had prepared for it, but she continued to resort to physical assaults instead. I couldn't for the life of me understand why when she had all that power at her disposal. Even then, I would have had her. I would've been able to contain her with my power. She would've been encased in my flames and driven back to me. I would've had her.

I hadn't counted on the damned royal guard and that stupid shield. I should have known sooner or later she would find the sorceress, but I hoped I had longer. Now she would be even more difficult to contain. The royal guard wasn't a problem per se, but she was a complication.

I hadn't been prepared for her today, but the next time I would be. I wouldn't make that same mistake again. I would get to the sorceress, or if I couldn't get to the sorceress herself, perhaps getting to her friends might be the next best thing.

TWENTY-ONE

Sadie

I had to admit this was weird, even for Portland. When Sabrina had said we were going to Church, this hadn't quite been what I pictured. Judging by the others' faces, it wasn't what they expected either.

The bar was separated loosely into two halves, one half was a dancefloor, the other half had the tables. The DJ was playing a weird mix of what I could only describe as Christian EDM. I was honestly surprised how far the bar leaned into their name. I hadn't expected the level of dedication.

Behind the DJ was a large neon red cross, about four feet tall. It gave the DJ an eerie backlighting, making him appear devilish and otherworldly. It had to have been on purpose. My eyes roamed over the rest of the room, quickly taking in the other people here, before noticing the ceiling. It made my jaw drop. The entire ceiling was dedicated to a recreation of Michelangelo's painting at the Sistine Chapel. From what I could see with the weird red bar lighting, it was a close replica. I would have loved to see it more clearly, but I doubted they ever made the lights bright enough.

I couldn't help chuckling when I noticed that Agatha was staring at the ceiling, too. I glanced over at Inez, expecting some reaction from her, but she just stood there unfazed. I don't know why I expected a reaction, especially when our whole world would have been confusing enough to her already. I couldn't help laughing at the thought that she probably thought this was what all our houses of worship looked like.

I was just glad she had joined us at all. When the bouncer made her surrender her sword to his care before entering, I thought she might leave. I didn't know what I would have done if she had. I probably would have followed her into the streets of Portland.

Knowing she was Inez, the real Inez, somehow here in front of me, impossibly here, I wouldn't have let her get away without talking to her.

I tried to remember what it was she had been telling me at the convention, but it was fuzzy. I hadn't paid as much attention as I should have. I was kicking myself now. I could remember something about her asking me to get Serena rescued, but not much else. I knew Serena's fate was already sealed; I had penned the ending myself. Could I change that? If I did, would it change anything for Inez? How the hell was Inez even here? How did she even exist? And if I couldn't save Serena, what would that do to Inez? What would she do to me? I gulped at the thought and tried to calm my racing mind.

I took a deep breath and braved the crowd, following Hanna to the bar. I was going to need a drink for this conversation, and I was sure Inez was probably thirsty after fighting Damien. Although maybe not. She was in peak physical condition and the battle itself had hardly lasted more than a minute. It was probably just a warm-up for her.

She asked after some mead and scoffed when they said they didn't have it. She turned to me, asking, "What kind of place doesn't serve a good mead? I don't know how you consider this a tavern without any mead. Unheard of. But from what I've seen of your realm, I'm not the least bit shocked."

Worried someone might overhear her, I quickly glanced around, but no one was staring. I shouldn't have been surprised, but I was. I expected her outfit to turn a lot more heads and raise more eyebrows than it had, but I had underestimated Portland. It seemed there wasn't much that fazed the locals anymore.

I ordered Inez and myself ciders. They came in silver goblets served by a bartender wearing the Halloween version of a nun's costume. I thanked him, took my glass, and steered Inez to the table in the corner. It was the quietest corner in the place, the furthest from the DJ. Quiet enough so we could hear one another, but not so quiet that others would overhear us, which was perfect. As unfazed as the locals had been so far, I still didn't want to risk anyone overhearing our conversation, even if they would just think we were all dedicated cosplayers, or discussing a book or something.

There was something about the crowd that soothed me. Eve, Mira, and Agatha were already sitting, but we waited for everyone else to get their drinks and join us. Partially because I didn't want to have to make Inez repeat the story more than once, but mostly because I needed more time to think of what to say to her and what I could possibly ask her and how the hell she expected me to help her.

Most people didn't disappoint Inez without garnering some sort of injury from the encounter. I gulped at the thought. I couldn't decide whether it was crazier to be intimidated by her, because she was my own creation after all, or crazier to not be. By the time the others all made their way over, I was still debating.

I had barely touched my drink, too lost in thought and worry to actually enjoy it. I took a deep breath and finally looked at Inez. She had been staring at me expectantly. I glanced away from her unexpected, intense stare, and noticed her own glass was drained. Without a word, I slid my barely touched glass to her.

She shook her head, so I said, "Really, take it. You'll enjoy it more than I would."

"Hardly. It's no mead, that's for sure," she said before proceeding to take a long swig that drained about half the goblet.

She put the goblet down with a *thunk* and turned to me. "Is this everyone?"

I did a quick headcount. Me, Eve, Mira, Hanna, Sabrina, and now Agatha were all here. Everyone except Naomi, but I nodded. Everyone from the garden was here.

I wondered for a brief moment how any of us could possibly explain this to Naomi. I doubted whether she would believe us. If I was in her shoes, I don't know if I would have. Hell, Inez had tried to tell me her story earlier, and even with her standing in front of me, I hadn't believed her. Naomi would question our collective sanity for sure.

Inez didn't waste a minute before saying, "We need a plan. Does anyone know what Damien wants?"

Everyone turned to me. I thought about our encounters, which were much more chilling now that I knew who he actually was. I can't believe I had, not once but twice, outsmarted and outran Damien. Never in a million years would I have thought I was capable of that. Most of the time, Serena, Inez, and Tristan barely got away, and here I was a normal powerless human and I somehow was able to get away.

"I have no idea. If he was just your average man, I would have said he was interested in me. He definitely has plans for me. First, he showed up at the airport, then at Kennedy's, and now in the gardens. I have no idea why he left me alone in the airport, though, or why he let me get away in Kennedy's. I would have said for sure he didn't have his powers until I saw his green flames. I don't know what would have happened to me if I hadn't tripped. Thank goodness for being clumsy." I chuckled a little before it hit me. "His powers! He was trying to charm me at the airport. He sort of did, a little. I remembered feeling weirdly attracted to him and some... other thoughts." I blushed, not wanting to elaborate.

Sabrina added, "No shame in that. We've seen him."

Inez wasn't amused. "He's a monster."

Sabrina might've been about to say something else, but I shot her a look quickly. Inez didn't take much of anything lightly, especially this. Damien had taken Serena captive and was planning to marry her. Inez and the rest of her world were convinced he had murdered his own husband, of course she would be worried. Even if she was starting to get over Serena, she had still loved her, and still did love her. That was her best friend. Now wasn't the time for joking about how handsome Damien was. Although, it would be a lie to say he wasn't. I knew he was; I had written him that way.

"Regardless, they were thoughts happening in my head, but they felt wrong. Not wrong like 'I shouldn't be having these thoughts since I'm demisexual' wrong, but wrong like they were the wrong flavor, almost? Like they were trying to imitate my thoughts, but weren't quite right."

I wasn't getting anything except confused looks. Inez looked thoughtful, but stayed quiet.

Eve put her hand on my shoulder and asked, "Wrong how?"

For lack of a better way to explain it, I stuck with my wrong flavor metaphor, but elaborated. "Like if my thoughts were watermelon flavored, those thoughts were artificial watermelon flavoring, close but not quite right. More overpowering and artificial tasting."

Inez nodded. "I haven't experienced it, but Serena said something to that effect. She wasn't really able to explain it either."

Well, of course she couldn't when I can't, I thought, but knew better than to say it out loud.

"So, he was definitely trying in the airport, but it faded quickly and he left me alone. It seems like he stepped things up in Kennedy's, though. It felt more powerful, but I was still able to resist."

Inez nodded thoughtfully. "Your power must surpass his. Celeste suggested it might, but we didn't know for sure."

"How does Celeste know about me?" I couldn't stop from asking. I probably should have been focused on her saying I was more powerful than Damien, but hearing Celeste's name surprised me.

"How does she know anything?" Inez said with a shrug.

When no one responded and continued to stare at her, she added, "Magic."

Sitting with Inez, who shouldn't exist in the first place, never mind be in our world, it seemed as good an answer as any. Even as the author of their story, Celeste was still a bit of a mystery to me. I didn't know nearly as much about her as you would think. Even with the series pretty much finished, she was still mostly a mystery to me.

Hanna started to ask her something, but Inez's already thin patience must have been waning, since she interrupted and told us, "You're focusing on the wrong thing. I need your help. At least while Damien is here, Serena must be safe, but it won't stay like that forever. Who knows what bargain he struck to be here." She turned to me hopefully. "Unless you know?"

I shook my head. I knew about how the magic of their world worked. The spells were very specific and often worked in ways the caster didn't expect. The wording had to be just right, and even still, sometimes the magic had a mind of its own and twisted things in ways you didn't expect. If we knew what spell had gotten Damien here, we would hold power over him. But, unfortunately, I didn't. Everything was getting more and more out of hand. I hadn't written any of this. Yes, I had written Damien and Inez, but Inez even being here was proof enough they weren't just off script, they had burned it and were dancing on the ashes. The Inez I had written in book three would have left Serena in Damien's hands. She wouldn't have risked herself to save Serena when Serena had just broken her heart. Inez wasn't that selfless and wasn't that good of a person, but maybe I was wrong.

"I don't know what brought him here. I wish I did, but I also don't know what brought you here."

She glanced around, eyeing the other patrons of the bar, but no one was paying us any attention.

She lowered her voice and said, "I can't divulge the spell that brought me here in a crowded place like this." She scrutinized me suspiciously, adding, "Nor should you expect me to, since you know so much about our world."

I nodded quickly. "No, no, not the spell. I was asking why you came in the first place?"

She tilted her head to the side, confused. "I already told you Serena was captured. Thank the gods Damien's here and not still there with her, but I need her safe."

"Safe in your arms?"

She blushed at that. "I just need her safe and happy."

I still wasn't following. What made this Inez so much more different, so much more willing to risk everything for Serena, her best friend, but also the girl who broke her heart? Why was she here after Serena destroyed her hopes and dreams? In the initial drafts, I thought Inez would try to rescue her, but the more I got to know Inez as a character and got further into the series, the more I realized she was just like Kay. She wouldn't lift a finger for someone else if it didn't benefit her. So why did she come? What changed?

"But she hurt you," I half-asked, half-stated.

Inez floundered for a moment before answering, "She never intended to, nor did she know she was doing it. I never told her."

"Do you think things would have been different if you had?"

"I did until I saw his amulet."

"And now?"

"Now, I would never ask her to pick me over her true love."

"But if you could be her true love?"

She shrugged. "I still don't know."

"So that's not why you came? You would have come anyway?" I asked, surprise showing on my face.

She looked outraged and responded without a second's pause, "If you know anything about me, you should know how much pride I take in my honor and loyalty. After all, I'm the captain of the royal guard."

Now it made sense. "Ah, I should have known. Of course you came because your duty made you."

By the glare she sent my way, I was sure I had offended her somehow. "If you think for one minute that I would have, under any circumstances, for any reason besides being dead myself, have left Serena to the mercy of Damien Bancroft the Murderous Regicidal King, then you don't know a gods-damned thing about me."

I was glad she had been forced to leave her sword outside, since even her glare had me cowering. "I'm sorry. I just assumed that since-"

"It doesn't matter. I don't care how all-powerful you are. Clearly, you aren't all-knowing."

I felt like she had slapped me. I looked around for some help from anyone, but it seemed they didn't know what to say either. Agatha offered me a sad smile. It crossed my mind that only a couple of them had probably read my books, so they must have been even more lost than I was.

Eve, sensing my distress, spoke up, "So what do we do about Damien?"

"I don't know," I said.

At the same time, Inez said, "Kill him."

I whipped around to stare at her. So did everyone else.

"You can't be serious."

"Deadly," she said with narrowed eyes.

"You may not understand the laws here, but you can't just kill someone. You'd be carted off to jail. Besides, he hasn't done anything wrong yet."

She narrowed her eyes at me and spoke deadly slowly, "Hasn't. Done. Anything. Wrong? What of Serena?"

"I know he kidnapped her, but he's here. She's safe."

"And can you promise she'll stay that way?"

I thought about it for a moment. If I told her about Damien's backstory and motivations, I doubted she would believe me, or care. She was incredibly stubborn and not liable to change her mind about him on her own. I knew he didn't plan to hurt Serena, but I couldn't guarantee he wouldn't to get what he wanted. I knew the villain I wrote and knew he long ago stopped having qualms about what he was and wasn't willing to do to get Cass back. He and Inez were alike in that way. He was willing to burn the world down to save him. It was touching and terrifying at the same time. But that was the Damien I had written. Inez was so far off script right now that I couldn't guarantee anything when it came to the other characters, either.

After a moment when I still hadn't said anything, she took that as an agreement. "I knew it! You can't. Because he isn't safe for her. If he's breathing, he poses a threat to Serena. I can't let him continue to live."

I gulped. I knew she was deadly and deadly serious, and as powerful as Damien was, she actually stood a chance. I couldn't have either of them end up dead. Now that Inez was living, breathing, and right in front of me, my thoughts went to the other people in my story. I couldn't have imagined for a second that what I wrote had more impact than just being words on a page. I couldn't see either of them wind up dead. They were both needed for the story. This Inez would play a bigger part in Serena's story than I had thought. She would fight to rescue Serena from whatever came for her. Everyone deserved a friend like that, and just because I didn't have any like that, didn't mean Serena shouldn't.

They both needed to go back. I could work up a new ending, but they both needed to go back. I couldn't have Damien running around Portland potentially hurting or killing anyone.

"I can't let you kill him here, but what if you take him back? In your story, anything can happen. In our land, killing would cause a lot of trouble, but in your realm, you would be hailed a hero."

She thought about it for a moment before saying, "And you could be sure he wouldn't overpower me?"

I raised my eyebrows at her. "Do you have so little faith in your own skill?"

She chuckled. "I don't doubt my skill in a fair fight, but I very much doubt it would be a fair fight. You and Serena are the only people I've heard of that can resist his charms."

"I wonder why."

"Your power must protect you, and I would guess the strong magic in Serena's bloodline protects her."

"That's quite interesting, but even Celeste couldn't resist him?"

"That's the weird part. She couldn't, so your power must surpass hers," she said, looking at me with a begrudging respect. "Even if you look inconspicuous and nonthreatening."

I smiled at that.

Sabrina asked, "So, what's the plan? How do we get them home? The sooner Damien's gone, the better."

"Yes," said Inez with narrowed eyes. "The sooner he's my problem, the more quickly you'll all be able to relax."

I hated that she was right, but that was the truth. I hated the shivers he sent up my spine when he looked at me. I hated the way his stare lingered. I hated the way I felt drawn to him. I knew there was more to him than met the eye, but when he met *your* eye, it was hard to remember that. When his green flames came into play, it was hard to remember that he hadn't wanted this for himself, that given the right circumstances, he would be happy to team up with Inez and Serena, not fight against them. He kidnapped Serena for his own gain; he needed her, but he didn't intend to hurt her. But I couldn't argue that he wouldn't. He needed her to help him, and he was desperate enough he would make her if it came down to that.

Now that I understood who he was, it was becoming clearer what he wanted from me. I was a pawn for him, the same as Serena. He wanted me—well, the power he thought I had. He wanted it and would stop at nothing to get what he wanted and needed from me.

I had never spent time and energy on regretting anything or any characters I had written, but I was now regretting giving him so strong a motivation and so much power. I was lucky I had a level of resistance to his charms. Otherwise, he would have easily overpowered my mind by now.

I shuddered to think he might be anywhere in Portland right now, stealing the will of any of the people who hadn't a clue what was happening.

The question remained, if he did capture me, what did he intend to do with me? I didn't have any power over him, or even really any understanding why Inez thought I had power in the first place. I was just a normal author, a normal person. Things like this didn't just happen to anyone, but they definitely didn't happen to me.

Everyone's eyes were on me still. I didn't know what to say, so when I did speak, I said the first thing to come to my mind. "I understand you're worried, and I will do everything in my power to help you and Serena." That was true; I simply left out that I didn't know what power I would have to help her, or anyone, for that matter.

"Thank you," she said with a nod. "So we need a plan to get him back, and make sure I will be able to master him when we return, and make sure the mist stops ravishing our land."

I was confused, and so was everyone else when they noticed my confusion.

No one knew what to say, but someone softly asked, "What mist?"

It was Mira. I shot her a grateful smile. Inez not killing Damien, and not hurting anyone else in the process, hinged on her continuing to think I was this all powerful magical sorceress. It wouldn't help my cause if I admitted my lack of knowledge about how things were going in her world. I wanted to help her, I really did, and I wanted to help Serena now that I knew she was real. I was really regretting the way I had ended her story.

Inez stared at Mira. Mira shifted uncomfortably but didn't shrink away from her stare. Inez turned to me. "Care to explain?"

I shrugged. "If I must, but I haven't been there or seen it for myself."

She sighed. "Fair enough. The mist first showed up a few weeks ago. We thought nothing of it at first. We were focused on finding a way to free Serena. But we started getting reports of the mist rolling through villages and leaving mass confusion in its wake. People were changing. It was like the last few weeks hadn't happened. We tracked down and questioned some of the citizens that made those reports, but no one else corroborated their claims, so we continued to monitor it until Astra came to us. She was in hysterics that Cierra didn't remember her. Well, rather that she didn't remember anything good about her. Astra had been with us trying to help us figure out how to rescue Serena when we got the report of the mist heading to their town. She raced home, worried about Cierra, even though we were nearly positive it was harmless. She plunged through the mist into the village and when it cleared, she found her way home, only for Cierra to refuse to let her in.

"Astra was in hysterics when she came back, telling us Cierra only remembered the battle we lost Serena in, but nothing after.

"Cierra and Astra had always been on opposite sides of everything until that battle. Astra saw Cierra struggling across the battleground and saw her take what should have been a fatal blow. Astra's scream gave way to a powerful magic that ripped across the battlefield and took out the creatures attacking Cierra. Shortly after Serena was taken, so I don't know the rest of what happened, but Astra says they travelled home together and really talked for the first time. By the time they finished the week's journey, Astra moved her things into Cierra's home.

Hoping Serena was okay and knowing she wouldn't forgive us if we didn't help her friends, we went with Astra to their village. When we got there, Cierra was happy to see the rest of us, but not Astra. She didn't remember Astra ... well, she didn't remember any of the good things about Astra. Astra had told us some," she blushed and cleared her throat, "rather intimate details about their time together over those few weeks, and it's not something anyone would forget, but somehow Cierra had. She got genuinely pissed off when we kept pressing her on it.

"We shouldn't have let Astra stay, since it pissed Cierra off more. Cierra got to the point where she told us that just because Astra saved her life didn't mean she owed her a damn thing and that if we continued to bother her about it, we could all get lost, too.

"Astra crossed the room to her and whispered something I didn't hear, but from the shade of red Cierra's face turned, I knew I didn't want to know.

"Cierra moved back, turned on her heel, and punched the wall with a loud crunch.

"I had never seen her that angry. She turned back and ground out, 'I don't know what kind of dark magic you used to find that out, witch, but I can assure you, you would be the last person I ever let close enough to me to know that. Just because you would whore yourself out to anyone who saves your life doesn't mean I would do the same.'"

I gasped and heard almost everyone else echo the notion. "That's horrible!" said Hanna.

Mira agreed. "Seriously, how could she say that?"

"Maybe she was scared," Sabrina shrugged. "If everyone was coming to me telling me they remembered me doing and saying things I didn't remember, I would be a little freaked out."

I had been too stunned to say much of anything. The mist came about right around when I finalized which ending I was using. Was it possible I caused the mist? I supposed anything was possible, since my characters were apparently alive. And since the story seemed to evolve on its own since I hadn't had any plans for Cierra and Astra. I hadn't even named them; they were just essentially more bodies in the story to form larger battle scenes. I couldn't think about the implications of what she was saying. I had no idea what to think. I was just trying to breathe. In and out. *I'm not the worst person ever.* In and out. I couldn't have possibly known I was ruining anyone's life. In and out. I didn't even really know if this was my fault. In and out. In and out. My breathing slowed a little, but I could barely concentrate on the others. I couldn't think of what I should have been saying.

Thankfully, Eve asked, "So what did you do?"

"We left with a heartbroken Astra and all of the belongings that Cierra threw out after her. We went back to the city and poured over the records we had of the interviews, trying to figure out why some people had been spared. Astra volunteered to go on the next mission to whatever town was hit next. She didn't care at that point what happened to her, now that Cierra didn't remember her. She wanted to forget, but it wasn't that simple. She raced out the next time the mist struck and came back with the same story. Some people were spared and others weren't. She was spared again. We figured that, in her case, her magic was a factor, but none of the others would own up to any magic or magical blood, so we couldn't be positive. All we know definitively is that the mist is changing things. It's changing people's memories and how they act. In Cierra and Astra's case, it's ripping people apart. I went to Celeste, hoping to find out the cause of the mist and how to stop it, how to save Serena, and how to destroy Damien's plans. It turns out she thought you," her eyes met mine with a pleading that made me almost tear up, "were the answer to all our problems, and I hope, gods willing, that she was right."

I didn't know what to say or what to do. I wanted to help, but I wasn't sure what to do. I certainly didn't have control over whatever magical mist was ravishing the Six Realms. I would scrap the new changes to the last book and go back to the original draft if it would change anything, but I didn't think it would.

I finally broke down and cried. I was sobbing, struggling to breathe. It took all my energy to calm my cries. Eve put her hand on my shoulder and Mira reached over and took my hand, giving it a little squeeze. Inez looked confused and worried, which only made me cry harder. I didn't know the first thing about how to help her. I wasn't worthy of her faith and trust. I wasn't worthy of being her creator; I wasn't worthy of being an author. Why had I ever thought I could build worlds when every decision I made had made someone miserable? No wonder Kay left me. I was a miserable person who made everything worse for everyone else.

Mira squeezed my hand again, and I felt Eve's hand soothingly petting my hair. The motion was calming and helped me to catch my breath a little. I started to calm, but I didn't know why they were all being so nice to me. Didn't they know this was all my fault?

I finally took a deep breath and said to Inez and all of them, "I'm so sorry, Inez, everyone really; you all deserve better from me. I'm a terrible author and, as I'm sure you would have found out sooner or later, a terrible person. It's why I don't have friends and why I came to Portland alone. I don't know the first thing about how to help you. It sounds like the mist might be my fault, but I don't know the first thing about controlling it, or stopping it."

They were all staring at me. Eve had tears in her eyes. Inez was wide eyed. Inez seemed about to speak, but Eve beat her to it. "You're far from being a terrible person. You're scared, and that's okay. We all are. But we'll figure this out together. You may have come here without anyone in your corner, but that's not how things are anymore. You have me." She gestured to the others, who were all nodding and smiling at me. "You have us," she finished. "Besides, no one blames you for not knowing how to control magic you just found out about. We can figure it out together, right, Inez?"

I turned sheepishly to Inez, who also nodded. "It will definitely make things more complicated." Eve glared at her, and she chuckled, putting her hands up in surrender, before meeting my eye again, "But Sadie the Just, I don't blame you. As long as you are willing to help, I'm sure we can figure it out together."

"But what about Damien?" I asked.

"Why don't we get out of town for a while tomorrow?" said Mira.

Everyone turned to her, surprised. "But what about Damien?" I asked again.

"Well, what better way to make sure we're out of his crosshairs for the day? If we aren't here, either he'll follow us or he'll sit in wait for us to return. I'm guessing the latter, since he knows we'll have to come back eventually."

"Well, I've always wanted to see the Pacific Ocean," I said excitedly. "It's only a couple of hours from here. We could rent a car and go to the beach."

"I heard there's a beach out there with rocks as tall as skyscrapers," said Hanna. "I'd love to see those!"

There was a chorus of agreement, and as they talked over the plan, I snuck a few glances in Inez's direction. She didn't seem overjoyed at the idea, but didn't seem opposed either. She was lost in thought, which was probably the best I could hope from her.

When I turned, Agatha caught my eye. I had almost forgotten she was here. She gestured to the bar, and I followed her. We stopped in front of the bar and she turned to me.

"I think I might be able to shed some light on the amnesia-causing mist."

I just stared at her, unable to form a coherent thought. She continued, "Well, slight confession that I'm thinking you're already piecing together. Your favorite novel of mine, the renaissance faire coming to life, well..."

She paused seeing Inez was watching the two of us closely from across the room. "Well, it actually happened."

I was stunned. "What?!"

She glanced around, shushing me. I blushed and lowered my volume. "You're telling me they're all real?"

She shrugged. "I'm honestly not sure. What I'm telling you is that they were truly of another land, trapped here. It was unnatural, and the longer they stayed trapped here, the more they forgot. They started to slowly believe they were from this world, to adapt to it and lose sight of who they really are."

"That's horrible! But what happened? What could have caused this?"

"I have a hunch. Tell me, did you make any drastic changes to their world?"

I gulped and nodded. I knew this was somehow my fault.

"That's what I thought. It sounds like the realm was starting to change, but some of the characters are rejecting it. It appears likely those with magic have been spared for now. It seems like the magic and the realm are waiting with bated breath for Inez and your villain to return, waiting to see how things will play out, what decisions will be made here, and what decisions you will make. The same was true with the renegades. It was almost like time stopped while they were waiting for something to change, something to happen. I had never seen anything like it, nor had I since until Inez.

"When she showed up at the book convention, I caught a bit of your conversation with her and saw some of the signs, so I followed her. I had to know for sure. She was forthcoming when she understood I believed her. I hoped she might have answers. I've been searching for any sort of explanation since, but haven't found any. Neither am I any closer now, since Inez didn't have any answers, but I've lived a long while, and it's enough to know I'm not crazy. All these years and I hadn't seen another single sign of magic. I was starting to think the book had been a vivid dream."

"But it wasn't? It was real? Everything actually happened?"

There was a twinkle in her eye when she laughed. "Well, not everything. I wouldn't be a very good fiction writer if I just recorded everything, but yes. It's true to the spirit of what happened. Why do you think it was so different from the rest of my books? I couldn't have made that up if I tried."

I swallowed hard, struggling to digest the truth, but grateful to not be alone. "So, they were your characters?"

She shook her head. "No. That part is new, but they weren't from here. I have no idea what kind of magic you have that you wrote yours to life, but I can imagine what a burden that must feel like."

She pulled me into a hug and I felt some of the tension in my body melt. She didn't know exactly what I was going through, but she understood enough.

"I just feel like this is all my fault," I muttered, unsure if it was even loud enough for her to hear.

To my surprise, she heard and hugged me tighter. "Honey, I'd love to tell you you're wrong, but with how crazy this world is, all I can tell you is that things happen for a reason. The renaissance renegades came into my life when I needed them most, and it seems like Inez and you are that for each other. I won't pretend to understand you or what's going on in your life, but I can say that you had that same look of being lost that I did back then. I know a fellow wanderer when I see one, and I saw that in you. Inez, too. And somehow, impossibly, after just a few days, I can sense the change in you and in her. No matter what happened to get her here, it seems you both needed it more than either of you knew."

I hugged her tighter and whispered my thanks, before pulling away and turning back to a very confused Inez.

To my disappointment, Agatha came over and said her goodbyes. I had assumed she was staying until after the ball, but that wasn't the case. She told us, "I'm an old lady now, ladies. I'll leave the partying up to you all. Have lots of fun for me."

She waved to everyone and pulled me into a hug before slipping me her business card from her pocket. "Promise you'll be careful, and promise to stay in touch."

I grinned. "Gladly to both. You can expect a full report after the ball."

"I would expect nothing less," she said with a parting grin.

The rest of us stayed a little longer, and had a couple more drinks. It wasn't until we were getting up to leave that I realized I didn't know where Inez was staying.

I glanced quickly at Mira for permission; she nodded. I was grateful she understood.

"Inez, where have you been staying? I'm not sure if you need it, but there's room for you with me and Mira if you need a place to stay, at least until we can figure out how to get you back home.”

“I was staying across town, but I don’t wish to let you out of my sight for longer than necessary. I’ll come with you if we can send someone for my things.”

I stared at her, confused for a moment before it occurred to me; she was used to being able to command others. I gently told her, “Here in Portland, we fetch our own things, but we’ll go get your things and get you settled with us.”

“What a weird place this is,” she said. She easily could have meant the bar, or Portland, but even before she continued, I knew she meant our world. “An all powerful sorceress who doesn’t know how to use her powers and fetches things herself. You’re an odd one, Sadie the Just, but I like you,” she said, ruffling my hair.

“I like you, too,” I said, smiling as Eve, Mira, and I walked with Inez to our waiting cab.

TWENTY-TWO

The rental we picked up was a shiny blue convertible, the ideal car for a beach trip. We broke into two groups. Since Eve, Mira, me, and now Inez were all staying together, we were all in one car. Inez had spent the night in my bed, which was strange, to say the least.

Before this trip, it had been a while since I'd shared a bed with anyone, but it hadn't been unpleasant having someone next to me. I liked the idea of knowing I wasn't alone if anything were to happen. I knew Inez was capable of protecting me against anything that might have entered the door or wish to do me harm, and that she would. Mainly because I was her key to getting home and her key to protecting Serena, but she would fight for me. I was thrilled she liked me, and she hadn't left, or even really complained when I had told her I didn't know the first thing about how to help her. She had seemed to value that I had given her the truth and trusted me, which made me incredibly happy.

Her choosing to stay with us in the first place was a testament to how much she cared about and wanted to protect me. I had been worried she might've been staying in a bad part of town or even staying on the street since she wouldn't have had any money.

To my surprise, when we got to the address she had given us, it was an even nicer hotel than ours. When I had asked her about it, she shrugged and said that gold spoke everywhere. She didn't need any of our weird paper currency with drawings of men on them when her gold was perfectly good.

She had led us up the elevator to the penthouse suite where her shield and a pack of her other belongings were dwarfed by the California king bed that they had been thrown onto. I had taken one look around and suggested we should stay there, but she shook her head, saying it was too conspicuous and that Damien had probably seen her come and go by now. So we ended up sharing my queen bed instead. It wasn't unpleasant, it just wasn't a California king in a penthouse suite.

I smiled over at Inez in the passenger seat, taking in her delight and surprise as I put the top down. When we hit the open road, I pressed the gas down halfway and the engine roared. I felt a rush of adrenaline that, when I glanced over, was mirrored on Inez's face. She threw her hands up with a yell of triumph. After a moment, she put them behind her head, leaning back against the headrest.

She grinned at me, yelling over, "This is much faster than Argo has ever ran. I could get used to this."

With Inez riding shotgun and Eve and Mira laughing and singing along to the pop throwbacks on the radio, my heart was full. I was leaving behind my troubles in Portland and was going to enjoy today, enjoy the time together with my new friends, and enjoy the crazy magic of being able to spend time with a person I had literally created out of thin air. It was truly a trip of a lifetime.

Once we got off the highway, we seemed to be in the middle of a dense forest. The trees reached to the sky with no signs of stopping. If it weren't for the smell of salt in the air, I would have thought the GPS had steered us wrong. In fact, even with the smell of salt in the air, when we were still in the middle of the forest twenty minutes later, I was positive we weren't going the right way. That was when I saw the forest opening up in front of us and the ocean waves crashing just beyond. It was breathtaking, but my jaw dropped when we rounded the next corner and saw the rocks of Cannon Beach loom up before us. There was a fog hanging over them that didn't appear to touch the rest of the beach. They were ominous in their majesty, and I couldn't wait to go see them.

TWENTY-THREE

I had to wait quite a while as we drove around most of the town searching for a parking spot. The moment we did park, Inez hopped out of the car, hurtling herself out the open roof, over the door, not bothering to wait for the doors to be unlocked. By the time I moved the seats forward to let Mira and Eve out of the back, she was halfway to the stairs that led to the beach.

When we caught up with her, she had stopped at the bottom of the stairs and was staring over at the rocks.

"Those are huge!" I exclaimed.

"Beautiful," added Mira.

"What a view," Eve said.

"How long do you think it would take to climb them?" Inez asked.

All three of us whipped our heads in her direction simultaneously. Eve and Mira probably thought she was joking. I knew from the tone in her voice and the excitement in her eye that she actually meant it. She could honestly probably do it, but why risk it? I didn't know what would happen to her if she was seriously injured or died outside of her story. Would her world rewrite itself around her? And what would happen if she never went back in the first place? What if I couldn't figure out how to send her back?

I started to panic, but felt Eve's hand on my shoulder. I took a couple of deep breaths and answered her worried look with a nod. I was okay. That was a problem for another day. Today's problem was trying to make sure Inez didn't kill or maim herself by doing a dangerous stunt for no reason.

"I'm sure you could easily climb them, but who knows what's in the water out here," Eve said.

She nodded thoughtfully. "You're right. If your sirens are anything like ours, it might be best to stay out of the water. I have no treaty with them."

None of us dared to correct her, but it was hard to see that the carefree Inez of a few minutes ago had faded. She was serious once again, and some of the joy had faded from her eyes. Talking of the ocean and sirens reminded her of home. I couldn't even imagine how homesick she must have been. She was stuck in such a strange land all alone, with no concrete way home, while her loved ones were waiting for her to return and save the day. I couldn't even imagine the weight she carried on her shoulders. My heart broke for her. I would've done anything to take some of that weight away, but I didn't know how. I didn't know how I was going to get her home. The best I could do was try. I hoped with everything in me it would be enough.

I didn't know what to say to bring her back, but Eve spoke up. "Why don't we look for the others, then we can come up with a plan."

Inez perked up a little at that and we started down the beach, searching for them.

We were supposed to meet up at the rocks, which I thought would be an easy meet up location. I hadn't imagined how big the rocks would actually be, and there was more than one group of rocks. Far off to our left, there were two rocks, to our right, there were three. None of us were sure which way was the right way. We ended up picking the group of three, saying it was because there were more of them, but me, Eve, and Mira had exchanged looks and picked the three because they were closer. The group of two rocks were much further away, and while Inez had the stamina to walk for miles at a time through the sand without a care in the world, the rest of us agreed that wouldn't be ideal or enjoyable.

Hopefully, the others parked somewhere near these rocks and were headed there as well. If they went to the other rocks, I didn't know how we would find them.

After ten minutes of walking toward the rocks, they still didn't seem any closer or appear to be getting any bigger. I was incredibly grateful we had picked the closer of the groups. I couldn't imagine how far away the further ones would have been.

As we walked, Inez continued to talk about how climbable the rocks were. Just the thought of her trying made me nauseous. Mira asked her a question I didn't hear about her homeland and that distracted Inez enough that she had stopped mentioning them. Instead, she started talking about Serena.

As wonderful as it was to have her distracted, I was struggling with hearing about Serena. I hadn't really been able to properly process that Inez and Serena were real. Every bit of pain they had ever experienced, every dark shadow that passed over Inez's face, every time her happiness was buried with worry, I was responsible. I had created her and given her that pain, that unwavering sense of loyalty and duty, and all the hardships in her life.

Not only that, but I had let her fall for Serena, knowing Serena wasn't the one for her, knowing that it would end in heartbreak for Inez. I had let her, because I thought it would be good for the plot. Readers loved a good unrequited romance. I let her suffer for the amusement and entertainment of others, and right now Serena was in the middle of enemy territory in Bancroft with who knows what happening to her.

It was both a curse and a comfort that Damien was here. Inez saw it as a comfort, knowing he wasn't there to hurt her, but she didn't know him like I did.

He didn't want to hurt Serena specifically; he wanted her allegiance and alliance. Well, it wasn't a want for him; it was a need. If she knew what he wanted from her and why, she wouldn't hesitate to help, but she couldn't possibly know. He hadn't tried to approach her with kindness, hadn't been honest and forthcoming with her, and had manipulated her realm. She wouldn't soon forget that and wouldn't be easily made to see his side, true or not.

Unfortunately, Damien was a lot of things but he wasn't particularly patient when it came to getting Cass back. In the original version of the story, he spent the time getting to know Serena and convincing her he wasn't the bad guy, but I had decided that wasn't the most realistic outcome.

In the final version of the story, he didn't try to convince her, just tried harder to manipulate her. The magic in her veins only protected her to a certain extent from his power, but he was patient enough to find a way around that. Tristan tried to battle his way to save Serena, and instead of trying to reason with him, Damien killed him. In that version, Inez didn't bother trying to rescue Serena. But with what Inez had described was happening in the Six Realms, things weren't conforming to my version of events. The truth was, I had no idea what might have been happening to Serena right now. At least if Damien had been there, I would have known she would be physically safe. I couldn't say he wouldn't try to warp her mind, but he wouldn't have hurt her physically. I couldn't say for sure what might have been happening to her in his absence, with his advisers in charge. I hoped he had them on a tight enough leash that they wouldn't go against him and hurt her, but I didn't know for certain.

There wasn't much I knew for certain about the Six Realms right now, but I knew I was to blame for all of it. I should've never become a writer in the first place. I couldn't believe how much pain I had caused to Serena and Inez—unknowingly, sure, but it was still my fault. I didn't know how Inez could stand to look at me. I wouldn't have been able to if I had been in her shoes. I didn't know how to deal with any of that. I would fall apart if I thought about it for too long, so I didn't. I took the easy way out and let Eve distract me, let myself be distracted by the majesty of Cannon Beach.

TWENTY-FOUR

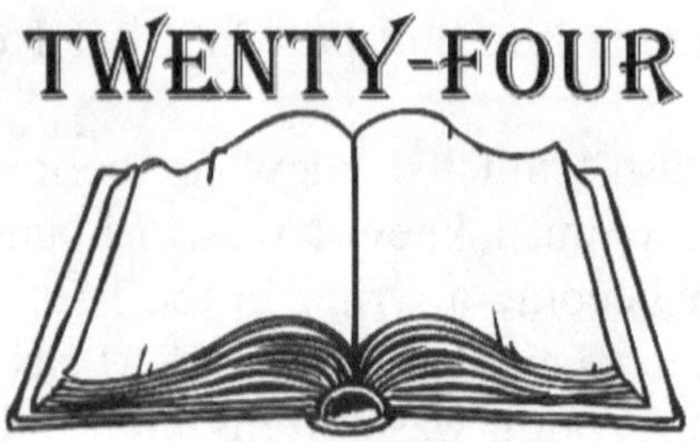

Surprisingly enough, we got lucky, and the others were already waiting when we got there.

We spread out a couple of blankets and settled in. Eve had brought a picnic basket with enough sandwiches to feed a small army, which turned out to be a good thing since Inez ate three herself.

Lying down on the blanket, surrounded by my new friends, listening to the sound of the ocean, I felt more at peace than I had for a long time. The world felt full of possibilities and I felt there wasn't anything we couldn't do if we did it together. We would figure out a way out of this mess, would figure out how to get Inez home, how to help Serena, and then I would put down my pen for good. I had already done too much damage. I wouldn't continue to make anyone suffer, not for any amount of money.

As the waves crashed against the rocks, I let myself imagine what it might be like to visit the Six Realms. I knew it wasn't possible, but until a couple of days ago, I wouldn't have thought it was a real place either, so I let myself imagine it.

I could feel the wind running through my hair as I raced horses with Serena, could hear her triumphant call when she won, and see the huge smile on her face at the victory. I could smell Delphine's cinnamon rolls baking while I lounged in the den curled up with a book she loved. I could see Tristan riding Serena's dragon through the skies, could hear his terror as she dove unexpectantly, could see the smoke clouds coming from the dragon's throat in short bursts that I knew was laughter.

I could feel myself twirling around the dance floor in a ballroom with Stella, could see Inez tap me on the shoulder to cut in, and felt my happiness at handing Stella off to Inez before being whisked off by Serena, who had abandoned Tristan in the middle of the dance floor to come dance with me. He held on to his feigned outrage for longer than I thought possible before bursting into laughter. His smile lit up his eyes as he watched Serena with such love, it felt like an intrusion to watch.

I could picture myself sitting around a bonfire, talking and laughing with the rebels from Miravale. I could picture myself sailing the seas with the pirates, could smell the ocean and hear the crash of the waves, could hear someone calling my name, could feel the spray of the ocean on my face as I peered over the side of the ship and came face to face with a siren.

She was calling my name, "Sadie, Sadie, Sadie."

I felt a hand on my shoulder and sprung up. My eyes darted around wildly and I saw my friends laughing at me. I must have fallen asleep. Inez had been trying to wake me. A smile was blooming on my face, but it died when I saw the serious expression on hers.

"What's wrong?" I asked immediately.

She stared at me, confused, and shrugged. "Nothing that wasn't wrong earlier today, but we should really start trying to work out a plan."

I nodded, watching as one by one everyone's faces turned serious and turned to me. I turned to Inez, but she was staring at me, too. "Why are you guys looking at me?"

"It's your story, your characters," said Naomi.

"But Inez lived there!"

"I lived in Sherbrooke for as long as I can remember, but I wasn't in town when Damien came. I should have been. I should've been there to protect her. Things might've been different if I was, but I wasn't. Until the day I met you, I hadn't even met him. I don't know more than our spies were able to uncover, which wasn't much."

"Face it, Sades, you know more about him than anyone. You know how he thinks, what he wants. You're our best bet," Sabrina said.

"I don't know the first thing about battling evil!" I cried.

"Well, don't think of it like that. Think of it as a story. If you were Serena, what would you do?" asked Eve.

"If Serena were here, her dragon would destroy him in less than a minute," Inez added.

Eve glanced at Inez, holding in laughter. She turned back to me and said, "Okay, well, then imagine you're Serena, only you can't shift here. What would you do?"

"Well, we'd want to know what power brought him here and for what purpose. He had to have used a spell or struck a bargain of sorts, like Inez did, but without knowing the wording, we're flying blind."

"Why would one fly blind? You would crash into all sorts of things," Inez added.

I laughed. "That's the point. It's less than ideal."

"So, how do we change things? How do we get our sight back?" she asked so seriously that I felt bad for almost laughing.

It was a good question, and I did have an advantage of sorts. I knew him and his motives better than anyone in the Six Realms, besides maybe Cass of course. Casimir! That had to be it. Everything he had done so far was just to get his freedom, to get him back. When Cass was taken, he lost not only his husband, but his own sanity, too. Damien used to be gentle and soft. Now he was aggressive and tough, and would stop at nothing to save his husband.

All of Zanaria believed Damien murdered his husband; no one believed his story, not even his own brother, the King of Somerset. Lost and alone, Damien lost his mind. He had lost the only person he cared about to the very clutches of evil and had been trying to claw him out ever since.

This had to be a new plan to do that, but how did these all connect? How could they? He was trying to marry Serena to gain an alliance with Celeste and have Sherbrooke's army at his disposal. With only his own, he didn't stand a chance against Altea, but with Sherbrooke standing with him, the odds shot up. With Celeste's powers and his combined, he hoped they would be powerful enough to undo the enchantment keeping Cass trapped.

But that was before. He had failed and then kidnapped Serena. There were two ways things could go. He would either convince her to help, or would try to control her. In the original, he spent the time to convince her, but he was here now, so there was no way to know what was happening to her there without his protection. No way to know when he would return or how things would go when he returned. No way for him to ensure she would be on his side when he returned. But why come in the first place? I wondered, knowing that would give us answers we desperately needed.

My best guess was that he found out Celeste was trying to change the past and make sure he didn't get Serena. No one there understood that it wasn't Serena he wanted. Even Serena had thought he was going to force himself on her. He wouldn't have, but it would be hard to convince anyone of that. It would be nearly impossible for him to convince people he was harmless enough for them to help him. So he travelled here to stop Inez, but also to try to make things better for himself. The sorceress, I thought with a gulp. Me. He was searching for me, counting on me to change things, to help him. I wasn't unwilling to help him. I just didn't know how to help, but he wouldn't know that. Ever since the King of Somerset, his own brother, declined to help him, knowing the stakes, he didn't trust anyone to help. Why would he when his own brother hadn't been willing to help?

So, he wasn't coming to ask, he was coming to take, and I didn't know if what I was willing to give would be enough. I was willing to change the story. I wanted to give him his happy ending. But would he believe that? And now he was going off the rails, and I didn't know how to stop him.

"I know he's looking for me. There's someone he means to save in the Six Realms and was hoping to use Celeste's powers to do so, but since he's here, I'm guessing he's heard of me. Inez, what was it that Celeste told you about me?"

"That you're the sorceress in charge of our fates with unfathomable power that surpasses even her own."

I gulped. "He's here for me, and to stop Inez, but he's here for me."

Inez's eyes narrowed. "I won't let him have you."

"Neither will we," Eve said.

Everyone nodded their agreement.

"I don't know how to stop him, though. I don't know what bargain was struck or what magic was used, but I have to assume he means to use my powers."

Inez met my eye and asked, "What evil is it that he wishes to wreak upon the Six Realms? What does he want to unleash?"

I shook my head. "Not a what, a who."

"So who then?"

"I can't say."

I shouldn't say. I had no idea how it would impact the trajectory of her decisions if I told her. I didn't know how it might change her world if she returned with knowledge she shouldn't have.

She nodded begrudgingly, before asking, "Well, if you can't tell me who, at least tell me this: would it harm the Six Realms if he succeeds?"

I didn't know how to answer that, but did my best. "What's good for one realm isn't necessarily good for the others."

"Would Sherbrooke be harmed?"

"No."

"What of Somerset?"

"I can say there would be consequences for Somerset. There are family ties there that have been neglected and bonds that have been broken. However, Damien gaining what he seeks wouldn't worsen things for Somerset."

Almost to herself, she said, "Damien rules Bancroft, so what's good for him is good for that kingdom, Sherbrooke wouldn't be harmed, and Somerset wouldn't be worse off."

"Since when do you care about the fate of Somerset?" I couldn't help but ask.

"Serena's happiness is tied to their prince. That's not a tie I can or would ignore. There isn't much I wouldn't do to secure her happiness, but you mean to distract me. So if Damien were to achieve his goal, there would be consequences for either Altea, Miravale, Santerra, or all three."

I didn't like that she was still pressing, but didn't deny it.

"We have always had good relations with Altea. I should hope they wouldn't be badly affected. We might have to step in if they were, but what of the consequences to Sherbrooke if Damien doesn't get what he wants? Would he keep coming for us?"

This time I could honestly say, "I don't know. His plan hinges on finding someone powerful enough to help him. He needed that to be Celeste, but now that he knows about me, I don't know what he'll do." Or what he might do to me if he thought I was lying about not knowing how to perform magic.

"So, the plan remains the same. Defeat his sorry ass, and kick him back to the Six Realms," Sabrina said.

"And send me back to deal with him," Inez added.

"And keep him far away from Sadie," added Eve.

"Far, far away," Mira agreed.

"That's hardly a plan," said Naomi. "How do we defeat him? And once we do, how do we send him back?"

"I don't know," I said quietly. "All I know is that he's looking for me. Him and everyone else are all counting on me, and the only thing I'm good at is letting people down."

They looked at me like I was a wounded puppy, and I couldn't say I didn't understand why. I felt helpless and hopeless. I wanted to fix all the problems I had caused, but I didn't know the first thing about how to.

"We'll figure it out," Mira reassured me.

"Together," added Eve.

Everyone nodded in agreement.

"And if it takes a while to figure out, I can keep kicking his ass until you get your magic back," Inez said with a grin. "That wouldn't be the worst thing in the world. This is turning into a rather nice vacation, if I do say so myself."

"With any luck, you'll be home right after the ball, but in the meantime, we might need to find you a dress."

She looked like I had struck her.

When we all started laughing, she scowled and mumbled something about not relinquishing her sword. She wasn't going to be at all thrilled about the ball's no weapons policy. Thankfully, I had roughly twenty-four hours to come up with a way to tell her.

TWENTY-FIVE

By the time we drove back to the city and arrived at the restaurant for our dinner, I still hadn't come up with a way to tell her.

Standing outside the restaurant, all I could think was we had made a mistake. We weren't in a great part of the city and besides a small sign saying the restaurant's name, the rest of the building was unmarked and the windows were blacked out. On a normal day, I would find that a little disconcerting, but on a day like today where I knew I wasn't being paranoid and someone literally was out to get me, I couldn't help the shiver that went down my spine. I turned to Eve to say something, but she was watching Mira, who already looked like she had seen a ghost.

Just when I had worked up the nerve to say we should probably leave, the door swung open, seemingly of its own accord.

Sabrina, Naomi, and Hanna walked in, leaving us to follow. Inez took up the rear, seeming to understand not to leave our backs unguarded.

When we got inside, I audibly gasped. The place was beautiful. The decor was gothic; haunted house chic. The windows were covered to add to the ambiance and our server grabbed and lit a candelabra before guiding us to our table and placing the candelabra on the table in front of us.

Inez sat on one side of me and Mira on the other, with Eve on Mira's other side. Now that we were inside, haunted theme or not, I felt much more comfortable. Eve seemed to relax as well, but Mira still looked a bit out of her element. Out of the corner of my eye, I saw Inez surveying the place, wide eyed.

She leaned over and asked, "Why did we choose to come to a dark place like this?"

I shrugged. "Some people like to be scared. They find it fun. Others like things they consider odd and unique like this."

She still looked confused. "No. Why did we come to a place without light? I thought all of Hawthorne had light?"

It took me a moment to realize she meant electricity. "They do have lights here. They're just choosing not to use them to make the place seem more eerie."

She gaped at me for a moment before rolling her eyes. "Your people are certainly odd, Sadie the Just."

I smiled at her. "They aren't my people, but you know you can call me Sadie. You don't have to add any sort of title."

She looked thoughtful for a moment before saying, "I suppose you don't call me Inez, captain of the royal guard, protector of Sherbrooke, defender of the innocent."

I gawked at her for a moment, and then she started laughing. "I jest, but it does have a nice ring to it." She grinned with a sparkle in her eye. "Maybe I can make that catch on."

The server came over with a round of jello blood shots on the house. They came in syringes and she set them down in front of each of us. Inez looked horrified when the server told her it was a blood shot.

She leaned over to me and whispered frantically, "You didn't say this was an establishment for vampires. Do they mean to turn us? I'll make a scene and we can-"

I grabbed her arm quickly and pulled her to me. "No; these are just a dessert made to look like blood. They have a strong concoction of a gross tasting mead in them, though, so you probably won't want more than one."

"So, they plan to get us drunk and then drink from us?"

"What? No. There are no vampires here."

At that moment, the server smiled at me and I saw her pointed teeth. Inez kicked me under the table. The moment the server walked away, she leaned over and said, "I told you so! They mean to steal your blood."

"They really don't. Those are false teeth."

"How can you be sure?"

"Vampires don't exist in Hawthorne."

"I crossed into your world. What makes you think vampires can't?"

"Vampires don't exist here," I repeated.

"Suit yourself, but I won't be having the sedative gifted to us by hungry vampires."

There was no arguing with her. She didn't touch hers, but the rest of us had ours. Once I did, I wished I hadn't. It had been years since I'd had a jello shot and I can't say I missed them.

Seeing the thinly veiled disgust on my face, Inez smiled at me and leaned over. "Told you so. You're lucky I'm here, but I'm feeling generous. I'll fight all of our ways out by myself if I have to. I won't let them have yours or any of your friends' blood." She gestured at herself smugly. "Protector of the innocent, remember?"

I laughed at that, and watched as Naomi took Inez's shot after making sure she didn't want it.

200

About halfway through our dinner, we heard screams coming from the basement. Before I could stop her, Inez had her sword in hand and charged the stairs. Not knowing what else to do, I ran after her. I had nearly reached her when I heard something bang.

We both whirled around, only to see it was a painting banging against the wall. I moved closer and it did it again, going quiet when I stopped moving. It must have been motion-sensored. Unnerving, but not dangerous.

We heard another scream. It was high pitched, and coming from the men's room. Inez didn't hesitate before barging in, sword and all, ready for battle. "Unhand them, Villain!" she yelled as the door crashed behind her.

I debated for a moment whether to follow her, but half a second later, I heard the indignant yells of men and another scream. A few moments later, a small group of men came running out, complaining about how the restaurant had taken things too far and that her outfit didn't even match the aesthetic. I couldn't help laughing as I heard them continue to complain about why the restaurant would hire a wild, sword-wielding woman to scare them and what was wrong with the classic chainsaw-wielding and axe-wielding scares, a sword was all wrong. Inez came out a few moments later, annoyed.

"No one was in danger and they all seemed annoyed that I was trying to help. There is a weird little voice in there talking about murder, but there isn't a soul in the room. I checked every possible hiding spot, so maybe there's an angry spirit living here. That was what scared the man who screamed."

I was curious, but not curious enough to enter the men's room to find out. I walked over to the ladies' room and opened the door. The moment I did, I heard a voice that sounded like a little girl. "Come play with me," and then there was a creepy giggle. A quick glance under the stalls showed, besides me and Inez who had followed me in, we were alone.

Inez's eyes darted around wildly. "The spirit followed us? First, it scared the poor men in the other room and now it comes here to terrorize us? I WON'T BE TERRORIZED, SPIRIT! DO YOUR WORST!" She raised her sword, looking for anything to swing at, but nothing happened.

The voice went through a couple of phrases before landing back on the original, "Come play with me."

I couldn't help laughing.

Inez gaped at me, horrified, and said in a hushed voice, "Don't taunt it!"

I met her eye, saw the serious look on her face, and doubled over laughing. "Says the woman who just told it to do its worst."

"Yes. Taking it seriously, showing I took it as a serious threat, but would not be cowed by it. Not disrespecting it by laughing in its face."

"It's okay. It's just a recording meant to scare people. That's what people come here for, to be scared."

"What a weird custom."

We heard another scream from the hallway and she rushed out and saw a group of girls crowded around an eye level mail slot. The girl who had screamed was backing away, and her friends were following her. Inez rushed past them and peered in for approximately five seconds before sticking her sword through the slot. My blood turned to ice when I heard something fall to the ground. By the time she had extracted her sword, I was already pushing her out of the way to look for myself.

Inside the room there was a fake severed head now bouncing on the floor. A glance up told me it had been dangling from a string. I thanked my lucky stars. I pulled back and turned to her, letting my face ask the question.

She didn't pause before saying, "Whoever hung that up thought it was hilarious to scare innocent maidens. Your lot might enjoy being scared, but where I come from, we don't go out of our way to scare others, and we don't enjoy being scared."

I smiled and put my arm around her waist. "So, Inez, the protector of the innocent, to the rescue."

"That really does have a nice ring to it."

"Mostly because it rings true. You follow a code that puts most others to shame. That's what makes you Sherbrooke's best, not the fancy title, not the strength and cunning, although those help, but your willingness to help others and dedication to doing so. It's why I know I can trust you to find a way to spare Damien's life."

She scowled at that and rolled her eyes. "Gods be damned, stupid code of honor." She gave me a small smile. "Why can't I be more rebellious?" I laughed at that, before she added, "Life would be much easier if I was less honorable."

I hated the sadness in her eyes as she said that, hated myself for having put it there, for having given her so difficult a journey. I wondered, not for the first time, if I might actually be able to change things for her. I knew now that if I could help her without hurting anyone else, I would. I would change the story for her if I could. I had no idea how, but if she could face her battles day after day and continue to have hope, then so would I. She was a hero worth rallying around. A girl worth fighting for.

TWENTY-SIX

When Sabrina said we were going for s'mores, this wasn't what I pictured. I couldn't really say what I had pictured, but it definitely wasn't this. The line was almost a mile long leading up to a storefront that looked like a bakery. A couple of times Inez asked if the line was worth it, but I assured her it was. Besides, I was fairly certain that if we tried to leave without getting s'mores Hanna would make us leave without her. She had been talking about s'mores all day.

Thankfully, the line moved quickly. When we entered the store, it smelled just like sitting around a campfire. Even Inez had a wistful expression on her face. The interior was decorated to look like the exterior of a log cabin in the woods. A forest scene was painted on the front wall and a canoe was standing against the wall, displaying some of the merchandise for sale.

Behind the counter, the women wore camp counselor outfits and were roasting marshmallows with handheld flame throwers. Inez's eyes lit up when she saw the flame throwers.

She leaned over to me and asked, "Can I buy one?"

I laughed and shook my head. "No. We're just here for the s'mores. They don't sell them. Besides, I don't think it would be able to make the trip home with you."

She sighed, longingly. "But just think of how much easier it would make life. It's like portable magic, and even more reliable and controllable."

I thought about the long trips she made and how cold the regions she travelled through got and wanted to indulge her, but it was in no one's best interest right now for her to have a portable flame thrower. But it was hard to get the image of her rubbing sticks together in vain in a cold, dark, damp forest while shivering. I knew there had to have been plenty of nights when she travelled that she hadn't been able to start a fire. If I found a way to set things right and send her home, I hoped I would be able to find a way to help her with that, too.

I didn't say any of that. I couldn't. Instead, I told her, "You'll love the s'mores."

When we finally had the treats in our hands, I took a bite and my taste buds exploded. The melting chocolate and marshmallow on the homemade graham cracker was out of this world. I watched as Inez took her first bite and moaned. By the time I had finished about half of mine, she had scarfed hers down and was left with chocolate all over her face and sticky hands.

Eve handed out wet naps from her purse. I don't know what we would've done without her, especially Inez, who had chocolate and marshmallow everywhere.

She looked at me with a chocolate grin and said, "It's a shame I can't take these with me. I know Serena would adore these."

"Well, actually," I said, but she cut me off.

"You know," she said quickly, "I bet I could roast marshmallows over a fire if we were able to make the marshmallows, graham crackers, and chocolate. We could probably do this outside."

I laughed.

"What? I know it's not nearly as fancy, but it would still be nice."

"No, no, that's not it. I was laughing because that's how it's normally done, everywhere except Portland anyway."

"So, in the rest of Hawthorne, you make these over fires? When I nodded she said, "I'll have to find a baker to make the ingredients and introduce these to the realm at once. Everyone would love them! That'll be the first thing I do when I get home!"

"The first thing?" I asked, surprised.

"Yeah. Why wouldn't it be?" she asked, and then a moment later, her face fell. "I got carried away for a moment. Of course it wouldn't be the first thing. Securing Serena's safety and the safety of the queendom would be the first thing."

I frowned at that and at the change that had come over her. "You know, it's okay to have fun sometimes. I know you have a lot riding on your shoulders and a lot of people counting on you, but it's okay to enjoy yourself sometimes."

She smiled a little at that. "Sadie the Just, maybe they should have called you Sadie the Wise. I appreciate the advice. I will take it under advisement. Today was certainly a nice break, but I don't like not knowing what Damien is up to. This feels like the calm before a big storm, like the calm will burst at any moment. I don't look forward to that happening, but I will be ready when it does." She wandered back over to the others, striking up a conversation with Sabrina.

Eve came up from behind me, having just thrown out the remains of her s'more. "That's good advice, you know."

"Thank you?" I half-said, half-asked.

She laughed and said, "You would do well to take some of your own advice. You aren't responsible for everyone's problems and you don't have to fix everything alone. You have us now," she said, smiling at the others.

I was five seconds away from crying at that, which she must have known because she wrapped her arms around me and pulled me in for a hug. I needed that more than I knew.

"Thank you," I whispered in her ear. When she pulled away a moment later, she linked her arm through mine and we headed back to the group.

TWENTY-SEVEN

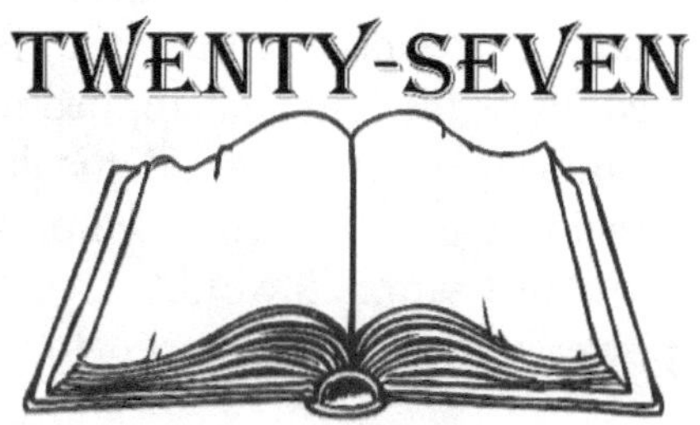

Damien

The whole damn day I had been searching for her, and nothing. It was like she had just vanished from the city somehow, or maybe she was getting craftier and was shielding herself from me. It didn't matter. Sooner or later, she would slip up and reveal herself. I grinned when I felt a tug at my power. It didn't feel as strong as it had before, but it was there. Either she hadn't mastered shielding or she had left her mark somewhere. Either way, I had to know.

The driver of the yellow carriage asked surprisingly little questions and followed my inexact directions until I arrived at another lodging, similar to the one I had been staying in. Albeit, the one I had been staying in was far grander.

I paid the driver and followed the pull of her magic into the metal contraption that had replaced stairs here. My magic knew where I was headed before I did, and the contraption followed my bidding, stopping where the feeling was the strongest. I walked down the hall and stopped in front of the door that was humming to me. I tried the knob. Locked. I applied some pressure, but still it remained closed. It appeared physical force wouldn't work. I would have to use magic. I hated wasting power when I didn't need to, but now it was necessary.

I sent some tendrils of my power questing under the door. Most of them hunted through the room for the source of power, but a couple stayed and unlatched the door. It swung open in front of me, and I stepped inside and stopped in my tracks, mesmerized.

I had never seen such raw power so haphazardly floating around. It was like everything she touched held a part of her power. I had never seen anyone able to do that, myself included. Maybe the rules were different here, or maybe she truly was more powerful than even I was.

I gulped. If that was the case, I didn't want to be caught unawares in her chamber. I needed to regroup and come up with a new plan. If I couldn't take her forcefully, I would have to make her come willingly. That would require more careful planning and a bit more time, but it would be worth it when I was back in his arms. I would do anything for that. For now, I should leave, but not without finding out what had drawn me here. I would need to be quick.

Without thinking too much about the implications, I let my power tear through the place. I gasped as clothing flew through the room as my power collided with hers. I ducked as a book went flying over my head, and was thinking of retreat when I noticed most of my power camped around a small metal device. It had a much stronger aura of magic than anything else in the room. I don't know how I hadn't noticed it before. I glanced around the room again, making sure nothing else stuck out, but nothing did. This was the answer; it had to be. It had to be an instrument of magic here, a way for her to channel her power.

I grabbed the device and felt a slight shock run through me, as if the device had a mind of its own and didn't want to be captured. I tucked the device in the inside of my coat, careful not to let it touch more of my skin than it already had.

Until I could figure out what made it tick and just what powers it had, I would need to be careful. I would give myself the night to figure out how it worked, and then I would either hold it for ransom or use its power against her. I hoped the device would be enough to draw her out, but a smile crept over my face as a plan-B came to me. It wouldn't hurt to have some assurance.

TWENTY-EIGHT

The room looked quite literally like a bomb had gone off. Inez pushed me and Mira aside, drew her sword, and swung around the room, searching for any sign of an intruder or what could've caused this, but she found nothing.

"Well, whatever it was is gone now," she said. "Check your belongings. Knowing if anything was taken should help us figure out what might've happened."

Mira rushed over to her corner of the room and began looking through her things. I was too shocked to move. Inez linked eyes with me and nodded to me. We were thinking the same thing then. It was Damien. It had to have been. But how did he know where we were staying, and what could he have possibly hoped to gain by breaking into our room? Besides scaring us, that is. Maybe that was his intent. Maybe. Inez quickly surveyed her things that she had stowed under the bed for safekeeping and saw nothing was missing. I watched Mira turn back and report that nothing was missing in her things, either. I felt numb as a creeping feeling rushed over me.

The feeling grew worse with each step toward my things, most of which were thrown throughout mine and Inez's bed and over the floor. There wasn't much that was still actually in my bag. I gulped as I kneeled down and my worries were confirmed. My laptop was gone.

TWENTY-NINE

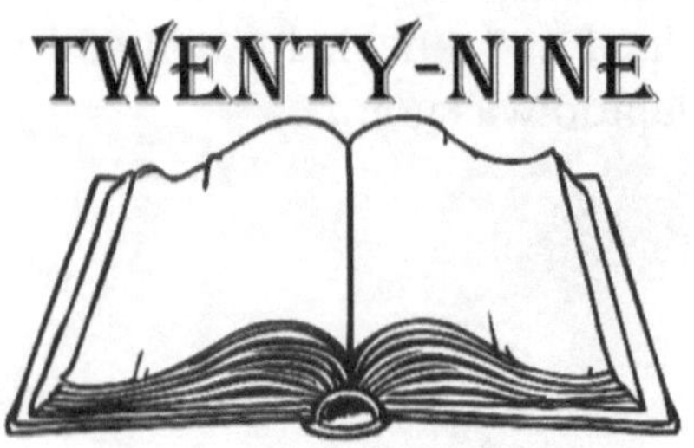

I had tried last night to trace my laptop's location, but I wasn't able to locate it any closer than knowing it was still in the city. That wasn't helpful or reassuring. If it was still in Portland, so was Damien.

I didn't know how he could have possibly known enough about technology to understand the laptop had a connection to their story. I didn't know what he hoped to gain by taking it. Maybe it had been a lucky guess. What remained to be seen was whether he knew what it was he had and if he found a way to use it, would the story change for him?

I had no understanding of how the magic worked in the first place, but he was quite powerful. Would he be able to use the laptop to change things? Would he want to, or would he want things to stay the same? Did he see a path to saving Casimir the way things were? If he did, then maybe changing things would be too risky for him. I could only hope that he wouldn't try to make any changes, since I couldn't even begin to fathom what that might do to his world.

Inez was equally on edge that morning, muttering about how he dared come to her home and mess with her things and her friends. I was happy she considered us friends, but I was as worried as she was about Damien knowing our location.

Not wanting to sit around for long that morning, we met up with Eve at the coffeehouse around the corner. Mira, Inez, and I didn't sleep much last night, so the coffee was welcome. Eve looked like she hadn't slept any better than we did. We had told her about the room, but we hadn't told anyone else. We didn't want to worry anyone else, but I knew Eve would've insisted on knowing, so we had told her.

She had called immediately and insisted the three of us spend the night in her room, but we all knew the worst of it was over. If Damien wanted to get to us last night, he would've stayed and waited for us to return.

We felt safe knowing he wasn't coming back that night at least, but in the morning light now, all I felt was anxious. Anxious about whatever he was planning next, because I knew for certain there was a plan.

When the others met up with us toward the end of our breakfast, I reluctantly told them about our night. They were all worried, but didn't seem surprised. After a full day of his absence, it wasn't surprising he had taken advantage of our absence to go through our things.

I was glad everyone knew now. Well, everyone except Naomi. She must have been enjoying breakfast with some of her other friends and hadn't had a chance to respond to our messages to her yet, but that was okay. We knew we would see her later for the ball anyway, and as long as she stayed with her friends, she wouldn't be in any danger.

None of us wanted to think too much more about Damien or what he might've been planning, so I was happy when Sabrina provided the perfect distraction.

"Did anyone else hear about the showdown between Gwen and Morgana yesterday?"

I had been waiting to hear something about them. From how explosive the energy was the first night we met them, I guessed something like this was coming. I hoped Gwen was able to handle it. Although I wasn't sure anyone could handle Morgana if she was anything like how she was the other day. She was on a warpath with a single goal; destroy Gwen. I would've hated to have been Gwen, and I hated that for Gwen.

From what I knew, she didn't deserve Morgana's rage. It didn't seem to me like she was dating Ollie, but even if she was, she deserved to be happy. Arty deserved the same, but it was better for her to end things than to string him along. Besides, it seemed like Arty wasn't nearly as upset as Morgana was. It was one thing to be protective of your friends, but she was taking it to a new level.

Eve asked before I could, "No. What happened? What'd Morgana do?"

Sabrina quirked an eyebrow at her. "What makes you think it was Morgana's fault?"

"What do you mean? Did you see her the other day? She's had it out for Gwen since the breakup," Eve said.

"You mean since Gwen cheated?" Sabrina said.

"Gwen didn't cheat!" I said. "There's no way she would have. That girl has such a big heart, she wouldn't hurt anyone, especially Arty, like that."

"I don't know. From what I've heard, it seems like she's been getting around," Sabrina said.

"Good for her!" I chimed in, not wanting to hear more negative things about her. "I doubt it's true from having talked to her for more than a minute, but if she is, more power to her. She deserves to be happy. The only one unhappy about everything is Morgana. Gwen has clearly moved on, and even Arty seems to have put things behind him, so why can't Morgana? Even if she can't be civil with her, she could stand to ignore her. It's not like Gwen didn't try to make amends. She really should leave her alone."

216

"You two might not wanna hear what actually happened." Sabrina said warily.

I met Eve's eye. She was just as confused as I was.

"We want to know," we both said at the same time.

Sabrina winced. "Well, don't say I didn't warn you, but I'd love to see how you explain away what your golden girl Gwen did. From what I heard, Morgana had given her space and kept her distance when they happened to both be at the same club, but Gwen wouldn't leave her alone. She wasn't talking to her, per se, but she wouldn't let Morgana out of her sight. Morgana was a relative saint and didn't say a single thing to her, until Gwen hit a nerve. Gwen had the audacity to drag Oliver out on the dance floor and start grinding up on him, right in front of Morgana. Morgana stomped over and asked her what the hell she thought she was doing. Gwen winked at her and told her she was having a good time and that Morgana should try it sometime. Morgana told her her idea of a good time didn't involve being a hoe, and then Gwen said, 'you haven't seen anything yet'. And guess what she did."

"What?" I asked quickly.

"Tell us," Eve added.

"She turned, leaned into Morgana, said something too quiet for anyone to hear, flicked her nose, and then turned and passionately kissed Oliver, right in front of her."

"No, she didn't!" I exclaimed.

"There's no way!" Eve said at the same time. "They aren't even together."

"Well, it certainly looked like they were last night."

I was afraid to ask what happened next, but, luckily, Eve had no such qualm. "So what happened?" she asked.

Sabrina shrugged. "Nothing, actually. Morgana stormed off, and Oliver took her by the hand and dragged her to a different room, whispering to her the whole way, probably to continue what she had started."

Eve and I exchanged looks of disbelief. That didn't sound like the Gwen we thought we knew. "That makes no sense," I said to her.

Sabrina shrugged apologetically. "Maybe you guys don't know her as well as you thought. There's two sides to every story. It sounds like you two should've given Morgana's side a chance."

She was right. We hadn't given Morgana much of a chance, but when you were drowning in Gwen's ocean eyes, it was hard to believe she could do anything wrong, especially when Morgana had thrown the first punch the night we met them. It was hard to not want to defend Gwen, but I couldn't possibly understand why she would have made out with Ollie in front of Morgana. It hadn't seemed like there was anything going on between them, but maybe I was wrong about her. I hoped I wasn't, but I supposed anything was possible. The pictures would be all over the internet right now. I gulped at the thought of what people would say about Gwen. I hoped she was ready for it, but I didn't know how she possibly could be.

Sabrina added, "I heard someone saw Gwen and Morgana talking later that night, but I don't buy it. You would've heard that explosion from a mile away."

I didn't know what else to say. I gathered from her silence that Eve didn't either. I was grateful when Hanna changed the subject and started talking about getting ready for the ball later tonight. After some discussion, we decided to meet up for lunch and then go to someone's hotel room to get ready.

"We really could've used your penthouse room right now," I said, nudging Inez playfully adding, "But we'll make do with the peasant rooms the rest of us have."

218

We were still laughing when I noticed some familiar faces. I turned to look closer and saw they were some of Naomi's friends. She wasn't with them, though. She must have slept in today. I couldn't say I blamed her. It was going to be a late night tonight, so it was a smart idea. I waved to them and they waved back.

After they got their orders, they made their way over to us. I was happy to see them until one of them asked, "Where's Naomi?"

My blood went cold instantly. Out of the corner of my eye, I saw the rest of the group had confused expressions on their faces, except for Eve and Inez. They both looked grim. So I wasn't the only one who immediately jumped to the worst possible conclusion. Good to know.

"She's not with you?" Hanna asked.

The girl shook her head. "No. She didn't come back last night. She didn't bother to tell us, but we assumed she was spending the night with you guys."

Last night. She had left sometime between dinner and s'mores, saying she was heading home. She hadn't felt like s'mores and wanted to get some rest. None of us had thought twice about it. But that was a little over twelve hours ago now. She had been missing for twelve hours and we were just now figuring that out? I was in full panic mode, but tried to take a deep breath.

Eve's face mirrored my own for a moment before she pulled herself together enough to say, "Well, we don't know there's anything to worry about. Maybe she's with some other friends. Do any of you know if she has other friends on the trip?"

Everyone shook their heads. If she did, we didn't know them.

"Has she responded to anyone's messages?"

We all checked our phones and shook our heads.

One of her other friends shrugged. "I'm sure she'll turn up."

I exchanged a wary glance with Eve; they didn't know what we did. They didn't know there might be a reason to actually have been worried.

I tried to smile but failed. "Yeah, I'm sure she will."

Eve asked for one of their numbers in case they heard from her. They exchanged numbers and then they moved to their own table, saying they would see us at the ball.

I turned to Eve as she turned to me. "Should we be worried?" she asked.

"I don't really know," I said carefully. "She's made a lot of friends so far. She's probably with one of them, right?"

I was more trying to convince myself, but Eve didn't seem convinced either.

"Would he have taken her?" I asked Inez.

She had a grave expression on her face. "I don't know. I don't know what he's capable of. You tell me; would he have?"

The more I thought about it, the more worried I got. "I really don't know, but I can't rule it out. If he did, he would want information from her. As long as she was willing to give it to him, she should be fine."

"Would she, though?" Eve asked Hanna.

Hanna turned pale. "I honestly don't know. If she thought it might hurt us, I don't think she would."

"Damn it!" I let out. "I hope she tells him whatever the hell he wants to know. No amount of secrecy is worth her putting herself at risk. Why would she make the stupid mistake of protecting us over herself?"

"Because we're friends," said Mira. "I think any one of us would've acted the same."

To my surprise, everyone besides me nodded. They couldn't mean that, though. Why would they possibly get themselves hurt defending me, defending the rest of us? We hardly knew each other. Why would anyone do that? I couldn't wrap my head around it. It was possible they were just agreeing with Mira because when she did speak up, no one liked to contradict her, but they all appeared sincere.

I glanced at Eve to see if she felt the same, and was surprised that she was nodding, too. She would pick us over herself, too. Was there something wrong with me that I wouldn't? That it wouldn't have occurred to me to do so?

Eve took my hand and squeezed tight. "But we don't even know if she's with him. Hopefully, she's off with some other friends and will be in touch soon. How about we wait things out until lunch? If no one's heard from her by then, we'll come up with a plan." I nodded weakly. She squeezed my hand again and said more quietly to me, "This isn't your fault, so don't get lost in guilt. You couldn't have possibly known or stopped this. But I promise you, we'll find her."

I gave her a weak smile. I was grateful for her comfort, but I couldn't help but feel like she was wrong. This was all my fault. His existence was my fault and him having possibly taken Naomi was my fault. He was trying to get to me. I could only hope I would be ready when he did.

THIRTY

Damien

In the inn's lobby, I ordered the peasant to call a ride and handed him a couple pieces of gold. I learned quickly, the quicker I handed over the gold, the quicker and better my bidding was executed. I was proven right when instead of the small yellow carriages I was used to, a long, sleek, black carriage pulled up in its place.

The servant, upon stopping, immediately jumped out and with a flourish, opened the back door for me. This was more like it. I handed him a couple of gold pieces and relished his widening eyes and the slight bow he gave as he hurried to the front. I was about to call him back, since he hadn't asked for a destination when two things happened. The first being that a window at the front of the carriage rolled down and there he was asking where he could take me to. The second was that a pull much stronger than the one that had brought me to this lodging tugged at my magic.

It felt achingly familiar. Knowingly or not, her magic sang to mine. I grinned. It wasn't her time yet, but wherever she went lately, her guard dog was likely to follow, so I bid him to follow my directions and we followed her magic's siren song.

We pulled up to the curb of a rundown building. What she and her friends were doing here, I couldn't guess, but it didn't matter. What mattered was getting the royal guard alone. I knew if I made enough of a scene out here, she would come racing out. She had a hero complex if I'd ever seen one. She would tell the others to wait inside and come rushing out herself. If I was quick enough in ambushing her, I could have her under my control before she even had a thought to resist. With her under my control, the path would be clear to the sorceress. I would finally get my hands on her. She seemed like the type to hand herself over to get me to leave the royal guard alone. If I was wrong, then I was sure the royal guard could make her come with me.

I told the driver to wait a little while and scanned the area for something that would make her come running. There wasn't anyone in sight. I would have to improvise. I was sure if I used enough magic and was loud enough, she would come, but it would've been easier if there were others around to scream in peril. I glanced around and saw there was a tall, heavy sign that was almost as tall as the building. If I struck that, she was sure to hear. Everyone was sure to hear, and she would come running.

I was about to get out of the carriage when the restaurant door swung open. Perfect. Someone to help me get the royal guard's attention. I turned to the door and couldn't believe my luck. It was the same girl from the bar two days ago. This might actually work better. She was a friend of the sorceress and while the royal guard had been the plan, this one would be easier to control. It was evident from our encounter at the bar that she already had some desire for me. It wouldn't be hard to get her to come with me, and then the sorceress would come willingly. She might not have for the royal guard, but she certainly would for her friend.

As I watched, the girl seemed to be waiting for something, probably a carriage to take her somewhere. I would need to act fast. I cued the driver to roll down my window and drawled, "Need a ride?"

I grinned as she took a couple steps closer, putting her within my reach if I was quick enough. Perfect. A flash of recognition came over her face, but so did a flash of fear. I didn't know how she knew to be afraid. I hadn't given her a reason to be at the bar. It must have been instinctual, and boy, was she right.

I already had my hand on the door handle when she shook her head. The hard way, then. I whipped open the door and before she could blink, I grabbed her arm and pulled her to me. I didn't need to speak the words to make the ideas take root in her mind, but I was in a hurry. My plan would work best if no one saw us yet.

I stared deep into her eyes and said, "You want to come with me. Don't scream, don't fight." Seeing the confusion on her face, I added for my own amusement, "You think I'm attractive and want to know where the night might go." I waited for a few moments for the suggestion to take root and watched as a range of emotions crossed her face before she blinked up at me through her eyelashes and moved past me to the car. She swayed her hips as she ran her fingers over my shoulder. I grinned. I had her.

I had been starting to doubt my powers, thinking maybe they didn't work the same here, but I was enjoying being proven wrong. I had half a thought of enjoying her tonight, but the hole in my chest ached for Cass and I heard his voice telling me not to go too far, only what was necessary. I might have thought it was my conscious if I believed I still had one. I was too far gone for that, but not too far gone to listen.

I ran my finger over the place where my ring had been and tuned her out as she giggled and flirted. She didn't seem to care or notice I wasn't saying anything back. I would send her to bed when we arrived and try to figure out the magic artifact. If I couldn't use it against the sorceress, I would use her friend against her.

By the time I shut the friend in the spare room, ordering her to sleep, I could have used some sleep myself, but there was work to be done. I could sleep once my husband was back home, safe and sound. Until then, I needed to push myself harder. The sorceress didn't understand what was at stake, couldn't understand. I had stopped trying to convince anyone after my own brother didn't believe me. *My own brother* had thought I had murdered my husband. I was the only one who knew the truth, the only one searching for him, and I would find him if it took everything in me.

A part of me wondered if Serena would help if I could convince her what was at sake, or if the sorceress might help, but I didn't have the liberty of time to convince the sorceress. Once I had her back home with me, Serena would be made to understand, too. I didn't need her help, but I knew I could use allies, true allies, unlike my good-for-nothing brother. Since Serena was imprisoned in my fortress, I had the luxury of time to convince her. I would even agree not to avenge myself on my brother if she willed it. Anything to have my husband returned to me safe, anything to keep him that way.

I opened the device and saw the top half was fully black and of no interest, but the bottom half held a spread of buttons with letters and numbers on them. I touched one of the buttons and was startled to see a white box pop up on the black screen asking for a password. Of course it couldn't have been that easy, but I knew I was on the right track. Why else would the device be protected?

I thought for a moment before saying "Sadie." Nothing happened. "Zanaria." Still nothing. I tried the names of all the realms I knew and still nothing happened. I yelled the names of every person and place I could think of at the infernal device and still nothing. I almost smashed the damned thing, but it would be a waste of such power.

I tried for most of the night to make it work, finally giving up when my eyes wouldn't stay open.

THIRTY-ONE

Morning came far too soon, and I would've liked to get more sleep, but I refused to waste time. The device was a dud, so on to plan-B. I would get as much information from the friend as I could, and then I would use her as a hostage; Sadie in exchange for her. The sorceress would make the trade, especially when she realized her friend was under my control.

I went to check on my captive, only to find her sleeping soundly.

She was so quiet and peaceful while sleeping. I knew the moment I woke her she would be back to the incessant yammering I dealt with on the carriage ride back. I thought for a moment about waking her and ordering her to stay quiet, but I needed information from her. I needed her to talk, but not quite yet. I could use some more quiet. I let her sleep longer.

When she came wandering out a few hours later, I was ready for her.

"Morning, handsome," she said, grinning.

I nodded at her. "Do you understand what's happening here?" I asked. I was never known for subtly.

"I understand you took me home," she said with a wink.

Maybe I had forced too much attraction. "Listen here and well, you are my captive. You are at my mercy, but as long as you tell me what I need to know and do exactly as I say, I will not harm you."

Not much anyway, I thought with a grin.

I watched a few emotions flash too quickly over her face before she settled on uncertainty. "What do you want to know?"

"Let's start with what you know of the royal guard of Sherbrooke."

"You mean Inez?"

Inez. I had heard her name before, but hadn't deemed her worthy of remembrance. After seeing how fierce and unwavering she was in combat, I wouldn't make that same mistake again. She was no match for me, of course, but she was noteworthy.

I nodded.

"She's strong, fierce, loyal, cares deeply about her realm and will do anything to protect it."

"Does she care for her realm or simply its princess?" I asked, barely hiding my smirk. I had heard the whispers.

She didn't flinch before saying, "Both."

I grinned and said more to myself than to her, "Good. It shouldn't be hard to leash her with Serena at my disposal."

"And what of the sorceress?"

"Who?" she asked.

"The sorceress. The one you call Sadie. Tell me all you know of her and her powers."

"There isn't much to tell. I haven't known her long, and she doesn't seem to have any sort of power." She shrugged before adding, "At least none that I can see."

I nodded. I had suspected as much. Even in my own realm, those with the gift of magical sight were few and far between. It was no surprise that in this realm, things weren't any different.

I breathed out deeply, hoping this hadn't been a waste of my time. "Do you have anything of interest to tell?"

She shrugged. "I'm not sure. How am I supposed to know what's of interest?"

I took another deep breath. Killing her wouldn't further my plans. Even if she was of no use information wise, she was still a captive and would be enough leverage to get the sorceress to do as I said.

"How long do you plan to keep me here, anyway?"

"Long enough that your friends start searching for you." I glanced out the window and saw it was close to midday. "I would say they likely already are. How would one send them a message quickly in your world?"

She just blinked. I pulled her toward me, staring into her eyes, pushing my power toward her. "How?"

She blinked again. "My phone, in my purse."

Neither of those words made sense to me. "Show me."

I released her arm, and she walked over to the bag she had been carrying yesterday and opened it. She took out a small metal device and handed it to me.

One glance showed it required a passcode like the other device. It was possible she might know how to use the other device as well. I thought for a moment about ordering her to open the device for me, but it was too unpredictable. If it were as powerful as I thought, she might have been able to use it against me before I figured out how to use it.

I handed the smaller metal device back to her. "Open it."

She unlocked it by tapping a few places on the screen. "Start a message to Sadie the sorceress."

When she looked up again, I added, "Now write what I say."

I watched over her shoulder, making sure she composed exactly what I requested, not that she could do otherwise. She was mine to command.

When she had, I had her put down the device and sit on the couch.

"So, you're using me as leverage? That's your genius plan?" she asked, rolling her eyes.

I thought about forcing her silence, but it had been a few days since I'd had anyone to talk to, and it wouldn't hurt any to tell her my plans. But if she continued that tone and her disrespect, I might just kill her myself.

Luckily, I had the power to change it. I stared into her eyes and told her, "You find me to be utterly charming and incredibly intelligent. You won't think for yourself. I will tell you what to think. You will hang on my every word."

A moment of indecision and worry flickered over her face before my power took root and she smiled at me. "You were telling me about your super smart plan?" she said, twirling a piece of her hair around her finger.

That was more like it.

"Yes; I was telling you how wildly brilliant I was to think of taking you last night and using you as a hostage at the ball you kept mentioning tonight. There will be enough people to keep us hidden until the right moment, and then I will make sure she bows to me."

"Make sure who bows to you? Why would you have to make them?" she asked, still twirling her hair and blinking at me through her long lashes.

"The sorceress, of course. I need her, but that damned royal guard hasn't let me close to her, but now that I have you, that changes."

She jumped up and clapped her hands together. "Yay! I'm helping!" After a moment, she cocked her head to the side and asked, "How am I helping?"

I chuckled. "You're my bait. The sorceress won't let any harm come to you, and is going to trade herself to me for you and then we'll be on our way back to Bancroft. Back to my fortress and the Princess."

"You're so smart!" she said, smiling. After a moment, she frowned. "But how do you know it will work?"

Because it has to, because I'm out of options, because I'm desperate. I didn't say any of that. I put on more bravado than I felt and said, "I know magic well, and as finnicky as it can be if you don't word it just right, I'm confident about the spell that got me here. It will keep me in this realm until I have enough power to change things back in my realm, or until I have a new crown on my head and a new realm bowing at my feet."

"So once you have her, you'll have the power you need?"

I grinned. "Exactly."

"That's so smart, but I think you missed something."

Unlikely.

"What's that?"

"I'm no one's puppet." She turned on her heel and walked out the door.

I stared at her, my mouth gaping. That wasn't possible. She was mine to command, and I certainly hadn't willed her away. Had I? I thought back carefully over my commands, every single one of them, but there was nothing that could explain it, unless maybe the trace of power I felt on her was her own power? That wasn't possible, though. It had been the sorceress's magic, and even if it wasn't, not just anyone could resist me, especially not when I was almost at full strength like I was now.

231

I thought about going after her and grabbing her. I thought about forcing her to her knees with the full strength of my power, showing her just what happened when someone defied me, but it wasn't worth wasting my power.

I needed to be ready for tonight. I would need every last drop of my power for the showdown I was expecting with the sorceress and royal guard, especially now that I didn't have leverage to keep them in line. I would have to improvise. Let the friend scurry back and tell them everything; it didn't matter. Nothing mattered anymore. I had the sorceress in my sights, and she would be mine. I would use her power, willing or not, and I would finally have my husband back and everything, everything I'd done to get to this point, every life I'd taken, every terrible thing I'd done, would be worth it. I would do it all over again; burn the world to the ground to get him back. It was time to prepare myself for war.

THIRTY-TWO

By the time we were leaving for lunch, we weren't any closer to finding Naomi. Between all of us, we managed to track down and contact everyone who went to dinner with us, but none of them had seen or heard from her since the night before. Most of them hadn't seen her all day yesterday, either.

Inez had even tried her compass, but she couldn't get it to point at anything else besides me. When I went to ask her why, she shrugged and explained, "You're the one I was seeking, the one with the power to help me and to send me home. Unfortunately for your friend, I don't want to find her more than I want to go home."

I put my arms around her and hugged her tightly. "I promise I'll find a way to send you home and to help Serena. After how brave you've been, I promise I will do everything in my power to help you."

As I pulled away, I saw she was smiling a little. At least I could do something right. I just hoped I would be able to keep my promise. When it was time to leave for lunch and we still weren't any closer to finding her, it was getting harder to stay hopeful. I was fighting to keep my thoughts from spiraling, but it was getting harder to think anything but the worst.

I had been holding onto hope all morning that by the time we met up for lunch, we would have found her, but no one had any news or anything new to share. Hanna had even tried tracking her phone, but it must have been dead, because she wasn't showing up anywhere. That was terrible luck, because even if Damien had her, he wouldn't have understood the danger of her keeping her phone.

We grabbed our sandwiches from the café, but no one touched much of their food. None of us had the stomach for it, or really knew what else we could do. We didn't have any way to track her, and unless I had developed magic powers overnight, we had no way of tracking him. I was just about desperate enough to try to tap into some of the power I may or may not have had, and was wondering if I should try meditation, tarot, or scrying, when my phone signaled a text.

Distracted, I pulled out my phone and literally jumped out of my seat when I saw who it was from. Naomi! I clicked on the message, glad she was okay, but my jaw dropped when I read: **Sadie of Hawthorne, I have borrowed this magical device from your annoying friend who goes by Naomi. She is under my power and my control. She remains safe, for now, but she will only stay that way if you agree to the following.**

She has been incessantly talking of a ball happening tonight. We will meet there and I will hand her over unharmed. In exchange, you will come with me back to my realm. If you refuse, I cannot guarantee her safety. I am sure you know of my power and that I will stop at nothing to get what I want.

I leave you with this piece of advice. Be wise and do not cross me, Sadie of Hawthorne. I shall see you this evening. I do not ask you to come alone, but do be sure to keep that Sherbrookian guard dog of yours on a tight leash. I would hate to have to show her my claws. Farewell for now, King Damien of Bancroft.

Well, fuck. I glanced up and saw Eve staring at me, worried. I knew I probably was as white as a ghost, which wasn't much whiter than normal, but from the concern on Eve's face, I knew I looked bad.

I didn't know what to say, so I just handed her the phone. She scanned it quickly, excited when she saw it was Naomi, and then worried when she realized who it was actually from, and downright terrified when she saw what it was he was asking for.

Everyone was looking at the two of us, concerned. I couldn't think of anything to say. There was nothing to be said. This was all my fault. He took Naomi, and she was in danger because of me. I had to save her; we had to save her.

Eve finished reading and turned quickly to Hanna. "Quick, try tracking her again!"

I was dumbstruck I hadn't thought about that. We all turned to Hanna, the text almost forgotten. A few heart pounding moments later, she called out, "I've got her! Quick, Sabrina, let me see your phone."

Sabrina handed over her phone, and we all watched as Hanna pulled up a map. "I can pinpoint her within a block. She's on the other side of the river, near the ball venue, actually, but I can't tell where. She has to be somewhere in this radius, though."

She held out both phones, showing us Naomi's phone's location and the map of the city. We compared the two, trying to pinpoint it any closer, but there wasn't any way to tell. As we watched, Naomi's dot went away. Damn. The phone must have actually died or been turned off, but we knew enough about where she was that we could start the search. She was in some sort of warehouse district. It wasn't much to go on, but at least it was something.

I wondered for the first time if maybe we should call the cops. We couldn't explain everything to them, obviously, but the fact that she was being held by a crazy man who thought he was from another world should have been enough to get them to raid the warehouses out there. But I shuddered at the thought of how that confrontation would go down.

I didn't know if he had powers here, or how they worked. I knew he had somewhat been able to influence me, but I had no idea if he could do that to others here. Judging by the fact that he had Naomi now, though, I had to assume he did. In that case, it would be a mistake to drag the police and their guns into the mix. I told the others as much, and they all looked grave but agreed. No one wanted to be held at gunpoint by a police officer under the influence, and Inez was confident we could handle him on our own. How she was so sure, I didn't know, but since she had held her own against him in the Gardens, I believed her.

We wanted to go right away, but Inez wouldn't go without her shield and some supplies. Luckily, we were only a block from our hotel, so we walked back quickly. On the way there, she explained to the others that her shield had the ability to repel magic. I was surprised and couldn't remember if I had written that or if the story had taken liberties with that. Either way, I was grateful. It was an incredibly useful item to have.

She grabbed her pack with all her belongings and the shield. I saw her pick up and scowl at the compass. She threw it down on the bed, before thinking better of it and scooping it up a moment later and putting it in her pocket.

When we went downstairs, the others had had the hotel call two cabs for us. They were sitting on the couch. I noticed with dismay that the pillows were all askew, but now clearly wasn't the time to say anything.

I plopped down on the couch with them, scooting over to make room for Inez and Eve, when a horn sounded from out front. One of the cabs was here. We quickly decided that me, Inez, Eve, and Mira would take the first one and Sabrina and Hanna would follow. I tried to tell them they didn't need to follow, but Hanna shut me down before I even finished saying it.

"Of course we're coming with you. You couldn't stop us if you tried. We're a team now. We have your back."

Everyone else nodded.

My heart soared at the gesture, but there was a pit in my stomach that said this was a bad idea. They didn't need to come, didn't need to put themselves in danger for me. They should stay. But I didn't repeat my concerns. I just thanked them and told them we'd see them soon. Inez, Eve, Mira, and I made our way to the revolving door.

I went in first and started to spin around when a curly head of brown hair in the other compartment caught my eye. It couldn't be! I kept spinning the door past the exit, back to the lobby, and ran out when the door lined up with the lobby entrance and I saw who it was. Naomi was back! I couldn't believe it! I raced over to her; she was in Hanna's arms, so I looped mine around her back and around Hanna. I couldn't believe it. She was safe and back! I thanked the universe she was okay.

When Inez asked her what had happened, I realized we were still in the lobby and weren't alone. I pulled away from Naomi, leaving my arm around her shoulder, and steered her toward the elevator.

"Why don't we go talk in our room?"

When the elevator opened, we all crowded in. The doors were about to close when a cane stuck in between the doors, prompting them to reopen. A grumpy looking old man adjusted his cane, scowled at us, and hobbled inside. His scowl deepened when the doors shut and he noticed the elevator was full of hip-hop music. Thankfully, he got off at the next floor, muttering to himself about how weird kids were today and how their loud music didn't make any sense.

When the doors shut again, we burst into laughter. Happy to be alone again and overjoyed Naomi was back, I couldn't help dancing along to the music.

A few floors later when the doors opened again to let us out, everyone else had joined in.

Once we were safely in our room, which, thankfully, was big enough to hold us all comfortably, Hanna immediately asked Naomi what had happened.

"Well, I guess he must have seen me go into the restaurant with you guys, cause when I left to go call a ride, he was waiting there. I didn't know it was him at first, though. A limo pulled up to the curb and the back window rolled down and he called out to me, 'Need a ride?'.

"I took a couple of steps closer to see who it was. I thought maybe it was someone we knew. When I got closer, I recognized him as the man I talked to at the bar a couple days ago. I thought it was super creepy he somehow knew where I was, so I shook my head. Well, it turns out I was closer to the limo than I thought, because he whipped open the door and in a flash was right in front of me. By the time I blinked, he had grabbed hold of my arm and pulled me to him. He leaned in close and told me, 'You want to come with me. Don't scream, don't fight. You think I'm attractive and want to know where the night might go.' I couldn't believe the nerve of the man until it hit me.

"It was Damien! Not only was he the same man who had chatted me up at the bar, but now he was here trying to use his powers on me! I had about five seconds to decide what to do.

238

In those five seconds, it occurred to me he thought he could control me. He didn't realize his powers didn't work here, or I was an exception. That didn't matter. What did matter was that he thought it would work, and that was a huge advantage for us. I had less than three seconds to decide whether it was better in the long run for me to go with him or not. I was a little worried about his plan, but if he thought I was under his control, he wouldn't restrain me, so I could always just run away. It was too big of an advantage to pass up. Too big of an opportunity."

"Wait, wait, wait," interrupted Hanna. "You went with him willingly?!"

She said what we were all thinking. I couldn't believe she would have done that on purpose just for us. She put aside her own needs and her own best interest for us, who she hadn't even known that long. Yet she was willing to put herself in danger for us. What had we possibly done to deserve that? What had *I* done to deserve that? When I thought about it, I knew it wasn't anything. I hadn't done anything in particular, but she cared about us and we were friends.

She shrugged. "I had to. It was what we needed. We needed to find out as much about him as possible; what his plan was. Besides, I could've run the minute things started to go south. I swallowed any of the fear I still had, and blinked up at him through my eyelashes and flounced into the car past him, running my fingers over his shoulder as I moved past him. I saw him smile and knew I had him. He bought it. Why wouldn't he? I am a flawless actress," she said, flipping her hair over her shoulder and batted her eyelashes at us. It worked to lighten the mood.

We all laughed before it hit me and I blurted out, "Wait, how did you know enough about his powers to know what to do?"

She looked confused for a moment. "I didn't tell you?" I wasn't sure what she was talking about, but a moment later, she explained, "This really cool author wrote an awesome book about it. You should check it out. You would like her." She grinned, nudging me with her shoulder.

I could've broken into tears right then and there. She had read my book. She had actually read it, and liked it! I was so incredibly touched she had cared enough to read it that I forgot what we had been talking about.

Thankfully, Sabrina asked, "So, what happened next?"

"Honestly, nothing really. We went back to his hotel room, or should I say, suite. It was probably closer to a penthouse, to be honest. It was huge! On the drive over, it occurred to me to worry about the sleeping arrangements. I had decided that if he said anything else creepy or insinuated we should spend the night together, I would have left, but he left me alone in my own room in his suite for the night, telling me I was tired and needed to get some sleep.

"I was going to let you guys know I was okay, but I had left my phone in my purse, which was still in the main room, and I couldn't go out without arousing his suspicion. Since his powers should've put me to sleep, but they didn't. It would've undone all my hard work. I'm sorry I didn't have a chance to tell you guys what I was doing, but I promise it was worth it."

"How could putting yourself in that much danger have possibly been worth it?" I asked.

"Well, I know his plan. He didn't think twice about bragging about it to me the next morning, after telling me I found him to be super intelligent and would be impressed by anything he said. It was a miracle I didn't crack, to be honest."

I wasn't sure what surprised me more, how casual Naomi had been, or how civil Damien had been to her. He hadn't needed to be, but he was. I knew he wasn't a bad guy, not really. In his mind, the ends justified the means, but he also seemed to be as civil as he could. When he could, he still cared for others, and didn't go out of his way to inflict pain on others when it could be avoided. His only crime was loving Cass so much he was willing to tear apart the world to get him back, and who didn't want to be loved like that?

"So, wait. He didn't just tell you his plan just like that, did he?" Sabrina asked.

She grinned. "You know he did."

"So, what'd he say?" Inez asked.

"His plan was to use me as a hostage until he could get hold of Sadie. He was going to bring me to the ball for the exchange, and then he was going to be whisked back to the Six Realms as soon as he had you. I thought quickly and asked him how he had orchestrated that so cleverly and he explained to me that the magic can be very finnicky and can be misinterpreted but that he was confident about the spell he used to get here. He had said he cast the spell to keep him in this world until he had found and secured enough power to change things in his world, or until he had a new crown on his head and the realm at his command. So, that's the good news. The bad news is I have no idea how to make either of those happen, but I was hoping you guys would know. I waited until I was sure he wasn't going to divulge any more info and I just got up and walked out."

"He just let you leave, just like that?" Inez asked.

Naomi nodded. "Well, yeah. I think he was too shocked to stop me. Who knows, but he didn't follow me. I just walked out. It was wild, really. I caught a cab back here. I was hoping you guys might be here getting ready. It was more of a hope than a plan, but it worked out!"

"I can't believe how simple that was. I'm so glad you're safe."

"Me, too," she said, smiling, but after a moment her face fell, "but what I learned wasn't nearly as helpful as I was hoping. I thought he was going to give us a way out of this mess, but his stipulations for the magic aren't really helpful, unless we can come up with a way to make either of those happen without Sadie going with him."

"Not even remotely an option," said Eve, nodding.

It hadn't occurred to me until that moment that I was even more so the root of our problems than I thought. Not only had I created the characters and the world that was now plaguing us, but I wasn't doing my part. I could have easily ended things by now by going with him. I knew he wasn't evil, not really. I knew I wouldn't be in much danger, from him, at least, if I went with him, and yet here I was being stubborn about keeping my friends in danger and being selfish when I had a way to right my wrongs.

I had created the Six Realms and Damien, and was the reason his story was as tragic as it was. If I sacrificed myself for my friends, I could probably do some good in the Six Realms, too. I didn't want to leave, I really didn't, but as I looked around the room at the people I'd come to know and deeply care about over the past few days, I couldn't help but think I could've done a lot worse with friends. They were certainly worth sacrificing myself for. They were worth saving.

THIRTY-THREE

By the time the others left to go get ready, they weren't any closer to a magical solution to our problem. They had been weighing out the options for hours, trying to twist his words in a way that would give us any sort of out. The more determined they were to find a way to save us without involving me, the more determined I was to make this sacrifice for them.

We took our time getting ready. The seriousness of the situation had sucked some of the excitement out of the night, but it couldn't take it all away. Eve was quieter than usual and Mira more talkative, so I could tell they were both nervous. Inez was lounging on our bed, sighing about how long women took to get ready in Hawthorne. She scoffed at me when I told her Serena probably took just as long to get ready for balls, but she didn't argue. She couldn't, because I wasn't wrong.

Mira's dress was a beautiful burgundy dress that clung to the right places, accentuating her curves. It was stunning on her, especially when paired with the elegant crystal headpiece she wore. "You look beautiful!" I gushed.

She waved off the compliment but smiled widely.

Eve was next. She wrestled her gown through the bathroom door to get ready before calling for help. I was still doing my makeup, so Mira went to help her. Her dress had a corset back like mine did, so there was no way she would've been able to do it on her own.

When she stepped out of the bathroom a few minutes later, my jaw dropped. She was wearing a black, shiny off-the-shoulder ball gown that swished when she walked. Her bright red hair and matching fairy crown with a red center jewel gave her a beautiful pop of color against the black. The effect was breath-taking.

"Eve, you look incredible!"

She grinned widely, doing a twirl. The dress flared out all around her and it was like time slowed. She was for sure the main character in that dress. As I watched her spinning in slow motion, I could almost hear music playing in the background.

When she stopped, she checked the time and told me I should hurry. I glanced over and realized with a start that she was right, it was later than I thought.

I slipped it the dress as quickly as I could and Eve started work on the dress's corset. Her fingers worked deftly over the back of the dress, pulling it tight against me.

I was grateful she was here and knew what she was doing, otherwise the dress would still have been practically falling off me since there was no way I could've laced it on my own. With one last tug, she told me it was done and took a step away.

"Okay, now turn around."

I had forgotten the mirror was behind me. As I turned, the skirts of my dress caught the light, sending sparkling green light dancing through the room. It was a magical sight, but it was nothing compared to the sight of the regal princess looking back at me from the mirror.

I looked stunning. Eve had done wonders with the lacing, and the off-the-shoulder forest green sequined gown clung to me at the top, cinching in at the waist, before flaring out to a full ball gown skirt.

"Wait, wait, wait," Eve said, moving across the room to where Inez was sitting on our bed.

I was confused, but she moved past Inez to my suitcase and picked up the box on top that held my crown. I grinned at her. She rushed back and dramatically told me to close my eyes. I laughed, but did as she said. I felt her put the crown on my head and reorder my hair a little.

When she told me to open my eyes, I audibly gasped when I saw myself. The crown had a large emerald at the forefront with a couple of smaller emeralds on either side and diamonds filling in the spaces between. It was as heavy as it looked, but it was worth it.

The crown completed the look in a way that stole my breath away and made me really feel like royalty. I could have easily believed that the girl in the mirror was a princess. It was harder to believe she was me. I smiled broadly and did a little spin. My ballgown flared out around me, catching the light and setting the room awash in a green glittery glow again. When I met Inez's eyes, the pain I saw in them startled me.

"What?" I asked, taking a step toward her, worried.

She shook her head. "Nothing, really, it's nothing."

"It's not nothing, and I care about you. Tell me what's wrong. Please."

She shook her head. "You're the spitting image of her."

It didn't take a genius to know she was talking about Serena. The sadness in her eyes reminded me of how homesick she must have been and just how much was at stake for her. That strengthened my resolve further. I would go with Damien, and I would right things in their world. I would make sure Serena was safe first and then I would fix the rest of the messes

I had caused throughout the realms, starting with freeing Casimir.

I hadn't the first clue how I was going to do it, but Inez and Damien agreed on one thing only: that I was capable of changing their world. Even Celeste had put her trust and faith in me. I would live up to their expectations and be the savior they needed. I caused this mess and I would be damned if any of my friends got hurt trying to help me fix it. I could and would handle this alone. I had gone through most of my life alone. This wouldn't be any different.

At least that was the lie I was telling myself. I knew it was different this time when I couldn't meet Eve or Mira's eyes as we finished getting ready and went down to the lobby to meet the others. I could already feel the guilt weighing on me. I didn't understand why. If it was the right thing to do, why did it feel so wrong? I couldn't meet Eve or Mira's eyes without picturing how upset they would be the moment he took me. They would feel like they failed me, but they hadn't. I had been failing them, letting them fight my battles for me, but not anymore. I couldn't keep hiding behind them and letting them risk themselves for me. Their guilt would fade eventually.

Still, I couldn't look them or the others in the eye when they came. Inez seemed to be the only one who noticed any change in me, but, thankfully, she didn't say anything, just watched me cautiously. I wondered if, on some level, she understood what I planned to do. I wondered if she would forgive me. I hoped she would. I hoped she would understand it was what I had to do, and unlike the rest of my friends, I would see her again.

If she wasn't pulled back to the Six Realms when we were, I would use whatever power everyone was so sure I had to pull her back where she belonged, and I would make sure to give her the happiness she so strongly deserved. I couldn't fix how things had already come to pass, and wouldn't even if I could. Where Serena and Inez were alike, Serena and Tristan were different. They brought out the best in each other; she helped him be more realistic, and he helped soften her rough edges. After everything Serena had been through, she was jaded and he helped with that. Even if I could change that, I don't think I would. There was someone out there for Inez, though. I knew that; I had written as much. Her amulet had worked, finally. I had written that into existence, so there had to be a woman out there for her, a match for her that would make her thankful that she had let Serena go. I would make sure she found her, and she would forgive me, eventually.

THIRTY-FOUR

In the lobby, the other girls were waiting. They all looked gorgeous, of course, but it was hard to be happy to see them, hard to be happy about them stepping into danger for me, hard to be excited about the ball with Damien hanging over our heads. I hadn't meant for any of this to happen, hadn't meant to ruin the ball for anyone, and I couldn't help feeling bitter about the fact that they couldn't enjoy it because of me. Well, really because of Damien, but he was my problem and my responsibility.

I didn't want this to ruin what should have been their perfect night. Especially when they all looked as incredible as they did. Naomi was wearing a blue and purple shimmery dress that had one shoulder strap and a glittery crown, but her smile and eyes sparkled brighter than the crown. Hanna was wearing a beautiful formfitting red dress, and Sabrina was in a sage flowing dress with glitter embellishments. They all looked beautiful. I hoped they would be able to enjoy the rest of the ball after I was gone. I glanced around at our small group and fought to keep the tears that were threatening to fall at bay. In the short time I had known them all, I had grown incredibly attached to them and had grown to care about them in a way I hadn't really cared about anyone since Kay. I hadn't known them long at all, so the sentiment surprised me, but I couldn't deny it. I loved these girls like I had known them forever, and I would've done what I was planning to do without hesitation for any one of them. I could only hope they would forgive me and themselves. This was my choice, and I hoped they would know that.

As my eyes roamed over each of them, I tried to picture what their lives might be like in the future, tried to picture them having happy futures. I hated the idea of missing out on getting to know them more and spending more time with them, but thinking about their futures strengthened my resolve.

I pictured Eve gliding down the aisle at her gothic themed fall wedding, a vision in her black lace gown. Being whisked away, happy and in love on a grand honeymoon before settling in to a cozy life with her own library and a cat or two, the real dream.

I pictured Sabrina and Hanna travelling through Europe from country to country, trying new foods and seeing the sights. I pictured them struggling to keep up with their trip schedule and then ditching it altogether to spend more time in a town they both fell in love with. I could picture them going on spur-of-the-moment day trips and laughing as they missed the train and had to wait for the next.

I could picture Naomi skydiving, screaming in delight as she hurtled to the ground. I could picture her hiking rainforests and swimming in secluded waterfall lagoons. I didn't know what else she might do, but that her life, without question, would be a bold one filled with adventure.

I could picture Mira volunteering her time to help children learn how to read. She knew how important of an escape reading was to herself and would go out of her way to share that with others. I could see her changing the world, one person at a time.

It helped me to strengthen my resolve. I would go through with this, for them and their bright futures. I would do what had to be done.

I would never get to get married. I would never get to see them experience the lives they deserved. I wouldn't get to go to Europe or do any adventurous things with Naomi, but I would have my own adventure and would be helping others. I would get to explore a new land with characters of my own creation. I would be an explorer of sorts, but I was struggling to hold back the tears. When I turned back to Eve, she was frowning. I quickly turned away, but I knew she knew something was wrong. In such a short time, she already knew exactly how to read me.

I was saved from much more scrutiny when our rides showed up. Thankfully, I was able to ride with Naomi and Inez. Eve, Mira, Hanna, and Sabrina took the other car. I was thrilled with the arrangement because even though the journey was only about ten minutes, I couldn't handle being alone with Eve for that long. She knew something was up and I worried that if she knew what I planned, she might try to stop me. I worried I would let her.

The closer time came for me to go with Damien, the worse I was feeling about it. It wasn't that he was a bad guy; I knew he wasn't. It was that I didn't want to leave. I knew a lot of people would feel ecstatic to be in my shoes and would take the chance to be whisked away to a fantasy world of their own creation in a heartbeat, and even a month ago I would've agreed. But now things were different. Now I had found friends that I genuinely cared about, and now I was going to have to leave them and I hated it. I hated the thought of missing all the milestones in their lives and not getting to experience my own milestones here, but I knew Damien wouldn't stop until I went with him, and I would never forgive myself if he hurt any of them. I couldn't bear it, and I wouldn't let it happen.

But when Naomi, Inez, and I slid into the backseat of our Uber, I couldn't help thinking maybe I should've gone in the other car. It wasn't that there was anything wrong with the driver. She was an older woman with gray hair and a warm smile, but in the front seat there was what appeared to be a cage covered with some sort of sheet and the entire car smelled terrible.

I couldn't put my finger on what the smell was, though, until she started to drive and removed the sheet from the object. It was a cage, holding a large colorful bird, who started screeching the moment the sheet was removed. The woman started cooing at the bird, telling him he was such a good bird and a pretty bird. I glanced at Naomi and saw she was just as confused as I was. Inez was the only one who wasn't fazed. She probably didn't have enough expectations about how these sorts of rides usually went to be fazed by this, but this certainly wasn't the norm.

After a couple of minutes talking to the bird, she turned to glance at us. "You ladies look lovely!" she said.

Inez had been forced into a cross between a dress and her training leathers. She was still wearing her arm guards, but she had let me braid her hair into a crown on her head. She was wearing her leather corset top, and her leather boots, but she was wearing a borrowed skirt. The brown skirt was renaissance faire style, borrowed from Sabrina, and had two high slits on either side. She had only agreed to wear it when she saw it wouldn't restrict her legs.

The driver took another look at us before turning her eyes back to the road. "You know, I normally let him out on these rides. People like it when he flaps around the car and says hi to everyone, but since you're dressed so nice, I'll leave him in his cage."

I squeaked out a thank you, just barely managing not to laugh. How was this reality? Thankfully, we made it the rest of the way without incident, and, somehow, Naomi and I managed to not burst into laughter as she talked to and soothed her bird.

We thanked her when we got out and Inez said goodbye to her and also to her bird. The woman grinned at that and told us to, "Run along, dears, and have a good time!"

We waved and thanked her, walking toward the rest of our friends. The moment she drove off, Naomi and I started laughing hysterically.

Our friends glanced between me and Naomi, confused. We tried to explain, but were laughing too hard. As we joined the line of people waiting to get into the ball, we told them about our ride with the bird lady. It was the tension release I needed, since my nerves were creeping up on me again.

Eve kept throwing questioning and concerned looks my way. Every time I saw her face, I felt a little more guilty about what I was planning to do, but there wasn't another option. When we got to the front of the line, the door person had horns attached to their head and had painted a deer's nose and freckles on their face. Even the staff were getting into the spirit. I couldn't wait to see the inside.

When they opened the door for us, a blast of fog hit us and we gasped. The fog was lit up green and purple and there was a twenty-foot tall man-made tree constructed off to the side of the lobby. We passed the coat room, making our way toward the tree. As we walked under the tree, we saw there was an archway constructed to look like a stone drawbridge. I couldn't wait to see what they had done with the actual ballroom, since they had absolutely killed it with the decorations so far and this was just the lobby.

We passed, one by one, through the stone archway, not because there wasn't room for more people, but because we all wanted photos taken of each of us going through the archway. Once it was my turn, I crossed under the archway and my breath caught. We were in a hallway lined with mirrors on both sides, but what really stole my breath was the cardboard structures that looked like stacks of books. There were about ten of them on each side of the hallway, but the mirrors multiplied them, making them seem infinite. The fog had carried over into the hallway, and it felt truly magical, like stepping into another world.

Just when I thought I couldn't be surprised anymore, the hallway opened up into the ballroom itself. There weren't many people there yet, we were some of the first, so I could clearly see every part of the room and the effect stole my breath. There was a string quartet playing in the middle of the room and projected onto the walls was a ballroom scene.

On one wall, there was a grand staircase fit for a royal ballroom. Over the dance floor, there were colored orbs hanging from the ceiling. Some of them looked like bubbles, others contained flowers and moss of some sort. Sabrina steered us toward the bar. At the bar, there were hanging candelabras that looked like they were floating. As I watched, the lights blinked on one by one. It was truly magical.

Once we had our drinks, we made our way to the dance floor. Inez kept scanning the room with her eyes, making sure we were safe. So far, so good. Damien wasn't here yet. I felt confident he would stick out enough that we would see him the moment he got here. Not only was he a tall man with a commanding presence, but there was maybe one man to every ten women in the room, so even if he were an average man, he would stick out.

Knowing Inez was alert and keeping us safe let me relax and lean into the feelings of wonder I couldn't help but have. My jaw dropped and gasps filled the room when the projection on the wall changed in time with the music. The wall was now covered in bookshelves from floor to ceiling. The effect was stunning; I felt light and airy, and as the music swelled, I spun. My dress flared out all around me and I let out a laugh, loving how much like a dream come true this felt. It didn't feel real.

After a few rotations, I stopped, needing to catch my breath and balance, and I saw Inez smiling at me. She stepped to my side as the music changed to a waltz. She took one of my hands in hers and put the other on her shoulder, putting her free arm around my waist.

"I don't know how to dance," I protested.

But she shook her head and said, "Don't worry. Just follow my lead."

She whirled us around the floor, and I felt like I was floating. We danced to the music, a few other couples joining us, but the dance floor was mostly empty, though I noticed the rest of the ballroom was filling up. I saw Inez was still scanning the room for Damien, so I relaxed in her arms. As the music swelled into a crescendo, she pulled me in tight before throwing me from her body and leading me into a spin. She then used the momentum from my spin to pull me back and dip me right as the music ended. She held me there for a minute before leaning forward and placing a gentle kiss on my forehead.

"I'm really glad to call you my friend, Sadie," she whispered.

I blushed at that. She pulled me back up and let me go; it was then that I saw we had an audience that started clapping at the performance I didn't know we were putting on. My blush deepened down my neck. Inez grinned and bowed, winking at me. Two could play that game, so I curtsied, and the crowd clapped and laughed with us.

I never enjoyed being the center of attention, but with Inez at my side, it was hard to mind. I was happy I would at least have her with me in Zanaria.

My friends and I spent the night dancing, glancing over our shoulders, making sure Damien wasn't lurking there. The longer we went without an appearance, the more nervous I became. I started glancing over my shoulder every ten seconds instead of every couple of minutes. I hoped maybe he wouldn't show, but I knew that wouldn't be the case. Part of me thought maybe he was forming a new plan now that he didn't have Naomi as a bargaining chip, but I didn't think we would be that lucky. Losing Naomi probably upset him. I couldn't imagine he would take that lying down and stay away. He knew tonight was an important night for us, so he would come, if just to make sure to ruin it.

We continued to dance, feeling safest in the middle of the dance floor. As time wore on, the projections changed into that of a mansion in spring, to a mountain scene at night, to a magical forest, to shooting stars. Every new scene added to the magic and wonder of the night.

About halfway through the night, I glimpsed a tall man in a suit out of the corner of my eye and froze up. By the time I had turned and searched where I thought he was, there wasn't anyone there. I must have been seeing things, or so I hoped. I hoped I might have been lucky enough to have a nice night with my friends without interruption, but I should've known better than to hope for that.

A few minutes later, there were gasps from the other side of the dance floor. A gap opened up, leading to us as the people stepped out of the way so we could see him clearly. Inez stepped in front of me, knelt down, and stuck her hand in her boot. When she pulled her hand away and straightened up, I saw she had a dagger in her hand. I rolled my eyes, but was grateful to her for how set on protecting me she was. Plus, she had promised no sword, so I knew she would say she hadn't broken her promise.

The others stood behind me and Inez, staring at Damien. Naomi stepped next to me when she saw him. I gasped when I saw her wink at and blow him a kiss. I turned back quickly and saw the rage on his face and had to fight hard to rein in my laughter. If he wasn't faintly glowing green, I was sure he would've been red with anger.

Wait, I thought as a moment later, my brain registered what I was seeing.

"Inez," I whispered. She didn't acknowledge. "Inez," I said louder. Still nothing from her. "INEZ!" I yelled. She finally turned. "Move back!" I said, trying to pull her behind me, but I was too late. He used her distraction against her, sending his green flames her way.

"Inez, watch out!"

She spun around a moment later, and I tried to pull her out of the way, but it was too late. The green fire engulfed her, surrounding her in his bubble of control. I saw the dangerous grin on his face when he captured her. Fuck. That wasn't good.

A moment later, the flames dissipated, and she turned around. I watched with horror as the green flames siphoned from the air around her into her eyes. They glowed green as she set her eyes on me. Her grin was almost feline and was, without a doubt, predatory. Horrified, I glanced over her shoulder at him and saw the same expression mirrored on his face. Fuck. This wasn't part of the plan. I didn't know how to free her.

She reached out a hand for me and I jumped back. I didn't know what she planned to do, but letting a possessed Inez with a dagger get hold of me didn't seem like the best idea. She swiped for me again, but Eve pushed me behind her. Inez tried to step around her, but Hanna slid into place there.

Damien glared at us, before smiling again. He patted his knee, saying, "Inez, come."

She turned and strode to him, taking her place at his side.

He's not evil, he's not evil, he's not evil, I chanted in my mind, trying to remind myself he wasn't really that evil, just misunderstood, but with that gleam in his eye, I was scared.

I couldn't say for sure what he might do to us and to her. I was scared for her. I had one thing going for me, though; I knew he wouldn't hurt me. I had to put an end to this, and quick. Who knew what he might do to Inez and my friends if I waited? I moved up between Hanna and Eve. I needed to save Inez, but I was afraid of what he might do if I took another step.

I watched in horror as he made Inez turn to him, smiling. He brushed a strand of hair that had broken free from her braid away from her face. I shuddered at her smile and at how she leaned into him. I hated knowing she was trapped in her own body, watching herself do these things in horror. I hated that for her.

"Let her go!" I called out to him.

His eyes tore from hers and locked onto mine. His grin widened. "Hello, love. Just the sorceress I was looking for."

The crowd glanced back and forth between me and him, recording and watching in awe. I heard someone whisper about how cool the special effects were, and that was when it hit me how much danger they were in.

They thought this was a part of the ball, something planned, something safe, when it was anything but. I needed to end this quickly, so no one got hurt. It wasn't even just about my friends anymore. I couldn't let him hurt anyone, and I needed to get his hands off Inez. I hadn't thought for a second he might've still had his magic strong enough to take control of her in our realm, but I should've guessed. She was of his world, and the magic affected her differently. I knew what it had felt like to me when he tried, so I could only imagine how much stronger it had felt for her.

Speak of the devil; I could feel the thoughts crawling in as he said, "Why don't you make this easy on everyone and be a doll and come here?"

I could feel my feet itching to move, but no. I planted myself solidly and felt the thoughts wash over me. *Go to him. You want to help him. Don't make him wait. You want to be near him. You want him to want you.* With that last thought, I met his eye and watched him lick his lips.

I knew I needed to go to him. I needed to end it, but not like this. I shook my head, trying to clear my thoughts.

"Be rational. You know how powerful I am. I'm sure you'd hate for your friends to see what real power looks like." He summoned a ball of green flame to his hand and held it aloft.

The crowd oohed and ahhed. How did they not know how real this was? How did they not understand the danger? It was as frustrating as it was understandable.

If I hadn't seen his powers firsthand myself and spent the weekend with Inez dodging his attacks, I might not have believed it myself. I hardly believed it now. When I didn't take a step forward, his eyes darkened, and he extinguished the flame, a dangerous expression on his face.

"Fine, the hard way, then. Inez, be a doll and show Sadie what real power looks like."

I flinched as she took a few steps forward, fighting not to retreat, fighting to stand my ground. I wouldn't give him the satisfaction of knowing I was afraid. But a moment later, my jaw dropped, and I involuntarily took a step forward. Inez had moved her dagger from her side to her throat. I winced as I saw a thin line of blood trickle down her neck from a nick she had made.

"If you want your guard dog unharmed, love, you'll come to me."

"Let her go! Stop! You're hurting her!" Naomi yelled.

I gulped, knowing what I had to do. I took a step forward and then another. I felt a hand grab my arm. I turned around quickly, afraid to tear my eyes from Inez for too long, afraid of what he might do if I did. It was Eve, and the pain in her eyes made me want to cry.

She gripped my arm tightly. "You don't have to do this," she said. A tear fell down her face.

I tried to swallow, but there was a lump in my throat. "I know I don't have to; I want to. To protect you all and Inez, there isn't anything I wouldn't do."

I tried to extract her hand from my arm, but she held tighter. "Please don't do this."

"Eve, I'm so sorry, but I don't have a choice. I can't let him hurt Inez or anyone else. I'll go with him and fix the mess I made of their realm. I can do this. Let me do this one thing right for once."

Her tears were falling in earnest now and my own were streaming down my face. "You don't have to prove yourself to me, or to any of us," she said, looking back at the rest of our friends. Naomi, Hanna, and Sabrina were staring between me and Inez with expressions of horror, but there was only one way out of this, and it wasn't going to be with Inez slitting her own throat. I stepped forward again; Eve followed rather than taking her hand off my arm. "I have to go, Eve. I'm so sorry. I hope you all have the best lives. You all deserve nothing but the best. Live well and long for me, and try to remember me."

I took another step forward, turning back to face Damien, who was grinning wide now. "That's right. Come to me, darling."

I felt a hand wrap around my left arm and yank me back. "The hell do you think you're doing?" Naomi asked.

"I don't have much of a choice."

"The hell you don't." She glared at him. "Such a big tough boy now that his powers work, huh? If you want Sadie, you'll have to come through us! Or are you too much of a coward that you have to hide behind your powers?"

He glared at her. "I have the power here. Unhand her and let her be a good little girl and come to me."

"Just what do you plan to accomplish here? Besides scaring a bunch of women? That's low, even for you," Naomi said.

"Once Sadie is mine, we'll return to Bancroft and you can go back to your insignificant little powerless lives, don't you worry."

I glanced at Naomi, who spat a retort at him, wondering what she was doing. She was buying time, but why? I glanced over my shoulder quickly and saw it was just me, Eve, and Naomi. Mira, Hanna, and Sabrina weren't there.

THIRTY-SEVEN

I turned quickly back to Damien, scanning the crowd, praying I was wrong, but sure enough, Hanna and Sabrina had made their way through the crowd and were sneaking up on either side of him. Fuck. I couldn't see Mira, but first things first. I made eye contact with Sabrina and shook my head at her, pleading with my eyes for them to stop.

He wouldn't show mercy, not tonight, not now, when he was so close to his goal. He would kill them both, or worse, make Inez do it. They would both be dead before any of us could move to help them. I kept tracking their path and realized it was worse than I thought; they weren't going to him after all. They were going to try to disarm Inez. There was no good way for that situation to play out. Either she would slit her own throat or she would stab one or both of them.

I tried to pull loose from Naomi, but she and Eve held tight. I scanned the room wildly for Mira, praying she might help, but I still couldn't find her. I hoped she was okay.

Before Hanna and Sabrina could make their move, a voice sounded over the loudspeaker. "Okay, everyone, it's time for the cosplay contest!" It was Kodie.

I wondered if she had seen any of the exchange and if she had, what she was thinking. She would've known it wasn't anything she planned. Maybe she thought we were just overzealous cosplayers? She swept over toward our group, and put her hand on Damien's shoulder. He looked shocked at the audacity, but she just smiled at him, before saying into the microphone, "I can see we have a couple of contestants here," glancing at him and Inez, "but I'm going to have to ask you to put away the dagger or I'll be forced to escort you out of the building." The crowd laughed at that. "You all know the rules. No weapons tonight."

Damien blinked a few times before Inez slowly removed the dagger from her neck and slipped it back in her boot. "Perfect! Now that that's settled, let's get you both to your places." She looped her arm with the microphone through Inez's, leaving her other arm on Damien, and started to coral them to the front of the room. "Anyone else who is participating in the cosplay contest, please make your way up now."

The crowd made way for a few men and women I didn't recognize, but my eyes landed on Gwen. She looked radiant in blue silk with little lace cap sleeves. It would be a good bet to say the dress was probably the same shade as her eyes, and from what I knew was almost an exact replica of the dress Ivy had worn to the Solstice Ball. She was a beauty to behold. The crowd parted for her and gasped as she seemed to float forward. There were more gasps, and I turned quickly to see what had the crowd's attention, worried it was Damien's doing, but it wasn't him. Instead, I saw Morgana coming forward in a dark navy, form-fitting gown that was topped off with a trailing cape of silk behind her. A dead ringer for Cassandra.

Most everyone in attendance knew the history between Gwen and Morgana, so the choice was one that would get people talking and send rumors spiraling. People loved gossip, and two incredibly famous cosplayers who were known rivals showing up dressed as a favorite enemies-to-lovers couple was making a huge statement people wouldn't soon forget. From the expression on Morgana's face, she had no idea, but from the sparkle in Gwen's eye, it seemed like this might've been part of a plan. I hoped for her sake that she knew what she was doing.

Morgana was glaring at her, but I was shocked to notice she seemed to be checking her out. I caught myself looking back and forth between Morgana and Damien, unsure who was more likely to cause a scene first. Kodie had wisely made sure Inez and Damien were separated, so they were both behaving for the time being, so I watched Morgana and Gwen. Gwen glided to the front, and tapped Kodie on the shoulder,

Kodie smiled and said into the microphone, "I know I said we were starting the cosplay contest, and we will in a couple of minutes, but first Gwen has something she wants to say."

I turned to Eve wondering if she knew what was going to happen, but she just shrugged. I hoped Gwen knew what she was doing. If she said anything that set off Morgana, the videos would be all over the internet, the showdown of the century. I hoped for both their sakes they would both keep their cool. I could already see people recording Gwen and a few of them had already gone live. Hopefully, Gwen knew what she was doing.

She took the microphone from Kodie and turned to the crowd. "Hi there, everyone," she said with a nervous smile. "For those of you who don't know me, I'm Gwen, and I hope you'll bear with me as I take a minute to bare my soul to you all. I've been quiet for way too long about this, and it's time I finally say something. I'm sick of hiding who I am. For those of you who don't know me, I hope you'll care to get to know the real me after this, but this speech is more for those of you who do know me, and really for a particular someone."

I saw Morgana cross her arms out of the corner of my eye. I saw a small frown cross Gwen's lips, before her plastered on smile returned.

She steeled herself and continued, "For those of you that do know me, you know I dated Arty for a long time. He truly was such a sweet man and an even better boyfriend. He was absolutely perfect. I know what you're thinking. If he's so perfect, why'd you let him go? I know the rumors say that I cheated on him, and those hurt the most. I would have never done anything to hurt him, and I hate that he has to live with strangers calling him clueless and stupid for having been with me. I didn't cheat on him. That's not what I'm here to tell you. There was another reason for our breakup, a reason that Arty has been so chivalrous to keep to himself, from even his best friend, and that's what I'm here to tell you today. He held up his end of the bargain and was more than willing to give me the time I needed, but I'm sick of hiding. We broke up because he wasn't my type."

The crowd gasped, and she laughed. "You didn't let me finish. I know, I know, you're thinking, Gwen, how could he possibly not be your type? He's tall, handsome, muscly, and such a patient, kind man. You're not wrong, and if I was at all into men, I'm sure he would've been the one." The crowd gasped as one. "I'm not done. You see, for a long time I was okay with being in the closet. I was too scared to tell the world my truth; I didn't feel like I could. I was worried that others would harass me for it, the way they had for me supposedly cheating on Arty. I worried my friends and family wouldn't understand. That the world wouldn't understand. I wasn't ready to be myself, to show the world those parts of myself I kept hidden. Until a woman taught me what it meant to be unapologetically myself. She is fierce, strong, and braver than I ever could be, but I'm trying. I actually broke things off with

Arty when I realized I was falling for her. Watching her unapologetically, boldly be herself inspired me. Her fire intrigued me, and her soul made me love her. I realized I would never be happy with just her friendship and that I hadn't had that same fire for Arty. As much as I love and care about Arty, I knew then that he wasn't my person no matter how much I had tried to make it work for mine and his sake; he just wasn't her. And I'm sure you're wondering who she is and why she didn't accompany me tonight. Well, unfortunately, we're still at the enemies stage of our relationship, but I would give the world to change that."

Another collective gasp sounded as she turned and met Morgana's eye. "Lanie, I'm so sorry I hurt you and that I hurt Arty. It was never my intention, and if you would ever find it in your heart to forgive me, I would be the luckiest girl in the world. I wasn't ready to be myself, wasn't ready to admit the truth, until you. Even if you never speak to me again, you changed me for the better and I'll always be grateful to have had you in my life. I don't know that I'll ever have another chance to say this, and this is a less than ideal a place for it, but I need you to know... I love you. I started falling for you long before I realized it myself, and I never stopped."

Morgana, Lanie apparently, was white as a ghost and looked like a bomb had dropped, not an inappropriate reaction to what she just heard. Gwen watched her hopefully for a moment, waiting for a response, anything, but Morgana continued to stare at her. She wasn't even blinking.

Gwen's face fell infinitesimally before she plastered her smile back on and said, "I know this is too little too late, but I needed you, and the world," she gestured to the crowd, "to know my truth. No more hiding." She was still smiling, but there was no hiding the sadness in her eyes. I don't know what she was expecting from Morgana, but she probably had expected some sort of reaction. Although, honestly, I thought her reaction was warranted and was probably better than whatever explosion I had expected.

Kodie took the microphone back, smiling at Gwen. "I am so proud to call you a friend, Gwen, and let me be the first to say, I'm proud of you."

"Welcome to the alphabet mafia!" someone yelled from the crowd, causing laughter to course through the crowd.

"You go, girl!" said another yell.

"Girls do it better!" another person yelled.

"Do I have a chance, Gwen?" a female voice yelled.

Gwen's smile was much more genuine, and I was warmed by the support of the crowd. You never really knew with things like this. Coming out was always scary and never an easy decision. It took an enormous amount of guts to come out at all, never mind to come out so publicly and to then admit her feelings for a girl who didn't feel the same. It took an enormous amount of courage.

My eyes moved to Damien and I was relieved to see he was still standing with the cosplayers, surprisingly not causing any trouble. He smirked at me, and I glanced in Inez's direction quickly, making sure she was okay. She was just standing there, waiting, like he was. I exhaled, relieved, before turning back to him. He raised an eyebrow at me; a dare, a challenge. I inhaled deeply, trying to borrow some inspiration from Gwen. I could do this. I could be brave and leave the only life I had ever known. I could make myself go with him and leave behind my new friends, who had become more like a family. I could, and would, to protect them.

Kodie turned back to the cosplayers and said, "Everyone up here is eligible to win our contest. I'm going to go down the line and have you announce who you are cosplaying and then we'll have the crowd vote on their favorite."

It was then that I saw Mira standing off behind the DJ booth with the sound technician and the projection technician. I met her eye, and she grinned. I couldn't decide if I should have been worried or not, but Mira was smart. Whatever she was doing, I was sure she had a good reason and hoped it would help us. We could use all the help we could get to make sure no one got hurt before Damien took me.

Kodie went down the line, Inez saying she was Inez Cyneward, royal guard of Sherbrooke. There were a few mutters of who? But to my surprise and joy, a few people yelled out, "I love her." Despite everything, I smiled.

I held my breath when the microphone was held in front of Damien, but he did the same, saying he was King Damien, the powerful, of Bancroft. There were a few boos from the crowd, which warmed my heart, especially seeing the glare he sent their way. But I was grateful he seemed to be biding his time until he could get closer to me again.

When they got to Morgana, she was still standing stiff as a board and barely coherently said she was Cassandra. When Kodie reached the end of the line, she turned to us. "Now I'm sure you're wondering how you're voting, right?" There were yeses from the crowd. "Well, if you will all pull out your phones and turn your attention to the walls, there's a number for you to text your vote."

We all collectively gasped as the screen changed to the number to text, along with everyone's character name listed and a percentage. They were all at 0% currently. I was voting for Gwen, and I would be shocked if it wasn't a landslide after her admission. I texted the number with Gwen's name and waited. As I watched, the votes filed in and Gwen's percentages shot up, just like I had expected. What I hadn't expected was that Damien's percentages were growing, too. Whether it was because of his good looks, people liking my story, or his display of magic earlier, I didn't know, but I hoped it was because people loved my story. Gwen's and his numbers continued to rise together, with Morgana trailing a little behind, but still above everyone else. I held my breath, hoping Gwen would win. She deserved the win right now. She needed it.

I audibly gasped when Damien's numbers rose quicker than hers. I heard a couple of cheers and a couple of boos. I found Gwen and was surprised to see she didn't look upset about it. I shouldn't have been surprised. I was thrilled for her that not only was she incredibly brave, but also gracious in the face of defeat. His numbers continued to rise.

I turned back to Damien, who was grinning cockily at the audience. He didn't have to understand much about our world to know what the rising numbers next to his name meant. He left Gwen in the dust. The final count coming down to him having 42% of the votes, Gwen with 26%, Morgana with 13%, and the rest were scattered between the others. I saw movement out of the corner of my eye by the DJ booth and glanced over in time to see that Mira had thrown her hands up triumphantly.

I didn't understand. Why wouldn't she have wanted Gwen to win? Why was she happy Damien won? My eyes moved to Kodie, who picked up the prizes for the contest and was walking them over to him, but my mind was hung up on Mira's reaction. Why would she think Damien deserved the crown? And then it hit me. The crown.

I tried to remember what Naomi had said about his spell, something about him getting a crown or ruling a new kingdom or something. I didn't remember the exact words, but it couldn't be that simple, could it? I didn't dare to hope it would. All that would happen was that he would have a shiny new accessory and another unneeded boost to his ego as he dragged me back to his kingdom with him. I watched his smug grin as Kodie brought the crown over to him. He knelt for her. I saw the confusion in her eyes; she had been going to hand it to him.

When she realized he meant for her to crown him, I caught her quickly rolling her eyes, before she turned to the crowd and shrugged as if saying she would indulge him.

She placed the crown on his head and he straightened up, took the microphone from her hand, and said, "Bow to me, peasants."

The crowd laughed and, one by one, dropped into a bow, indulging him. I dropped myself, worried about what might happen if I didn't. My friends did the same.

After a moment, I went to straighten up and saw a green light coming from the stage. I whipped my head up, worried about what magic he was doing, worried about who would get hurt now, but I couldn't quite comprehend what I saw. He was engulfed in a green haze, and from the way he was beating his fists against it, it didn't seem to be his. I heard him scream, "NOOO!" before the green haze turned opaque, swirling around until I could only see his fists beating against it, and then the bubble vanished and where he had been standing a moment earlier, there was nothing.

The crowd gasped and then broke out into applause. I heard people saying it was the best special effects they had seen tonight, even cooler than the projection walls. I heard someone else say he was a magician. I was still staring at the place he had been. Could it actually have been that simple? Could it really be over? Maybe it was a trick, but his anger had been pretty convincing.

I glanced over at Inez, who was holding her head and scanning the room, confused. Her eyes locked with mine and I could see from here that all the traces of green fire had fled. She gave me a questioning look. I could see her asking, *Is it over*? I smiled at her, happy she was back and okay. Since she wasn't under his spell anymore, I dared to hope it might actually be over. But I didn't want to give her any sort of false hope, so I shrugged. She nodded, scanning the room, and then relaxed a little, not seeing any immediate threat.

When I glanced over at Kodie, she was still staring stunned at the place he had been standing before regaining her composure. "Well, I suppose the rest of the prize can go to our runner-up Gwen."

She turned to Gwen, smiling. Gwen shook her head softly. Kodie looked at her questioningly, leaning toward her with the microphone, sensing she had something to say. "I really appreciate the votes. Thank you all so much from the bottom of my heart, but I can't accept this. I feel like it would cheapen what I did tonight. I don't want anyone's pity or to be rewarded for finally doing and saying what I should have long ago. It's important to me you all know I didn't do this to win some contest, so I don't accept, but I do thank you all." She smiled at the audience, and Kodie shrugged with a smile before moving over to Morgana.

She stood in front of Morgana, glanced at the crowd, and said, "You're not gonna refuse the prize, too, right?" She laughed, but her face dropped when she looked back at Morgana, who wasn't laughing but was instead eyeing a certain redhead a little ways away. *There's no way*, I thought, but I hoped for Gwen's sake that maybe I was wrong.

Morgana smiled with a gleam in her eye, before saying to Kodie, into the microphone. "I'm sorry, but there's something more important to me than winning the contest. There's something I have to do, so you can give it to someone else."

With that, she closed the distance to Gwen, who was staring at her in surprise, took Gwen into her arms, dipped her low, and kissed her. The audience gasped before applauding louder than it had done all night. When Morgana came up for air, the dazed smile on Gwen's face lit up the room. Morgana righted her and Gwen quickly took her hand, seeming to need physical assurance this was real.

I was thrilled for them and cheered with the rest of the crowd. After a few minutes, the crowd dispersed, although a lot of people were making their way toward Morgana and Gwen, probably to offer them congratulations.

I saw Inez making her way over here and crossed the remaining distance, throwing myself in her arms. "Thank goodness you're okay! I was so worried about you!" I said.

She held me tight for a moment, not saying anything. When I pulled away, she scanned me for any sign of injury and was relieved to see none. "Thank the gods you weren't hurt."

"Me?" I asked, genuinely surprised. "I wasn't the one with a dagger to my throat."

She shrugged it off, but I could see the shadows that passed over her face. "That's not the first time and probably won't be the last." I cocked my head at her. She seemed to read my thoughts and said with a false lightness, "It is the first time it has been by my own hand, though. That is definitely an experience I don't wish to repeat."

"But you saw what happened to Damien? What do you make of it?"

"I wish I knew. I hoped you would. It looked like he was sucked back to the Six Realms, but that wouldn't make sense unless the magic was on our side. Even with the most liberal of interpretations, the cosplay winner's crown was hardly the crown he meant in his spell."

"That's the beauty of it. He didn't suspect it for a minute," Mira said from over my shoulder. I was startled since I hadn't heard her approach. "Had he been more cautious or less vain, he might've suspected, but he didn't."

I took her into my arms. "I was so worried about you when I couldn't find you! What were you doing over there, anyway? How did you know it would work? And how the hell did Damien, one of *my* characters, win the cosplay contest?"

"That's a funny story actually. So, I had been thinking about the wording of his spell all afternoon, and when I found out one of the prizes for the contest was a crown, I knew it had to be our way out. There had to be a way out that didn't involve you going with him. I wasn't willing to accept anything less. I didn't tell anyone because I didn't want to get their hopes up, but I think Eve knew I was up to something."

Eve rushed over, pulled both me and Mira into a hug. "I'm so glad you're both okay, but don't you dare ever scare me like that again, either of you! But now that the day has been saved, spill, Mira. What were you up to all day? How'd you know that would work?"

She shrugged, but before she could answer properly, Hanna and Naomi came racing over with Sabrina in tow. They pulled us all into a group hug. I couldn't stop the tears from falling. I hadn't felt this loved, or this cared for, in a long while. My heart was so full, especially when Eve and Mira pulled apart, making room for and gesturing for Inez to come join us.

She hesitated for a moment before Naomi yelled, "Get your ass over here, girlie. You're one of us."

We all laughed at that, and Inez smiled widely. I couldn't help but feel a pang of sadness looking at her, though. If everything worked out how it should, she would be leaving tomorrow. I had known in the back of my mind the whole time that she would be leaving, but I had gotten used to the idea of leaving with her. I hadn't really thought all day about being separated from her.

But as I looked around the circle at everyone else's faces, I realized I wouldn't have to say goodbye to any of them.

I could leave Portland saying 'until next time' to them. I would see them again and would get to be around for their special moments. I would get to travel the world if I wanted. My future was wide open before me, waiting for me to take it, and for the first time in a long time, I felt hopeful about how it would turn out.

The rest of the ball passed in a blur of dancing and laughter. I was grateful for each moment I was getting to spend with each and every one of them. I had a few people come up to me and congratulate me for my character winning the cosplay contest. Some of them asked me more about my book and said they were going to check it out. I even saw one person reading my book in the corner of the ball. I thought for sure that was going to be the highlight of my night, until Jordan A. Day herself tapped me on the shoulder.

I spun around, thinking it was going to be one of my friends, but my jaw dropped when I saw her. Jordan freaking A. Day herself!

"Hi! I'm Jordan!" she said, smiling.

"I-I'm Sadie," I stuttered out.

She grinned. "I know. I heard it was your character who won the cosplay contest! That tall, dark, and gorgeous man with the badass special effects, right?"

I nodded, too stunned to say anything. "That was so ridiculously cool! Definitely made me want to check out your work! Do you have a business card or something?"

I nodded, incredibly thankful I had brought some in my clutch. "I do! Here you go! And not to fangirl for a second, but you're Jordan A. Day. I love you so much! Your writing is incredible. You're indie author royalty!"

She laughed at that. "Really I'm just an author who loves her own characters a little too much, but here." She reached into her clutch and pulled out a card of her own. "Here's my card; reach out anytime."

Someone called her name from over her shoulder. She glanced over and waved before turning back to me. I was clutching the business card like my life depended on it. I still couldn't believe this was real life.

"Well, it was great meeting you! Definitely reach out sometime so we can talk!" With that, she turned and was gone.

I couldn't believe it. I had just talked to Jordan A. Day! And she was excited about my work! How was this real life?

People kept congratulating me on Damien winning the cosplay contest. I couldn't believe he had won in the first place, so when Mira told us a little later that she had hacked the voting and blustered Damien's votes to surpass Gwen's, I wasn't surprised. He hadn't actually won. I would have felt guilty if Gwen had been sad about it, but Gwen had her own happy ending.

I watched them dance, and saw Morgana's genuine smile for the first time since meeting her. Gwen's ecstatic face told me she still couldn't believe this was real and was trying to take in every detail. I was so happy for them both.

By the time the ball ended and we made it back to our hotel, I was fighting to keep my eyes open. As quickly as I could, I removed my makeup, changed out of my dress, and fell into bed, falling deeply asleep the moment my head hit the pillow.

THIRTY-EIGHT

Damien

"NOOO!"

I was still yelling myself hoarse when the damned bubble burst and the smoke cleared. With a sinking heart, even before the smoke dissipated, I realized my fears were right. I could smell the cold mountain air, ice and pine, the smell of home. I let out a scream that faded into sobs as I sunk to my knees. The sobs wracked through my body, feeling endless as I drowned in my grief.

All of this had been for nothing. I was no closer to getting my husband back safely. I had no plan, nothing that I could do. The Realms thought he was dead, but I refused to believe it. I knew Altea still had him. I would do anything, anything to see him again, but would he even still like the man I had become? I sobbed harder at that. I felt the grief and despair pulling me under harder, deeper.

I felt like I could and would lose myself in it, but that was the thing about being alone. There was no one there to save you. If I abandoned myself to my grief and let myself drown, there would be no one there to save me, no one to throw me a lifeline. I had to save myself, pull myself back, if I wanted any chance of rescuing him. I wasn't completely hopeless. I still had the Princess.

I knew time was short, and I didn't have time to try any of the usual tricks on her, magic or otherwise. She'd shown time and time again through my stay in Sherbrooke that she could see right through me, and with her newly unlocked powers, she was a force to be reckoned with, with Celeste at her disposal and an army at her command. She would be a powerful ally; possibly even more powerful than the sorceress would've been. I knew it was only a matter of time before Inez returned and came for her, and I had a lot of damage to undo to win her over. It was my own damned fault, and I didn't know if it could be done, but I had to try. For him, I had to try to thaw her heart to me. She resisted my magic and charms, so I would have to resort to the truth.

I shuddered even thinking it. Vulnerability didn't suit me as well as it used to. That part of me had died when I saw him dragged away, but now I needed it. I knew the Princess well enough now to know that she would know if I was being dishonest with her or using her. I would have to tell her the truth and would have to find a way to make her believe it. I could only hope I somehow would have the patience to wait out her stubbornness. I could only hope I had enough time to change her mind before Inez rammed down my door.

I didn't have a minute to spare. I glanced down at my suit and wrinkled my nose. Well, perhaps I had a few minutes. It wouldn't do for anyone to see me in these otherworldly clothes. I would change, perhaps take a nice long bath, and then I would start work on the Princess.

THIRTY-NINE

Sadie

When I woke the next morning, I felt arms around me and was confused for a moment before I remembered where I was. At some point through the night, either I or Inez must have crossed to the other side of the bed, because she was holding me in her arms. I smiled at how peaceful she was sleeping before extracting myself from her. I didn't want to. I would have loved to lie there all morning and block out the world, would have loved to ignore the rest of my problems and laid in bed, close to her.

She was a comforting presence, and I enjoyed being near her. She made me feel safe, and as much as I didn't want that to end, didn't want her to leave, I knew she had to. She had a life and her own friends waiting for her back in Sherbrooke. Plus, Serena was now stuck with an angry Damien whose plans had been thwarted, who would now see her as a last resort to getting what he wanted, what he needed, and I didn't think he would take the time to convince her.

Inez needed to get back there as soon as possible, and I needed to fix things. Things had gone off course the second I decided Inez wouldn't go rescue Serena and Damien wouldn't try to convince Serena to help him but would instead force her to. Knowing Inez for more than a few minutes, there wasn't a single doubt in my mind that it didn't matter what had happened between her and Serena, she would be there for her, and I hoped Serena felt the same.

I knew Serena didn't love Inez in the way Inez wanted her to, but she loved Inez and I felt secure that she would try to protect Inez, too, if the roles had been reversed. Hell, Inez had gone out of her way, time and time again, to help me since coming here, and she hadn't even known me. It was my turn to do this for her, and to try to right the wrongs I had caused. I didn't know for sure that changing the story would change anything, but I was going to have to try.

Without my laptop that Damien had stolen, I had to get dressed and make my way down to the lobby to see if they had any computers I could use. I hadn't seen any, but maybe they did. The woman at the front desk apologized, shaking her head, and told me that there was a library and cafe within walking distance that had computers, but that they wouldn't open for another couple of hours. I thanked her and returned to the room.

I tried to enter quietly, but must have made some sort of noise, because Inez started awake and glanced around quickly. When she saw Mira still asleep and me standing by the door, she relaxed again. I thought she might lie back down, but she stayed sitting up and alert. She patted the bed next to her, and I crawled into the bed and over to her. She put her arm around me and I leaned into her.

"So, today's the day, huh?"

"It seems like it," I said solemnly.

"Don't be so excited about it. You're only going to exhibit power beyond the 'Six Realms' wildest imagination and change my fate and the fate of everyone else in my world with a power you didn't even know you had and don't really know how to wield. What's there to be worried about?" she said with a laugh.

I laughed, too. When she said it like that, the whole situation sounded too ridiculous to be scary. It didn't feel real.

"Well, when you put it like that, I'm a fool for worrying at all," I said with a chuckle.

It must not have touched my eyes, because she still looked concerned. She stroked my hair from my face, asking, "What's really wrong?"

"It's nothing."

It wasn't, but it didn't feel right letting her know I was going to miss her. I didn't want to burden her with my feelings. I was sure she was happy to be going home, that is, if she wasn't too worried about my ability to send her home. I was trying not to dwell on that too much, hoping it would be as simple as changing the story, hoping that would reverse time and take care of the mist.

That was asking for a lot of trust on her part, and it would make sense if she were worried. I had a hunch that the mist had been triggered by my changes to the story, but that once I changed the story back to my original ending, the mist would go away. I hoped. I wished I could feel more confident, but it was hard, and all I really had to go on was my hunch. But none of that was what was bothering me.

Despite the insurmountable odds, I felt pretty sure that once I changed the story, the magic would be satisfied and she would be sent home. What was bothering me was the thought of not being able to see her ever again, not being able to communicate with her or see how she was doing. Realistically, I knew I would have some insight into how she was, but after my story ended, I would have no idea what was going on in her world.

I would make sure to give her a happy ending—if anyone deserved it, it was her—but I had no idea what that looked like, and didn't know the first thing about how the magic would affect any story line I tried to give her. At the end of this new story, she ended satisfied with the hope for a happy ending, but she wasn't any closer to that happy ending than she had been at the start of the series.

Realistically, I knew I would be spending a lot more screen time with her, trying to figure out her perfect ending and crafting the perfect woman for her, but I wouldn't ever get to see her smile again or be this close to her again. I would make sure to open new doors for her and her future, but in doing so, I would have to slam the door between us shut.

She seemed to have read some of that on my face, and said, "I'll miss you, too, Sadie."

"I know you have to go, and even when I thought I was going to have to go with Damien, I didn't really want to, but at least you would've still been there. The thought of never being able to see you again isn't one that I'm fond of."

She pulled me a little closer and said, "I know. I don't like it either, but whenever I look up at the sky, I'll know I have the most kick ass goddess watching over me, crafting my fate, and pushing me to happiness. You may not be there with me, but you'll always be in here." She pointed to her heart, and my tears fell in earnest. She sniffled before adding, "And I'll know who to blame when something goes wrong," she said, shoving me playfully.

"You know it wouldn't be a good story if there wasn't a little bit of difficulty."

"You know I can handle whatever you throw at me," she said with a challenge in her eye and a playful smirk. "But knowing you'll be looking out for me is comforting, anyway."

I burrowed a little more into her. "Always. Promise you'll think of me from time to time."

"Always," she said, smiling. "Besides, once I tell Serena about you, she's going to have so many questions that I'm sure I'll be talking about you for the rest of both of our days."

We both laughed at that.

"You think she will?"

She nodded enthusiastically. "She'll be curious enough that by the time she's finished with her questions, I might be begging Damien to take her back," she said with a laugh before realizing a moment later what she had said and her face fell. "She's with him now."

I nodded.

"But she'll be okay until we can fix things?"

I nodded again.

He wouldn't have hurt her or done anything more than tried to scare her into helping him. He wouldn't have had enough power after controlling Inez and getting transported home for much else. I just had to change things and get Inez home before much else could happen. I had to make sure the changes sent her home. No matter how much it would suck to see her go, I needed to send her home.

"You still won't tell me what you know of him?" she asked.

I sighed and shook my head. "I can't, and even if I did, you wouldn't believe me until you saw it for yourself, but yes, once you return and rescue Serena, you'll find things have changed."

She nodded. "So I'll still have to launch a rescue mission?"

"I can't change anything from before she was taken, that's written in stone so to say, but you and Tristan won't meet much resistance storming his fortress to take back Serena, and once you have her back, things will be different. You'll see."

She swallowed, took a deep breath, and said, "About that, I thought a lot about our talk and your offer, and I changed my mind. Not that I had really given you an answer before, but I'm ashamed to admit I had considered it. I don't want anything to change between Serena and me. I do love her and a big part of me always will, but loving someone means respecting their choices and wanting them happy. She's happy with Tristan, and he's really a good enough man. As good as anyone could be for her. He doesn't deserve her, but then again, I don't know that I would feel like anyone did, including me. Even when I hoped she might notice me like that, I knew I wasn't worthy of her."

I frowned at that and said, "Inez, I hope you know you're quite the catch."

She frowned, too. "Who's catching me? I don't want to be caught."

I laughed at that, shaking my head. "No. I meant you're quite special and anyone would be lucky to have you, Serena included. You were more than good enough for her, but you weren't meant for each other."

She nodded. "In the short time I got to see her around him, I was starting to understand that. He brings out a side of her that I had only rarely seen. He softens her in a way I don't think I could. She does that for me and I love her for it, but I don't think I could ever really be what she needed. I just hope he will try his best to be worthy of her."

I smiled at her. "I can promise I will do everything in my power to make sure he does. He has nothing but love and good intentions for her."

"And I trust you'll find a way to steer me in the right direction to the woman meant for me." She put her hand to her neck, feeling the loss of her amulet.

"I will do everything in my power. I can't say it won't be a little messy and chaotic getting there, but I promise she's worth it and promise the future you have waiting for you is everything you could want. I want that for you and will make sure you have it."

She kissed the top of my head, holding me tight. We stayed like that for a little while longer, basking in the comfort and closeness, savoring our time together.

FORTY

Only when Mira stirred did I suggest we get up and get ready for brunch. We had arranged to meet with the others at a restaurant a couple blocks away, and we had about an hour before we were supposed to be there. From there, we had the author's farewell brunch with some of the people who attended the ball. I was ecstatic my friends had all made the cut with their VIP tickets and that, as an author, I had the privilege to bring Inez as my honored guest. I wouldn't have gone if she couldn't have come. I would've skipped it in a heartbeat to spend a little bit of extra time with her.

We both knew her time here was dwindling. A part of me kept worrying she might disappear at any moment now that Damien had been sent back, but deep down I knew she wasn't finished with me yet. Her mission wasn't finished. The story still needed to be changed.

Walking over to brunch, I linked arms with Inez, while Eve looped hers through mine and Mira's on her other side.

What an odd group we made walking down the streets of Portland, with Inez in her battle leathers. Not that anyone gave us a second glance. When we passed a "Keep Portland Weird" mural, I took out my phone and gestured everyone in close and took a picture of us with the mural. I didn't know what would happen to the picture when she returned, if it would be like she was never here at all, but I hoped I would get to keep it.

We made it to brunch, still arm in arm, and saw the rest of our group sitting at a table in the corner. When we walked over to them, I wasn't surprised to see they all looked as tired as we did. It had been a long night.

The moment I sat down, Naomi grinned at me. "Guess what?"

"What?"

She frowned, giving me a mock pout. "No. You have to guess."

"Ummm..." I took in her smile and asked, "Did you meet someone?"

She blushed. "Well, that wasn't exactly what I was going to tell you, but you're not wrong."

"But we want to hear all about you meeting someone!" Hanna said.

"Seriously, though!" I added. "How could that not be the thing you wanted to tell us about?"

"This is even more exciting, though!" Naomi insisted, reaching into her purse. When she pulled out the object, I couldn't believe my eyes. "Is that what I think it is?" I asked, my voice high as I reached for it and examined it. It was! Without a doubt, it was actually my laptop. "How'd you find it?"

She shrugged. "Well, it's a funny story. When Damien kidnapped me, part of his plan involved destroying it, since he believed it was how you channeled your power or something like that. He thought that destroying it would hurt you and ruin your plans to change things to make sure he lost. He planned to destroy it right before leaving for the ball, so when he was distracted, I snagged it before taking off."

"Just like that?" I asked.

"I can be sneaky when I want," she said with a laugh.

"Thank you so, so much!" I said, gratefully. "This makes things so much easier."

Inez looked at me in wonder. "Does it really contain some of your power?"

I went to shake my head, but instead shrugged. "You know about as much about my powers as I do, but it does contain yours and Serena's story, every draft of it as I've made changes along the way. I have it backed up, of course, so he wouldn't have actually destroyed the only copy or anything, but it feels right to have it back. It feels right to be able to fix things with the same computer that started it all. It's much more personal."

I thanked Naomi again, before turning back to Inez. "I know you have to leave soon, and I know I said I needed until after the farewell gathering to send you home, but if you would rather leave sooner, there's time for me to give it a shot before the gathering." I hoped she would be okay with staying. I really wanted to spend a bit more time with her, but I wouldn't fault her if she was too worried about Serena and her world and needed to return earlier.

She examined me, read as much in my eyes, and said with a shrug, "What's a few more hours?"

I threw my arms around her shoulders, pulling her close, incredibly grateful she was willing to extend her stay a little longer.

FORTY-ONE

Walking into the farewell party, there was a red carpet rolled out, leading down the hallway to the entrance, and we were handed champagne with a strawberry slice on the rim. I took a sip of the champagne and sighed, content. It was sweet, just the way I liked it. By the time I moved my glass from my lips, Inez had already downed hers. I laughed and handed her my glass. I wasn't much of a drinker, anyway. She eyed it happily before asking if I was sure. I chuckled and nodded. She took and downed my glass in a heartbeat, too.

"Whatever this concoction is, it's delicious, and by far the closest thing I've had to mead since I've been here."

I was glad she enjoyed it.

We walked in and made our way to the table marked with my name. All the tables had been named for authors. My friends took their seats with me. Inez sat next to me and took up another glass of champagne that they had set on the tables for us.

"You might want to slow down. I don't think the magic that brings you home will also take away your hangover."

She laughed heartily. "It would take more than a few drinks to reduce me to that state."

I grinned back at her, sure we were thinking of that same thing. "I should know better since you put half of Altea's royal guard to shame, drinking them all under the table."

Her eyes widened. "You know about that?"

"Know about that? I wrote it. I'm the reason you didn't have a hangover the next day."

She burst out laughing, and I joined her.

When my laughter stopped, I couldn't stop the sad smile from taking its place. "I'm going to miss you dearly."

"I'll miss you, too. I feel like I've known you all my life. You know and see every part of me."

"Something like that. Things will definitely be more boring around here without you, but I'll have to start working my magic on getting you your happy ending," I said with a wink.

She grinned at that, picked up her champagne, clinked it with my glass that was still sitting untouched in front of me, and said, "I'll drink to that," before emptying the contents.

FORTY-TWO

After letting everyone know I would need a couple of hours to work my magic, Inez and I went back to our hotel room. Eve asked if I wanted extra moral support, but I was okay. I knew what I needed to do and I could get through this. Mira ended up going up to Eve's room with her. They said it was to hang out and read, but I knew they were giving me some space and time with Inez, and I appreciated them so much for it. Although a part of me worried she would be watching over my shoulder the entire time, impatiently waiting for me to finish and asking questions about what changes I was making. But I shouldn't have been worried because the second we entered the room, she flopped down on our bed, and by the time I was sitting in front of my laptop at the desk, she was already snoring.

I smiled to myself and got to work. I had my original version all edited and ready to go before I had made the changes that ruined everything. I didn't need to do anything else. I could just void out the changed version and resubmit the new version for publishing. That was what I had done last time and Inez said that was when the mist came, so I was hoping that was all that was needed to send her home. But if I sent her home with the original version without any changes, things would change back to the moment Serena was taken.

The mist never would have come and Inez wouldn't have teamed up with Celeste to figure out how to stop it and save Serena. Inez would have just saved Serena without ever having come here. I could let that happen, but I had another option.

I knew enough about her experience after Serena was taken before Inez came here to recreate it the way it had happened for her. I could add in the mist to the story, make her disappear from Celeste's tower and reappear a few moments later with the knowledge she had gained and the ability to save Serena. The mist would vanish and she could start her quest to save Serena.

I knew that was what I had to do. I told myself I was doing it because I didn't know what would happen in the real world or the story if I wrote out Inez and Damien coming to Portland, and that was somewhat true, but it was truer that I didn't want Inez to forget me.

I wanted her to remember our time together. She had changed me and I wouldn't change that for the world. Besides, it wasn't just me. She had changed, too.

She had gained a lot of perspective and had come to terms with things with Serena and was ready to move on, and after saving Serena and maybe the Six Realms, too, she was going to find her true love and her happiness. It wasn't going to be easy, but she would get there. I wanted her to remember that, to remember that I was here looking out for her and that every challenge I threw at her, I was right there beside her, helping her. I wouldn't let her fail and knew she could handle the struggles coming her way. Maybe it was selfish, but I wanted her to remember the hope she had found here.

A couple hours later, with the rewrites done, combed over for issues, spell checked, and grammar checked, I felt like I was as ready as I would ever be. I felt a pang of regret that I didn't have time to send it to my editor. It wasn't my best work, but it would have to do. It was only two small new chapters; I was sure my readers would forgive me if it wasn't completely perfect.

Ready as I would ever be, I turned to wake Inez, only to see she was already awake and watching me. "How long have you been up?"

"Long enough to see how adorable you look when you're concentrating. What'd you do to the story?"

I shrugged. "I probably shouldn't say."

"I know, I know, I'll find out when I get back." She rolled her eyes, shoving me playfully..

"I can tell you, the only change I made this time was making sure to include you going to Celeste and getting here," I said quietly.

Her eyes widened. "I thought things were going back to how they were before?"

I couldn't meet her eye. "I only had the ability to change things after Serena was captured, and I promise this version ensures her safety, but I couldn't write out you coming here. You would've gone back to being the heartbroken Inez who came here, and," I swallowed, struggling with what I needed to say, "I didn't want you to forget me."

I heard a noise and slowly glanced up, relieved that when I did, she was grinning. "You really had me worried for a second there. I don't think it would've been possible for me to forget you, but I'm happy you made sure of it. As strange as this journey was, I learned a lot about myself and wouldn't trade that for the world."

When she held open her arms, I went to her and let her wrap me up in them. I hated knowing it was the last time I would feel the safety of her embrace, but I knew she had to be going. She had some realms and a best friend to save.

After a few minutes, I pulled away from Inez and reached into my pocket. I had been reaching for my phone, but I found the moldavite. Well, I guess I didn't need it anymore. I pulled it out of my pocket and handed it to her.

"I want you to have this."

"A talisman?" she asked, surprised.

"Yeah, a talisman of sorts. To remember me by."

She grinned. "As if I could forget you." But she ran her fingers over it, caressing it gently before slipping it deep into her pocket.

I took my phone out of my pocket. "I'll let the girls know it's time."

She nodded, and we sat there together for a couple of minutes, enjoying each other's company, until there was a knock at the door. That was quick. Inez got up and checked the peephole, and opened the door. Eve and Mira came in.

"Hey guys," I said, forcing a smile onto my face. "You could have used the room key."

Mira shrugged. "I didn't remember to bring it. Sorry about that." She always kept it in her wallet, so either she had actually taken it out, or they didn't want to intrude.

Inez walked back over, sitting down next to me again, and said, "That's okay. With the spyglass in the door, I could see it was you guys. I don't know why all doors don't have those installed."

Eve, Mira, and I exchanged a look before breaking into giggles. "What?" asked Inez. "It's really a security oversight that most doors don't have a way to identify who's on the other side unless you open it." We started laughing harder. I was struggling to catch my breath. Inez seemed like she was going to say something else, but there was another knock on the door. Eve was standing closest to the door, but Inez jumped up and rushed past her to check who it was.

She opened the door after a moment; it was Hanna and Sabrina. That made sense, since their hotel was closer than where Naomi was staying.

While we waited for Naomi, they tried to keep things light, but I was struggling to keep my emotions in check. I was struggling with Inez leaving. She seemed to feel similar because she was quiet, too, which wasn't usual for her. I knew she was anxious to get home, and probably nervous this might not work, but I knew she was going to miss me, too. I was surprised by my own lack of anxiety about this working. I really had no reason to think it was going to besides blind faith and trust in the magic that I wasn't anywhere close to understanding. I just knew it was going to work because it needed to. As much as I was going to miss her, she needed to get home, and if this didn't work, I didn't know what else would.

There was a knock, and again Inez, even though everyone else was closer, bounded over to the door to look out the peephole before opening the door. Naomi came in and our little family was whole. At least for the time being, until Inez left.

I took a deep breath and asked, "Okay, how do we want to do this?"

Everyone was quiet for a moment until Eve said, "This might be a little too funeral-like, but I thought maybe we could all go around and say a few words about Inez and one of the things we'll miss about her."

Inez grinned at that, and everyone else nodded. I didn't know if I would be able to keep the tears in, but I nodded, too. It was as good a send-off as any. Besides, Inez had perked up at the idea.

"Are we sure we want to give her a bigger ego?" Naomi asked teasingly.

Inez chuckled loudly at that.

"Okay, okay, I'll go first," Naomi said. "I'll miss your spirit of adventure. You live life untamed and I admire that. I'll miss you."

Inez smiled. "And I, you."

"Me next!" said Hanna. "I'll miss your energy and kindness."

Inez's eyes widened in surprise, before she broke into a grin. "I'll miss you, too."

Sabrina went next. "I'll miss your badass style. I could use a pair of those leather arm guards for sure."

Inez went to slip them off her arms, which shocked me to the core. She had had those since she was first appointed to the royal guard and besides her now destroyed amulet, they were probably her most treasured possession.

I was going to say something, but Sabrina held up her hands quickly. "No, no, you keep them. You need them more than I do where you're going, but I might end up getting a pair of my own someday. If I ever do, I'll make sure they would be ones you'd approve of," she said, smiling. "I'll miss you and won't ever forget you."

Again, Inez smiled sadly. "Nor I, you."

Eve went next. "I'll miss the way you can make order out of chaos, the way you always seem to know what to do in any situation, and the way nothing ever bothers you." I was shocked. I glanced around, but if anyone else was surprised, no one showed it. That was how I thought of Eve. I wondered if she knew that was how she came across to other people.

"You're my mirror image in that way. Don't let yourself forget it."

Eve reddened a little and replied, "I'll miss you."

"I'll miss you, too. Try to keep these ones out of trouble for me?"

I saw a tear roll down her face, but she nodded with a little laugh. "Of course I get the hardest task."

Inez smiled and said with a shrug, "Well, you can handle it. Look out for our little family."

Eve nodded. "I will."

Mira stepped up next. "I'll miss how you command a room and respect, but never look down on others. I'll miss how kind you are to animals and how much you care about others."

Inez smiled widely. "Your heart is a thing of beauty. You are incredibly clever, and see things differently from other people. Don't let anyone change you. I'll miss you."

Mira blushed. "I'll miss you, too."

By then, I had stopped trying to hide my tears. They were streaming down my face and wouldn't be stopped. When Inez turned back to me, I saw her eyes were watery, too. I gave her a shaky smile.

"Well, it's back to the two of us now, huh?"

"It looks like it," she said.

"I don't even know where to begin. Inez, even though you've only known me for a short time, I've known you for years now. When I first started my journey with you, you were a completely different person. You were young, wild, undisciplined, and could be a little selfish at times. I watched you grow and go on adventure after adventure, slowly getting older and wiser. I was there for your first drink, your first horseback ride, I experienced every first with you, and it has been an extreme honor. I loved the girl you were, but to watch you grow into the woman you are now has been such a privilege for me. You brought back my faith in friendship and in goodness in general. I am so proud of how much you've grown, but I hope you know all the ways you've changed me. You gave me back my hope in people and helped draw our little family together. You are wise beyond your years, and I'm incredibly lucky to have met you. In the short time you've been here with us, you've grown even wiser and more mature. I know your path at home won't be easy, but I promise you can handle it. It will test you and push you, but never beyond what you can handle. You have already grown up so much, but you still have a little way to go. Just know I'm holding your hand the entire time. When you're tired, scared, or lonely, know that I'm there and that the hard times won't last. They might seem like there's no end in sight, but believe that they will yield to the light. I will always be there for you and I will never stop thanking the universe and my lucky stars for the time I got to spend with you."

I had to stop to catch my breath. I was crying too hard to breathe. Inez pulled me into her arms and squeezed me tight enough I thought I might actually suffocate. When she loosened her grip a moment later and I was able to move back enough to look up at her, I saw she was crying, too.

"I won't soon forget you, Sadie of Hawthorne. Every time I look up at the stars and wish, I'll be thinking of you. Anytime I am struggling and can't find anything positive to think of, I'll think of you. When things are so hard I feel like they'll never get better, I'll blame you," she said with a laugh. I laughed a little before she said, "No, really, bring it on. I know I'll be able to take whatever is thrown at me because you're looking out for me. And when I finally get my happily ever after with whomever is unfortunate enough to become my wife, I'll tell her all about you. When our children ask for bedtime stories, I'll tell them of our adventure. When they're scared, I'll tell them about the kind, lovely sorceress who helped their mother through all her hardships and helped their mothers find each other. I will talk of you my whole life. The way I will talk of you, don't be surprised if Sherbrooke builds you a temple or two."

I laughed at that, before seeing she was serious, and then laughed some more.

"I won't ever forget you. I will carry you with me for the rest of my life," I told her, tears free-falling again. She wiped them gently away with her thumb, smiling sadly at me.

"I couldn't forget you if I wanted to. You are a light in the dark and a powerful force. May others recognize that strength in you and flock to you. You would make a great leader."

I blushed at that. "I'm fine with just being someone's friend."

"Lucky you have us then," said Eve, squeezing my shoulder.

"Thankfully."

"Alright, alright," said Inez gently. "I should probably be going. Besides, I hate crying."

I extracted myself from her arms reluctantly and took a seat in front of my laptop. I had the website up and ready to go. All I needed to do was delete the old file and drag and drop the new file in there. I took a deep breath and turned around. I saw everyone crowded around Inez, holding onto her. I didn't know how the magic worked, but I didn't want to take any chance. I took a deep breath and with a heavy heart, asked them to step away from her.

"I don't know how the magic works, but the last thing we need is anyone else jumping worlds."

We all laughed, but they quickly moved a foot or so away from her, clearing space for her.

I took another deep breath. "Okay, are we ready?"

"As we'll ever be," said Eve.

Inez nodded, concentrating on holding back tears. She was trying to keep it together for our sake. I turned back and deleted the file. I felt a hand squeeze my shoulder and turned around to see it was Inez. She pulled away a moment later, and I already missed her.

I was prompted to upload a new file. With shaking hands, I dragged the file from my desktop to the website. I turned back quickly, not wanting to miss Inez fading out, but she was still there. I was stunned. Why was she still there? What had I done wrong?

I didn't have another plan; I had been so sure this was going to work. Seeing the fear on my face, Inez's smile faded. She reached out to me, putting her hand on my cheek. I leaned into her touch.

"It's okay," she told me, putting on a brave face. "We'll find another way."

I nodded, but I didn't know if I believed it. As much as I hated to see her go, I didn't want her to be stuck here, isolated from her world and her friends who needed her.

There had to be something I was missing. I turned back to my laptop to see that the file was only 50% uploaded. I exhaled, relieved. "It's okay, guys. It hasn't finished uploading yet."

There was a collective sigh of relief, and when I turned back to Inez, I saw her smile had returned. "With any luck, I'll be home any minute. Farewell, fair maidens. My friends. I won't forget any of you."

I turned back to the laptop. 95%. 96%. 97%. Any moment now.

I turned back to Inez, holding my breath. The others were standing a little off to the side, huddled together. Everyone was tense watching Inez. She looked hopeful, and I hoped she was right to be. I held my breath for another few seconds and then there was a faint light forming around her. I blinked twice, hoping I wasn't imagining things. The glow got stronger, turning a bright blue and surrounding Inez. She was glowing, but her smile glowed even brighter. She mouthed, "Thank you," and waved to me and the others. A few moments later, just like it had with Damien, the blue shield turned opaque before fading, leaving empty space where she had been standing.

I stared at the spot, not daring to take my eyes off it for a few more seconds. Nothing happened. She was gone. We had done it. I had done it. Right now, she had appeared on the floor of Celeste's study right where she had left, hopefully a few minutes after she had left. The mist should lift in the Realms, along with the effects it was causing.

I had done it.

Inez was back and would save Serena. When she found Serena, together they would change everything and save the Six Realms. She was going to do it, and I was going to have to get started on the next book, and the next after that. As many as it took to get Inez her happy ending. I wouldn't be giving up my pen anytime soon. I had a job to do and a friend to protect.

I smiled through my falling tears, and a moment later, Eve was there, pulling me out of the chair and into a hug. Mira joined in, and then I felt the others surrounding me. I felt a pang at the hole Inez had left in our little group, but I knew she was where she was supposed to be, and I was in good hands.

FORTY-THREE

It was a long night, and as much as I knew I should have been exploring the city, I hadn't felt up to going anywhere. We ordered room service and watched old episodes of *Xena: Warrior Princess* and *Buffy the Vampire Slayer*.

When we were all getting tired, Naomi, Hanna, and Sabrina left and Eve went back to her room. I got ready for bed, and when I came out of the bathroom and saw the empty bed, the tears came back. I backed around the corner, hoping Mira didn't see.

I had been crying most of the day and didn't want to make her continue to feel obligated to take care of me. I leaned against the wall and sank to the floor, the tears free-falling now. I felt like I was being ridiculous. She was fine. I knew exactly where she was and what she was doing and knew that she was happy to be back, and I was happy for her, too. Relieved, really, that I was able to send her back, but I missed her so much already. Knowing I'd never get to see her again was a lot for me to handle. It would get easier; I knew it would. It would have to, but for now, there was an ache in my chest and an empty bed.

I didn't know how I was possibly going to sleep. Maybe I would tire myself out from crying, hopefully.

When I heard a soft knock on the door, I picked myself up, tried to wipe my face as best as I could, took a deep breath, and went to the peephole. It was Eve. She must have forgotten something. I eased open the door, not sure if Mira was still awake, and saw that Eve had changed into pajamas and had a bag with her. Maybe I was more tired than I thought if I missed that through the peephole.

I gave her a questioning look, and she just shrugged. "I took one look at you when I was leaving and thought you could use a sleepover. I got my things, but I hoped maybe I was wrong and you'd be asleep when I got back. You must be tired after today and could use some rest, so I knocked quietly just in case, but since you're up, I'm glad I came back."

I was stunned and speechless. It took me a good minute to say, "Thank you, but you really don't have to stay."

"I know I don't have to, but I want to. You're not alone anymore, and I want to make sure you know that. You're worthy of being loved, and a phenomenal friend. You would do the same for me in a heartbeat, so of course I'm here."

If I hadn't already had tears streaming down my face, that would've done it.

She pulled me into a hug and squeezed tight until the tears finally stopped. When I pulled away, I noticed she had been crying, too. "I know it's been a tough day. I won't tell you it hasn't, but I'm proud of you."

I stared at her. "I'm a mess. What's there to be proud of?"

"It might not feel like it right now, but you're incredibly strong and, as much as saying goodbye sucks, she'll always be a part of you, quite literally."

I giggled at that. "I'm glad you're here."

I don't know how I would've possibly slept on my own that night, but with her by my side, I slept soundly.

I didn't want to get out of bed the next day, but didn't really have much of an option. It was our last full day in Portland, and I wasn't going to make anyone miss it on my account. I had already taken up the whole night yesterday, not wanting to get out of bed or do anything. I would get up and deal with things today. I had to.

We went back to the bookstore, and I bought a couple of books and actually managed to enjoy myself. We explored the city, going to all sorts of tarot and witchy shops, before making our way back to the same crystal shop I had bought the moldavite in.

I hadn't been the biggest believer, but with everything that had happened on the trip, it was hard to be skeptical anymore.

When the woman recognized me, she blanched before quickly saying, "No returns. I don't know what the moldavite has done, but it has to run its course."

I laughed at that, putting my hands up in an 'I come in peace' gesture. "It has run its course, actually."

"And?"

"And you were right. I wasn't ready, but it was what I needed."

She smiled at that. "Well, what brings you back? Looking for anything in particular?"

I figured there was an empty feeling space in my pocket where the moldavite had been, so another crystal couldn't hurt.

She ended up helping me pick out a moonstone, which I was incredibly happy came in the shape of a crescent moon. She said the moonstone was perfect for what I was looking for, remembrance and new beginnings.

I hoped it would help me to keep Inez in my heart and to move on. When it was almost time for dinner, I asked Eve what the plan was, but she wouldn't tell me. With a wink, she told me it was a surprise, but that we would need a change of clothes. We said goodbye for now to the others, and Eve went to her hotel room. Mira didn't change, instead packing a bag and saying she was going to change when we got there.

"What should I wear?" I asked her, glancing down at my suitcase. I had no idea what kind of occasion we were dressing for, but I didn't want to be under or overdressed.

Mira just smiled and shook her head. "Eve will tell you when she gets here."

Eve knocked a minute later, and I bounded to the door, excited to see what she was wearing, excited for any clue about where we were going, but she only had a bag, too.

"You didn't change?"

"And ruin the surprise? Absolutely not."

"So, what do I wear?"

"Leave that to me. You just turn around and don't look." She rushed past me to my suitcase.

"But-"

"No buts. I promise you'll like what I pick out."

"Okay, okay, fine, but hurry at least," I said jokingly. "I wanna know where we're going already. The suspense is killing me."

"It's worth it, I promise," Mira added.

"Definitely," said Eve, "so no more complaints."

With that, she showed up behind me with a bag for herself and a bag for me. "See? Painless. I'm already done. Let's get going."

We laughed at that and went down to the lobby to catch a ride.

FORTY-FOUR

When the car pulled up to a part of Portland I hadn't been to before, I was a little nervous. I tried to remind myself that the gothic restaurant hadn't been in a great part of town either, but we had pulled up to a random set of stone stairs that went down from the sidewalk into the dark. I was skeptical, but I trusted Eve and the girls. Although maybe she was messing with me and we weren't actually getting out here, but when I hesitated, she urged me to get out and thanked the driver for the ride.

I got out, still thinking that I'd turn around and have Eve and Mira telling me to get back in the car to go to the actual location, but no, they both got out after me. When Eve urged me to go down the stairs, I looked at her skeptically.

"I know how this looks, but I promise the place is worth it. Trust me."

Okay, okay. I trusted her, and it couldn't be that bad.

When we got down the stairs, there was a wooden door that looked like it was taken from a medieval castle. Interesting. Odd. It had what looked like a sliding opening at eye level. The door also had a large brass knocker. I was getting major speakeasy vibes from the place, or medieval jail, so I was hoping for the speakeasy. I waited for a minute, but nothing happened.

I turned back to Eve who motioned to the door. "What are you waiting for? Go ahead and knock."

"Knock? Like with my hand or the brass knocker?"

"Whatever you're feeling," she said smiling.

I took hold of the knocker, rapping against the door three times. I was sure the other two times were unnecessary, but something about the door and the weirdness of the situation made me feel like three knocks were warranted. At the end of the third knock, a man with a hood covering most of his face appeared in the opening, having slid the wooden slot to the side to be able to see us.

"Password?" he asked.

I turned back to Eve, who smiled before saying, "Zanaria."

As I turned back to the man, the door was opening. "I can't believe that worked!" I said. "How much did you have to bribe the place for that to be the password?" I asked, joking.

"I'm quite compelling when I want to be if you haven't noticed," said Eve.

"I've noticed," I said, grinning.

When the door opened, my jaw dropped. I took a tentative step forward, sure I was dreaming somehow. Another step forward and I heard, "Surprise!" and out jumped Hanna, Sabrina, and Naomi. I jumped a foot into the air before squealing. I recognized their outfits as renaissance faire inspired, which was perfect for the place.

"What even is this place? How did you possibly find it?"

"We figured this was the perfect place to have our last hurrah, to make you feel a little closer to Inez before we all left."

Tears welled up in my eyes. "Thank you all so much. This is perfect."

The more I took in, the more perfect it became. I couldn't believe they had found a place like this in the middle of the city.

The walls were wooden with axes and swords hung on them. The place was dimly lit, but there was a roaring fire welcoming travelers to sit beside it and rest their feet. The floor had fake stone tiles that added to the ambience. This felt like it could've been a tavern straight out of the Six Realms, a tavern where friends gathered to plan their next adventure. It was perfect, but I couldn't help but wish they had told me about it since I had the perfect outfit for a place like this.

That was when Eve cleared her throat behind me and handed me my bag. I had forgotten she packed me clothes. I hoped for a moment that she might somehow have been enough of a mind reader to have picked out the outfit I was thinking of, but I had brought quite a few renaissance inspired outfits, so it was a long shot. Except, when I looked into the bag, I actually squealed before throwing myself at her. She caught me in a hug, and I could hear her soft laughter in my ear. A moment later, I pulled away, excited to go change. Sabrina pointed me in the right direction.

Eve had packed a perfect mix of my Serena and Inez cosplays. The only thing that was missing was the arm guards, but realistically I didn't need arm guards at a bar.

The outfit itself was perfect. I wouldn't have thought to combine them in this way, but I loved it so much. The top was a homage to Inez's training gear that she had been wearing for most of her time here. It was a cross between a corset and armor, and looked to be fashioned out of leather. The bottom part was designed to look like dragon scales, fitting for Sherbrooke.

The skirt was a reddish-brown, multilayered, uneven renaissance faire inspired skirt that was fashioned after Serena's favorite skirt. It was short enough she could move around in it, but long enough that she could fight without being indecent. She loved the way it swirled when she danced or when she was sparring; it made no difference to her. It had taken her a long time to convince Inez to stop throwing pants at her when she showed up to train in it and even longer for her to figure out how to use it to her advantage and fight in it, but she was nothing if not stubborn.

I felt every bit a badass, especially as I pulled out the purple dragon's eye choker. It was a perfect homage to Serena's dragon.

I walked back out into the main room and did a little twirl. My friends cheered, and I did a little curtsey. Laughing, I told Eve, "This is literally perfect. Thank you. Thank you all. This is just what I needed."

Sabrina stepped forward with her hands behind her back. "Speaking of just what you needed, close your eyes and hold out your hands."

I looked at her curiously before following her instructions. I held my hands palm up to hold whatever she was going to give me.

She laughed. "No, not like that."

"Like a zombie!" Hanna said.

Feeling ridiculous, I raised my arms into the air, straight out, palms down like a zombie.

"That works," Sabrina said with a laugh. "Now stay still and keep your eyes closed."

I felt cool leather encircle my wrists and part of my arms and grinned. I should've known they wouldn't forget my arm guards.

As Sabrina fastened one and talked Hanna through fastening the other, I realized they felt a little different than mine. Stiffer, sturdier, maybe? They didn't actually buy me new ones, though. There was no way. Maybe mine were just stiffer than I remembered. I had certainly never paid this much attention to the feel of them before, so I was probably just noticing now.

A moment later, they stepped away, and Sabrina told me to open my eyes. I did and was speechless. Not only were they not my arm guards, they were clearly new, but they had the crest of Sherbrooke etched into them perfectly. They were an exact replica of Inez's. My eyes were watery as I stared at my friends. They were grinning back at me.

"Thank you all so much! This is too much. You really didn't have to!" I laughed before adding, "But I'm so grateful you did!" I twisted my arms back and forth, getting a better view. They were perfect. "Where did you, how did you, when did you..."

I couldn't finish a question. I was too stunned. I looked at Eve, but she shook her head. "It was Sabrina's idea. She noticed how much you loved Inez's arm guards."

"Who wouldn't? Those things are badass," Sabrina said, grinning.

"We searched all over the city for someone who could do leather etchings. We were going to have yours etched with the Sherbrooke crest, but when we found this place, the owner took one look at the picture of Inez's arm guards and your arm guards and refused to etch it. We were crushed, until he explained he was going to craft a pair to exactly match Inez's."

"Yours were too costumey for him," said Sabrina with a laugh.

Eve added, "He wanted them to be a perfect replica when we told him how heartbroken you were about one of your best friends moving away."

I was ridiculously touched and felt a tear slip down my cheek. Sabrina and Hanna pulled me in for a hug, Mira, Eve, and Naomi quickly joining the group hug.

A moment later, we pulled away when Naomi said, "All right, enough of the mushiness. Let's have some drinks!"

Eve and Mira took turns changing into their renaissance outfits, and then we all sat at a roundtable close to the fire, laughing and talking.

When the bartender, who was dressed as a Viking, with locs, war paint and all, brought over our drinks, I was again surprised. Most of them came in silver goblets, but Naomi's came in a long Viking horn, about the size of my forearm.

I stared at it before asking, "How are you possibly going to drink that?"

She laughed. "It's ale. I would've preferred mead, but the second I found out ale came in a Viking horn, I knew I needed it."

I watched as she tipped back the horn and took a sip. When she pulled the horn away, her mouth was puckered and her nose wrinkled.

"Enjoying it?"

She grinned. "Not at all, but I look ridiculously cool."

We all laughed at that and put up our goblets for a toast.

"To Inez," said Eve.

"To us," I said.

"To the Saviors of Sherbrooke!" Naomi said, clinking her horn enthusiastically against ours.

"To the Saviors of Sherbrooke," we all cheered.

It was crazy to think of us like that. I certainly hadn't, but she was right. Everyone in their own way had played an important part in helping Inez and saving Sherbrooke, and the rest of the Six Realms. I had always longed for adventure; we all had. We had all pored over fantasy books, losing ourselves in the worlds and longing for adventure, and here we had been lost in our own fantasy adventure. Although lost wasn't really the right word. Some people lose themselves in books; I found myself in one. We all did, one way or another. We were all irrevocably changed by this and bonded for life. Us, the Saviors of Sherbrooke, our own little sisterhood. I could've never imagined a more perfect ending to a more perfect getaway.

I saw Eve riffling through her bag and watched as she came away with a hand full of something that caught the light and sparkled. When she brought her hands up to the table, she held them closed for a moment before saying, "I got everyone a little something."

"Stop it. You didn't have to do that!" I said.

"I know, but I wanted to."

"Did everyone know we were doing gifts except me?" Naomi asked.

We laughed at that. "I love you ladies, but I don't have any secret gifts for anyone."

Mira nodded. "Me either, but I wish I had thought of it."

"For real, though. I'm so lucky to have you all in my life. You all are gifts to me," I told them.

I meant it, but that didn't stop the laughter at how cheesy it sounded. Everyone else laughed with me. "But seriously, I mean it."

"I know, I know," Eve said, "But I wanted to do this. Quit protesting before you even know what it is."

Fair enough. "Alright, alright. I can't wait any longer," said Hanna. "What is it?"

Eve slowly opened her hands, revealing six necklaces that had potion bottles hanging off them. Each had a different colored sparkling potion inside. They were all beautiful, but the one that immediately caught my eye was a mix of purple, blue, and pink that looked like a galaxy. I would be extremely happy with any of the ones she gave me, but I wondered if she knew which one each of us would want.

I wasn't sure if she had gotten the colors randomly, or had a specific one in mind for each of us, but wasn't left wondering long since she started to pass them out to each of us. She handed Naomi the cerulean blue one. For Hanna, it was the cotton candy pink. Next was Sabrina's light iridescent pearl white with a splash of purple. Mira's was a sunshine yellow. With only mine and hers left, I wasn't surprised the galaxy one was still there.

The other was a fiery mix of yellows and oranges that reminded me of the beginning of sunset or of the first dawn light. They were day and night; exact mirrors of each other. She smiled before taking the orange and yellow one and holding out the midnight galaxy to me. When I took it in my hand and spun the mixture, the colors swirled and danced before my eyes.

I gaped at her, awed. "Where did you find these?" I asked.

"I made them," she beamed.

My jaw dropped. "You made them?!" I exclaimed.

"Cool, right?"

"More than cool. They're perfect!" Hanna gushed.

"Definitely perfect," agreed Mira.

Everyone said their thanks, and Eve was starting to blush. "It really was nothing, guys."

"It's so far from nothing," I said. "I love this so much, and will cherish it. A perfect memento from a perfect trip with the best of people."

"What, we're not perfect people?" Naomi chimed in with a grin.

With a laugh and a shrug, I said, "What can I say? Perfect's overrated. I'd take you guys over perfect any day."

"Hey!" Naomi said, still laughing.

I playfully nudged her before pulling her in for a hug. Not long after, everyone else pulled themselves in. "But, seriously, I'm so grateful for you all," I said.

More grateful than I could express. I wanted to take that weekend and capture it in a bottle to revisit down the road. I wanted to relive that weekend over and over again. I wanted to be able to bask in that feeling, because for the first time in a long time, I was at peace.

I was surrounded by people I loved that loved me fiercely in return. I missed Inez, a lot, but looking around at the smiling faces of the sisterhood I had stumbled on, my found family, my Saviors of Sherbrooke, I knew I was going to be okay.

EPILOGUE

As Inez cuddled up by the fire next to her wife after kissing their children goodnight, she couldn't help but think about how lucky she was. How grateful she was for everything that had happened that led her to this point. As she held her wife close, she whispered a thank you to the stars that Sadie the sorceress had blessed her.

She pulled her wife closer, holding her tight, grateful for the peace in the Realms and the quiet life her wife had chosen for them.

They still saw Serena and visited the castle often, which Inez was grateful for, but her loyalties had shifted. She had pledged her unwavering loyalty and given her heart to a new Queen, her wife, and would worship her for the rest of their days.

And they would live happily, peacefully, ever after.

I stared at the words, struggling to comprehend their meaning, the finality of them. A tear rolled down my cheek as I realized I was done. I was putting a lid on that chapter of my life, closing that story. I wasn't ready to say goodbye, but she was ready for her happy ending. Every ending was just a new beginning. Maybe I would meet her again in another story or in another life or another form. I hoped so.

Finishing her story let me keep her close to my heart, and it was hard to really be done. Hard to admit to myself that she didn't need me anymore. In a way, that she would hate to hear, she was like my child and it was hard to see her no longer needing me, hard to see her grow up and be fine on her own. I was ecstatic she was happy, but it was hard to let go. So hard, in fact, that I had dragged out finishing the story for a good few more months than it should've taken because I wasn't ready to move on.

But she was ready. She had fought hard her whole life to get to this point and seeing her happy, knowing she was curled up cuddling with her wife and their little family, knowing she was smiling most of her days and had a future that didn't involve having to constantly watch her back for threats was reward enough for me.

Knowing she remembered me and thought of me with gratitude every once in a while was enough for me. I was happy for her, I really was. I smiled down at my last words and thought about her with her wife and their kids. Maybe sometime, when I missed her and Serena too much, I would take out the story and write something else. Maybe I could write about their children someday, if there was a way to do so without putting anyone in danger, but for now, this was enough.

I couldn't help thinking about how grateful I was for everything in my life that had gotten me to where I was. I was even thankful for my experience with Kay. For the longest time I had wished I could have changed things with her, or even wished we had never been friends, but I realized now what I hadn't back then.

Our friendship wasn't meant to last, and Inez helped me see that even though things can be fleeting, it doesn't mean they aren't important. Even though things ended badly, it doesn't mean they didn't matter. Even though she broke my heart, it doesn't mean she never cared. Was she some big villain who tried to hurt me? No. She was just a flawed person, like the rest of us. If my adventure had taught me anything, it's that everyone's the villain in someone's story.

My reverie was broken by Naomi yelling from in the house behind me, "Come on, Sadie! We're gonna be late!" I glanced at the clock on my laptop and started. It was a lot later than I thought. I barely had time to get ready.

I saved and backed up the file before closing the laptop. I sighed, pushing myself off the lounge chair and staring longingly at the pool in front of me and the ocean beyond that. The ocean was calling me, but it would have to wait. White villas as beautiful as ours lining the cliff side glowed in the sunlight. It was a breathtaking view that was hard to look away from. It didn't matter how long I'd been here or how long I stared at the view. It would never get old and I would certainly never get sick of swimming in the clear blue Aegean.

But not today.

This was more important. Still, it was hard to walk away from the crystal clear pool and beckoning of the deep blue Aegean Sea, but it would be there when we returned. Tonight was about celebrating; tonight was about the long time coming reunion of the Saviors of Sherbrooke.

It had been a crazy year and a half. I published the end of Serena's story and had just finished Inez's story, and it was due to be published early next year.

I would love to say that the end of Serena's story was a sweeping success, but it didn't hit record sales. It didn't make any bestseller lists, but I couldn't have been happier with it, knowing how Inez and even Damien would have been feeling about it. I didn't write to sell books; I wrote to tell a story, to make people feel things, and I knew I had done that.

Even if no one had ever read it, I knew I created a very real world, and that I had a duty to those people. But as it turned out, my readers loved it. I thought they might think it was too much of a happy ending, but they didn't. Most agreed that it was just what was needed. I was grateful for that, because I wouldn't have given any of the characters I had grown to love and think of as friends anything less than the happy, peaceful ending they deserved.

Attending the first Book Ball had gotten me more exposure. People in attendance were still talking about the Damien cosplayer and his badass special effects. It had caused an increase in sales, especially when the videos hit *TikTok*. One of the videos even went viral. I spent hours scrolling through comments about people speculating about how he did it.

The exposure got me invited to a few more book balls and conventions. Mira travelled with me to a couple of them. I was incredibly grateful she was willing to. She was my righthand woman, and I was incredibly grateful for her.

Now, I was taking some much-needed time off, and some rest and relaxation was just what I needed to finish Inez's story.

I had been staying in paradise for the last three weeks. Together with Naomi, Mira, Hanna, and Sabrina, we were renting a villa in Santorini. They all had shown up about a week and a half ago, but today Eve was getting here with her new husband. We hadn't seen her in the month since her wedding. A month wasn't that long of a time, but she had been so busy with actually getting married that we didn't get to spend much time with her. Before her wedding, we hadn't seen each other in a few months either and I couldn't wait to see her now.

They were meeting us after their grand tour of Italy and Athens before heading to the island. We had offered them the Master Suite and were overjoyed when Eve and her husband agreed to stay. It was going to be a perfect few more days in paradise. I couldn't think of a better way to celebrate finishing Inez's story than with our reunion.

The Saviors of Sherbrooke were back together again. Santorini didn't know what it was in for.

Sadie's story may be over, but this is hardly the end for Inez, Serena, and the rest of the crew, and this won't be the last time you see Damien.

Inez and Serena's story is in the works, but for now for more from Zanaria, check out the novellas:

Under Lock and Key
and
The Lost Princess

Also coming soon is Gwen and Morgana's story.
They were supposed to be just a subplot but I fell in love with the girls and their story. You watched their story play out in the background, but now they'll have the spotlight.

So, what did you think of Off Script?

I would love to hear any and all of your thoughts! If you would be so kind as to leave any review it would be greatly appreciated. Any review, good or bad, short or long, is always welcome.

For updates on my next book or to tell me what you thought about this one, you can find me:
Visit my website: Thelibraryofsarahzane.com
Or follow me on TikTok or Instagram: Libraryofsarahzane
Like my Facebook page: Sarah Zane (libraryofsarahzane)

My TikTok is hilarious if I do say so myself.

Please come find me on any of those platforms, I would love to hear what you thought about my book!

ABOUT THE AUTHOR

Sarah is an author of happy endings for traumatized queers.

She is a bisexual feminist and a licensed therapist. Her stories deal with themes of feminism, trauma, sexuality, and mental health.

She lives in New England with her husband and 2 black cats named Gatsby and Mr. Darcy. When she isn't writing, she can be found perusing a book in her home library that features over 400 books, making chaotic book themed videos for TikTok (aka Booktok), or cuddled up with one of her cats crying over fictional characters or yelling at them about how badly they need therapy.

For more from Sarah Zane, check out *Beautiful Little Fool.* A sapphic, feminist retelling of the Great Gatsby from Daisy's POV.

Forbidden Love. A reputation in ruins.
How much will she risk for a happy ending?

Sequel coming soon...

ACKNOWLEDGEMENTS

First and foremost, I want to thank Jordan and Kodie for making so many peoples dreams come true by throwing Books, Gowns, and Crowns, a Fantasy Book Ball to give fantasy readers a chance to wear ball gowns, crowns and dance the night away.

Thank you both for making it a welcoming space for new authors to showcase their work and thank you both so much for taking a chance on me and including me in the lineup. I'm so proud to be a part of the Books, Gowns, and Crowns family.

To Jordan, I've been so proud of watching you grow in your author journey and am so happy to be able to call you a friend.

To Mags and Beth, thank you both for being there for me, your support means more than I can express. I'm so glad to have both of you in my life. Thank you both for being there for me through all the ups and downs of life since we've met and for supporting me and for helping inspire this story.

To Heather, Jocelyne, Amanda, Zoë, Emily, Cindy, and Shannon, thank you all for helping to inspire this story and for making Books, Gowns, and Crowns Chapter One a memorable, amazing experience. I'm so glad to have met you all.

To my husband, thank you for continuing to support me in my author journey and encouraging me to go after my dreams.

To my parents, thank you for believing in me and for throwing me a debut party for my first book. Thank you both for continuing to support me in everything I do.

To the rest of my family and friends, thank you all so much for the love and support. It means more to me than I can express.

Thank you to my beloved Booktok community of wonderful authors, readers, and new friends. I have so much love for you all and am incredibly happy to have found such a great community that makes me feel so at home.

Last but not least, thank you to you, dear reader, for reading this and helping support my crazy dream of being an author.

From the bottom of my heart, I love you all.